HOW BIZARRE

HOW BIZARRE

SIMON GRIGG

PAULY FUEMANA AND THE SONG
THAT STORMED THE WORLD

AWA PRESS

First edition published in 2015 by Awa Press, Unit 1, Level 3,
11 Vivian Street, Wellington 6011, New Zealand.

ISBN 978-1-927249-22-2

Ebook formats
Epub 978-1-927249-23-9
Mobi 978-1-927249-24-6

Cover photograph by Carmen Kemmink
Cover design by Greg Simpson
Author photograph by Stuart Page
Typesetting by Tina Delceg
This book is typeset in Minion Pro, Berthold Akzidenz
and Helvetica Neue
Printed by 1010 Printing Group Ltd, China

Find more great books at awapress.com.

Produced with the assistance of

ARTS COUNCIL OF NEW ZEALAND TOI AOTEAROA

SIMON GRIGG is a music industry professional and writer. His career has included artist management, music publishing, label ownership, clubs and radio appearances. Between 1977 and 2007 he released or was behind over 150 New Zealand-produced records, of which three-quarters entered the charts. 'How Bizarre' and subsequent singles and albums by Pauly Fuemana were released on his Huh! label. In 2012 he became creative director of *AudioCulture*, a website that works with artists, historians and music industry people to tell the stories of New Zealand popular music culture, from the first vinyl recording in the 1920s to digital streaming today. He lives in Auckland and Bangkok. This is his first book.

For Brigid and Bella

Introduction

IT WAS A STRANGE FUNERAL SERVICE for someone so famous and so young, and seemed only to multiply the sadness. It started forty-five minutes late: the hearse had apparently got lost on its way in from South Auckland. The venue, a Pacific Islanders' church near Karangahape Road in Auckland's inner-city underbelly, was in a backstreet known for its late-night hookers. I had assumed the church would be overflowing but it was only about half full. The family was there of course, and Pauly's kids looked both proud and, for want of a better word, regal. The Fuemana clan was as close to South Auckland music royalty as it was possible to be. These young people were the heirs apparent to all that Pauly and his brother Philip had played a pivotal part in creating.

Pauly's sister Christina stood and sang. The song's lyrics were a little too close for comfort to Luther Vandross's heart-tugging swansong 'Dance With My Father' but tears flowed across the aisles. I was close to crying myself as I remembered Pauly leaning on a railing by the Seine, somewhere near Notre Dame, on a stinking hot Paris day in July 1996, saying with a massive grin on his face, 'We're in Paris, bro. Paris!'

We had looked at each other silently for a moment, reflecting for the first time where, after months of chaos, recent events had taken us.

Going to Australia had been just doing what thousands of Kiwi musicians had done over the years, but having a huge hit there had been thrilling and given us an inkling of the possibilities that lay ahead. We had then found ourselves being feted in the United Kingdom. Now the song we had released so hopefully in New Zealand just seven months earlier had brought us to the famous left bank of France's greatest river.

After the end of that year the grin would disappear as the demands of record companies overwhelmed us, lawyers circled us with stopwatches firmly in fee-charging mode, and Pauly took the missteps that would eventually destroy his career.

I stood in silence in the church, thinking in a scattershot way about what had been, but mostly about a man who had, despite all that had happened, been a mate. For all the big ups and huge downs – the darkness, the violence, the mistakes – I still had a strong affection for Pauly and hated that his life had ended with him penniless and with few friends. But I had not been surprised when I took the call that Sunday morning telling me he had gone.

The media would later say there were two hundred and forty people at the service. Realistically, the number was perhaps half that. As well as Pauly's extended family, there were parishioners of the Newton Pacific Islanders Congregational Church, some of whom may have known Pauly as a kid from the years when his grandmother, who raised him as a boy, took him to services there.

'I grew up in that church,' he once told a journalist for *Pavement* magazine. 'As a child I watched the place being built. Although I'm not a practising Christian I still believe in the values. I believe in compassion.'

Others at the service, many of them elderly, probably knew his family from the days when they had lived in the city suburbs of Parnell and Grey Lynn: it seemed unlikely they had known him during the last decade, when he had lived among the mostly white and Asian residents of Auckland's North Shore. I guessed they were there as a token of respect for the passing of Niue's most famous son. Pauly would have liked that.

He had always been staunchly vocal about his roots and his bloodlines, both Niuean and Māori.

In the centre of the church the recording industry contingent clustered together. The twenty or so people included a fair smattering of those who knew the truth behind the OMC story – the meteoric rise and the slow, messy fall. Discretion, respect and protocol demanded they remain silent but outside, as the casket left, other 'friends' of Pauly gathered voraciously around the cluster of media microphones. Over the next few days their noise, opinions and often confusing accounts would fill the TV screens, radio waves and newspapers.

Missing was the former PolyGram New Zealand boss, Victor Stent. I guessed he would not have dared show his face at the funeral since Pauly and his family had long regarded him as a prime villain, the evil grasping architect of all that had gone wrong. I didn't like Victor and understood where the enmity came from but I knew it was unfair. For all his wrongs and the wide dislike for him within the company, Victor had merely provided a useful scapegoat. He had taken a fall so others wouldn't have to, and there were people who had benefited from his forced departure.

Missing, too, were Grant Thomas and Bill Cullen, Pauly's managers from the end of 1996 to 2000, when he had publicly fired them. Pauly and I had talked of this several times over the years that followed. As late as 2007 he still referred to Grant as his manager when the mood took him. He had fewer kind words for Bill Cullen, although after early 1997 Bill had been one of the few who had taken the time to think about Pauly beyond the business. He had been one of the better people to come into Pauly's life after his initial success, but his attempts to push the recording artist into a traditional rock 'n' roll template had been doomed to fail. At times Pauly himself wanted that. He could never work out whether he wanted to be a singer-songwriter, or a drum 'n' bass producer like Goldie, or New Zealand's Jobim, the Brazilian who had written 'The Girl From Ipanema', or just Pauly Fuemana. His management had offered no inspired guidance when it was most needed.

Pauly, born Paul Lawrence Fuemana, had in 1995 found himself at the beginning of a tumultuous rollercoaster ride for which he was neither mentally nor emotionally equipped, and in which his worst enemy was often himself. Journalist Rosemary Mcleod would write in *The Dominion Post* a few days after the funeral: 'Something his brother said conveyed a touch of both pathos and an unwillingness to accept reality. "He went from nothing to having all this fame dumped on him and he was meant to cope with it all himself," said Tony Fuemana, as if a doubly bad thing had happened. And yes, that would be what would happen, and at the same time it's what happens to us all. We have to cope with life all on our own, winners and losers, and in this case one-hit wonders included. It's tough, and rotten, and not fair, but there it is.'

1

THE CORNER OF SOUTH AUCKLAND where Pauly Fuemana spent his teenage years was one of Auckland's 'new suburbs'. While the village of Ōtara dated back to the 1850s, it was not until after the Second World War that it had begun to take off. In the late 1950s the settlement was officially designated a state housing sector, which more or less meant it was a place to cordon off the poor people – rural Māori looking for jobs in the city and the large number of workers arriving from the Pacific Islands – from the more affluent and established suburbs to the north. Over the next three decades it grew rapidly as more and more lookalike state houses were built and the government encouraged families such as the immigrant Fuemana clan to move in.

By the late 1970s, Ōtara was 80 percent low-income Pacific Islanders and Māori and boasted the worst crime figures in the nation. Pauly and I several times talked about the harrowing 1994 movie *Once Were Warriors*, which was set in the gang-dominated streets where he had grown up. As the film had been globally successful, it was sometimes the only reference point that overseas journalists had for Auckland and came up when they interviewed him. One day, walking through London, Pauly looked at me and said, 'Bro, that film wasn't a drama, it was a documentary.' Over the next few weeks he would repeat the phrase to bemused interviewers. Uninterested in anything beyond a quick celebrity-filled couple of inches for their tabloids, they would swiftly drop the subject.

Pauly's personal history, as he related it to record producer Alan Jansson and me in the hundreds of hours we spent together, was at best confused. One day he'd tell us he'd spent years in jail, the next he'd claim he had managed to avoid any long-term incarceration. One day he'd been working for organised crime in Sydney as a hitman, the next he'd visited the city only once or twice. From the bits I pieced together I worked out that he had lived in Sydney for about three years from his late teens, then returned to Auckland when he was about twenty-one to escape some brewing trouble and worked as a car salesman out west.

He told stories of being assaulted as a young child, of facing weapons charges in his mid teens, of enduring boys' homes and foster parents. He said his mother had left him when he was a kid. He himself had fathered children in South Auckland. All the stories seemed to have some basis in fact.

Sometimes his experiences would be woven into long intricate stories. Other days they would be blurted out without warning in conversations or media interviews. The stories were often contradictory and details ever mutating. He told us several times about a spell he'd spent in a state boys' home after being inadvertently caught up in a robbery at a fast food outlet. As a young teenager in a car, more or less along for the ride, he had been told by an older man to wait while he went into the food store. When the store had no money in the till, having just opened, the man had locked the owner in a walk-in refrigerator, opened the doors of the shop, and served customers long enough to get a handful of cash before leaving. The storekeeper had eventually suffocated.

Pauly claimed to have had absolutely no knowledge of the crime until long afterwards but had been sent to the boys' home as an accomplice. Meanwhile, the perpetrator of the robbery and murder had gone to jail. After the success of 'How Bizarre' the man contacted him, wanting a payout for 'covering his back'. Pauly sent him a colour television set for his cell and received in return a carved OMC plaque and an invitation to visit the prisoner at Cell Block 5 of Auckland's high-security Paremoremo.

Pauly's father was Niuean. After he arrived in New Zealand from the tiny Pacific island – population 1,500 – in the 1960s, he had skipped off the boat on which he was working and moved in with a Māori woman from the Tūhoe tribe. Pauly was his fourth child. According to Pauly, his mother had run off to Sydney shortly after he was born. He wouldn't hear from her again until he was in the Australian charts and she, too, contacted him asking for money.

His father's mother raised him in what were then the racially mixed suburbs of Parnell and Grey Lynn until he was in his early teens, when he moved to Ōtara to be with his siblings. Once there, like other kids his age he found trouble relatively easily.

Despite his grandmother's best efforts, it was clear education had not played a big part in his early life. His literacy and reading skills were weak. This would become increasingly obvious as we took on the world beyond New Zealand and Australia: his upbringing had given him few clues about how to behave in a different social milieu and he struggled with simple things that many people take for granted.

He may have been better equipped to deal with the pressures that came his way if he'd not been so obviously and painfully damaged by his childhood, by the trauma of early abandonment, and later by foster homes. His attachment to his past – to his family and the society he'd grown up in – was mixed. Pride and a strong love of family seemed to clash with the deep pain and anger he felt. The irony was that his often traumatic and broken past had built the person able to co-write and front the music that producer Alan Jansson constructed for him. Pauly's history drove his uniqueness.

Pauly Fuemana did not possess extraordinary musical talent, at least not in the way such talent is usually defined. He played no instrument proficiently, and he was unable to write a song without collaboration: his input consisted of elements, words, phrases and broad concepts. He couldn't coherently arrange music, nor could he produce or satisfactorily assemble musical elements in the studio. The countless home demos he recorded after his break from Alan Jansson underlined that. They were, without exception, snatches of ideas roughly thrown together without any real structure or logic, waiting for a compiler to take the best and, adding the necessary elements, make them into a workable whole.

Nor was his singing voice strong. Alan compensated for this by manoeuvring his vocals in the studio towards the safer, semi-spoken style that became his trademark.

He also lacked the skill to stand back and analyse his music with an objective ear, or to accept the advice of others who could. But he was talented – hugely so. His talent lay in his powerful persona, charm, allure and charisma. He had the X factor. In a room, without a word being spoken or a note sung, and long before he was a pop star of any sort, Pauly stood out. In a bar, people looked.

Alan Jansson had instantly recognised this when the two of them first met and it drove Alan's desire to make records with him. He had a grand plan and he knew instantly that Pauly was the person he needed to turn it into something tangible.

For his part, Pauly knew he was unique, although I don't think he ever quite understood what it was that made him that way. Instead, he tried to be everybody else. Depending on his mood and who was in his ear that week, he was the introverted singer-songwriter, the drum 'n' bass DJ, the South Pacific Antônio Carlos Jobim, the traditional touring rock 'n' roller, the aching torch balladeer, the techno wizard.

When he began working with Alan, his vocal delivery was still a snarl. At Pauly's request Alan consciously smoothed the edges, and so tempered the threatening quality that in an earlier song 'We R The OMC', recorded by Pauly, his brother Phil and Paul Ave in 1994, had sounded very real indeed. When Pauly first barked, 'Are you a friend or a foe?', the opening line on that very first, quite brilliant Otara Millionaires

Club single, it wasn't a question meant to be taken lightly. It was one that dominated Pauly's world.

In his one movie role, in which he had a small role as a character called Mr Scary, he had to repeatedly ask the other characters, 'Who da man?' Alan and I wondered if he had scripted his own words, because for Pauly there was always 'the man'. The designated 'man' would change all the time without notice, in a matter of days or even hours, and often without any perceptible logic. Alan was the first 'man', then me, PolyGram's Victor Stent and Paul Dickson at Polydor Australia, followed by a seemingly endless flow of people in Australia, the United States and the UK, until in 2005 Pauly sent an email that seemed to anoint me as the man once again.

Pauly was extraordinarily handsome. He coupled this with an arrogance that punched heavily across a room and was evident every time he looked at a lens, spoke to a journalist, or just stood around. Even in the last decade of his life when he was down, he had an unyielding belief in his own talents and destiny. It took that to do what he did.

He also had unerring style. He could go into almost any second-hand clothing shop, rummage around, find an item for a few bucks that most would think stylistically worthless, throw it on and walk out looking as killer as Elvis ever did in his pre-army days, or like a young Jobim, the Brazilian musician he idolised.

Once in Los Angeles, killing a few hours, he and I wandered into a vast second-hand clothing store off Melrose Avenue. Pauly picked out an old leather jacket. 'This is you, bro,' he smiled. It was. Despite having to have it resewn a few years back I wear it to this day.

2

I FIRST NOTICED PAULY FUEMANA in the late 1980s. Tom Sampson and I were running a nightclub called Cause Célèbre & Box on Auckland's High Street. In the narrow street beyond the club a thriving street party exploded. It was not something we intentionally created, but the presence of our club, together with two other fairly hip ones down the street and the large rambling Hotel DeBrett with its various bars at the northern end of the street, provided the late-night atmosphere that drove it.

Tom and I had owned or run several other nightclubs over the previous few years. Each had opened with a big bang then closed within a year when its 'hot' factor seemed to wane. We had begun in 1986 with The Asylum in suburban Mount Eden and then moved into the central city with The Playground on Nelson Street. In 1988 we had bought the once upmarket Club Mirage, which was struggling badly because of the '87 economic crash. We renamed it The Siren and later, after renovations, Cause Célèbre. In April 1990 it expanded into the disused Returned Services Association Club's basement next door, a room we named Box.

These nightclubs, together with ones previously run by my friends Peter Urlich and Mark Phillips and where I had deejayed, were the first in the centre of Auckland to comfortably and consciously mix races. Before them there had been Polynesian clubs and Pākehā clubs and the patrons of the two had rarely mixed. When they did, the clash of cultures was sometimes messy. Street brawls outside nightclubs between brown and white, disco kids and punks were common and often brutal.

We worked to change that. Our clubs were inspired by the global post-punk style explosion documented in magazines such as *The Face*, and the embracing of Black American dance music by style gurus in the UK and New York. In the UK a new generation of British-born young people of immigrant Caribbean parents were growing up and changing the rules, integrating both the clubs and the music played in them.

Similarly, New Zealand in the 1980s saw the coming of age of the first generation of Polynesian children born there, the offspring of the steady wave of migrants who had come to Auckland in the decades after the Second World War. These sophisticated, stylish and increasingly urbane young people first started to appear in the city's entertainment zones from the mid '80s. In their sharp suits and street wear, they were often better dressed than many of the white kids. And they had been exposed to and adopted large parts of the African-American street cultures that were filtering through the media – and, in the case of many Samoans, coming from their relatives in California.

The funk and soul music, and their offspring hip hop, mixed comfortably with the Polynesian rhythms with which these young people had grown up in their family homes to produce a fusion that would become known as Urban Pacific. Our club was among the first in the city to welcome this vibrant new mixing of races as a matter of policy.

As Cause Célèbre became increasingly successful, other clubs opened in the rectangle bounded by O'Connell Street to the east, Shortland Street to the north, Queen Street to the west, and Victoria Street to the south. Each night of the weekend the cluster of clubs, bars, record stores and fashion shops turned the area into party central. Hundreds of young people congregated on High Street, the 300-metre lane that formed the axis.

It was here that the young Pauly Fuemana could be found most weekends, alternating between the street outside our club, turns on the dance floor in Box, and Cause Célèbre, where a band fronted by his sister Christina was resident at various times in the early 1990s.

The Fuemana family was well known in South Auckland. Philip, the eldest and clan leader, was a dominant figure in the local youth culture and the music that helped define it. Christina possessed one of the great voices from the South Auckland suburbs that had become notable for producing great voices.

It was Christina's voice that dominated the stunning family album *Fuemana – New Urban Polynesian*, written, produced, directed and mostly played by Philip and released on Auckland entrepreneur Kane Massey's Deepgrooves label in July 1994. Three years earlier, in September 1991, the family band, then known as Houseparty, had released a single called 'Dangerous Love' on Murray Cammick's Southside label and this track appeared on the family album. The sleeve of the single had credited Pauly as drummer but big brother was offering a helping hand: according to the album's credits Pauly's only contribution had been as a backing vocalist.

'Dangerous Love' would become something of an international underground DJ hit later in the 1990s when several British soul DJs picked it up. It was eventually bootlegged in Britain as a 'rare groove'.

Pauly became one of the regulars at Cause Célèbre, turning up two or three nights a week. He and I often talked. I liked him: he had a musical background and always looked the part. I was happy to encourage him and, as I did with many regulars, gave him a small bar tab on the condition it was paid off each week.

Unfortunately he blew it in the first week, running up a bill that remained unsettled after three weeks despite constant requests and reminders. Finally we offered to let him work off the debt. He was given the job of porter. The lowest position in the club hierarchy, a porter clears glasses, washes them, carries beer from bar to bar, and does whatever cleaning up or dogsbody work the floor manager orders.

As an employee, Pauly was hopeless. He arrived dressed in his club best. He then spent far more time talking to his mates and girls outside at the club's door, worrying about how he looked, and protecting his clothes from accidental damage than doing any work. Eventually we gave up and asked him to do a couple of nights as an assistant doorman. The bar tab was effectively wiped, and the staff were given an inflexible instruction that Pauly Fuemana was not to be given credit under any circumstances.

3

I FIRST ENCOUNTERED ALAN JANSSON, who would come to play a leading role in the Pauly Fuemana story, in 1980. Alan was the guitarist and songwriter for a Wellington band, The Steroids, which had just released a self-financed single on its own indie label, White Light Records. The post-punk track was called 'Mr Average', but despite the self-deprecating title the band clearly had something going for it as the disc was in demand, as was the case for all of the tiny number of New Zealand releases filtering out of garages after the independent label explosion of 1979.

The Steroids had pressed and distributed the record themselves in Wellington but had no way of getting it into record stores in Auckland. One morning I received a call from their manager asking if I could help. I had set up an independent label, Propeller, and achieved modest success with the first few singles I had released. I was now using the valuable contacts I had made with retailers to help some of the fast growing number of independently released New Zealand singles into those Auckland stores whose managers had worked out there was a growing demand for them. The stores were finding these funny-looking, roughly recorded and often amateurishly packaged 7-inch singles sold quite well – to the bemusement of the major record labels. It was easier for me to sell my own records if

I had a catalogue of indie records, since retailers in Auckland found it convenient to order through a single wholesaler.

I also set up a direct-to-customer sales service. At the time I was sharing an apartment with Murray Cammick, who co-owned and edited New Zealand's hugely influential music monthly *Rip It Up*. Murray offered me a free ad in every issue of the magazine to sell independently released New Zealand records. The operation, which we called Indies Mail Order, took off with a roar and I was soon sending singles and albums all over the country, and later all over the world.

I quickly sold the first 50 singles I received from The Steroids and needed a few more. I rang their number. The man who answered said his name was Alan and, yes, more were on their way. I didn't have a lot to do with The Steroids' next two singles as the band jumped to a major label, CBS. After this it quietly split – or rather took a breather and changed radically. A few months later the remnants of the last line-up re-emerged as The Body Electric, a synthesizer-driven, heavily electronic act whose debut single 'Pulsing' arrived in 1982 on 12-inch via Wellington's independent Jayrem label. Its sheer catchiness and novelty value – New Zealand had not produced anything like this before – saw it sit in the Top 40 for nine months.

The residual punk elements in Auckland hated 'Pulsing' but I was fascinated by both the record and the band and encouraged them to play Auckland as soon as possible. It took a month or two but eventually they came north. My friend Marcus Wells, a lawyer and briefly a wannabe band promoter, handled the gig, which took place in a space on the corner of Wellesley and Albert Streets that had until recently been A Certain Bar, a successful weekend club hosted by Peter Urlich, a former pop star, and *Rip It Up* writer Mark Phillips.

It was an uncomfortable gig. For the first half there was quite a strong crowd, most of them increasingly confused by the lack of traditionally structured songs and the dominance of the unconventional machine-like synthesizer and drum-machine rhythms. After about half an hour there was a noticeable drift to the bar, and, worse, to the door. Finally a rather drunk man muttered something about musical trespass, walked backstage, turned off the power and stormed out. His name was Barry Jenkin and he was the prominent presenter of an alternative radio show on Auckland's mostly pop radio station 1ZM.

Surprised by the negative reaction, I immediately told Alan and the rest of the band how I felt. A bond of sorts was tentatively formed. Alan liked the fact I seemed to understand what they were trying – I felt with some success – to do. I was mystified as to why most of the Auckland crowd didn't get it. I bought that first Body Electric single, then their album and their next single.

In 1983, frustrated by Auckland's conservatism, I folded my label and moved to London. Two years later, having indulged myself in dance music, I decided to return home. Before I left I stopped off in the South London suburb of Borough and managed to fast-talk my way into picking up New Zealand rights to an act produced and released by the songwriting and record-producing team of Stock Aitken Waterman. Over the next decade this trio would have dozens of hits, including with Mel and Kim, Rick Astley and Kylie Minogue.

Back in Auckland I dragged in Peter Urlich and Mark Phillips to form a new label, Stimulant. I convinced Gilbert Egdell, A&R[1] manager at CBS New Zealand, and the company's managing director Murray Thom to fund and distribute our releases. Our debut release in 1986 was by a South London vocalist named Princess, the Stock Aitken Waterman-produced artist I had licensed that day in Borough. Princess's anthemic soul record 'Say I'm Your Number One' made number two in New Zealand – only a local band, Peking Man, kept it from the top spot – and sold extraordinarily well: the album went gold and the single easily made platinum.

Stimulant's early success – which included producing another four Top 20 singles and a couple of popular street-level dance music compilation

---

1 Artists and repertoire (A&R) is the division of a record label or music publishing company charged with finding new recording artists and overseeing the artistic development of recording artists and/or songwriters. It also acts as a liaison between artists and the record label or publishing company.

albums, firsts for New Zealand – provided us with the impetus to visit Alan Jansson. Following the demise of The Body Electric, Alan had moved north to Auckland. After working briefly out of another studio, he and a couple of partners, including another former Body Electric member Garry Smith, had set up a recording studio called Module 8 in almost forgotten Waverley Street, off the upper, less commercially desirable part of Queen Street. Alan had hocked himself up to the eyeballs and equipped the studio with a Fairlight CMI^2 processor.

At the time studios were moving away from the old multi-track reel-to-reel analogue tape to a digital format, and in the process redefining how and what could be achieved in a recording studio. The Fairlight digital recording machine, designed in Australia, was state-of-the art and unmatched in New Zealand at that time. A hugely expensive piece of very complex machinery, it was being used by the likes of Peter Gabriel, Brian Eno, Stevie Wonder and Paul McCartney. Many more would jump on board as the system was enhanced by add-ons and major upgrades.

Alan borrowed time and again to invest in these upgrades. In 1996 he told the magazine *NZ Musician* that the decision to invest in the new technology had come about when he worked out in the early '80s how the UK bands that inspired him were achieving the sounds they were putting on vinyl. 'A light went on in my head,' he told the interviewer, Andrew Polson.

His aim was not for the machine to become a rig for hire by any advertising hack who wanted to use it, but to allow him to make the sort of music he felt driven to make. For years, he would walk a tightrope between finding the money he needed to cover the large loans he'd taken out and being true to his vision. Despite financial pressure, he would turn down far more work than he accepted, including several massive commissions that would have allowed him to be debt-free years before he finally managed this. He was setting himself up to make genre-defining recordings that would go around the world.

---

2 Computer musical instrument.

Alan knew where he was going – he just needed the tools. And he was happy to break the rules, or didn't know the rules existed. Of Greek and Scandinavian heritage and imbued with a radical individualism and refusal to conform, he simply followed his heart and his instincts. He frequently told me he was going to record a US number one record. I smiled: we were, after all, in New Zealand.

It was clear that the only way to take a record into the charts beyond New Zealand would be to create an aberration, a record that sounded likė nothing else and so could not be nailed down as a poor cousin to whatever had crawled up the billboard charts the month before. I quickly worked out that despite the seeming impossibility of the task, if anyone could pull it off Alan Jansson might just be the one. His unwillingness to follow musical fads and trends, the way he sat outside the whims of fashion and tracked his own self-determined path, gave him a massive advantage over many of his peers.

Peter, Mark and I had a crazy idea. We would make our own club-oriented records for our new label. They would be recorded by New Zealand acts but not be replicas of UK or US dance records: we were into creating local recordings first and foremost.

It made sense to approach Alan. He was one of the few – perhaps the only – producer or studio in New Zealand who would understand what we wanted to do. I arranged a meeting and the four of us sat and talked over options and ideas at great length.

After a few days Mark and Peter drifted off but Alan and I went on talking. Later we were joined by James Pinker. James, a close friend of mine, was the drummer in the first band I'd recorded for my Propeller label. The days turned into weeks as we tried to work out how to make a releasable record that was somehow different.

We first worked with a vocalist, Taisha Khutze, who had been introduced to us by Dave Bulog. A talented keyboardist and composer, Dave was a member of one of the great Auckland bands, Car Crash Set, a synthesizer fanatic and a like-minded soul. The record we made with

Taisha, which had the working title *Love Is An Ocean*, was never released. Somehow we lost momentum and other things took over. However, the collaboration had made us think more about projects on which we could work together.

For a few months things drifted. The Stimulant label stalled and then collapsed after I fell out with Mark and Peter over what seemed major at the time but was in retrospect minor clubland politics. Alan and I needed a label to release whatever records we were going to make so I revived Propeller, which, apart from an occasional reissue, had been in hibernation since 1983.

Eventually Alan, James, Dave and I worked out the sort of record we wanted to make. It would be a club one but a particular kind – a house record inspired by the underground sounds coming out of the clubs and indie labels of downtown Chicago and New York. House music was a new revolutionary international movement. Still alien to most New Zealand club-goers, it had originated in the US but was taking the clubs of Europe and the UK by storm. We wanted our record to be in the house style, but not a direct copy of any other record.

'Jam This Record', an eponymous cut and paste 12-inch single, was made on Alan's expensive new equipment at Module 8 over a week of midnight-to-dawn sessions and became New Zealand's first house record, albeit with our own twist. We sold a few hundred locally and shipped more than a thousand to the UK, where the record got extensive club play, achieved strong sales, and entered the London club charts as an unknown white label[3] in early 1988.

The record established an enduring professional working relationship between Alan and me. With Dave, we worked on several projects and ideas, but mostly we talked and schemed with little concrete result. Crucially, though, Alan promised I would have the first look at anything interesting that came his way.

---

3   A white label is a promotional 12-inch single. Its name derives from its white centre label, which usually contains only minimal information.

Most of these things I turned down. We came close to releasing a single by one of the early Auckland hip-hop crews but I backed off because the tracks were too reliant on several samples by major acts that had not been cleared for use.

Meanwhile, Alan would often ring and ask me to come in and give my opinion on a mix or a sound he was thinking of using, and I sat in on many mixing sessions. Sometimes, too, he would ask my view on where to put elements in a mix; this could involve my taking the mix back to my club and running it through our large dance-floor-tuned sound system.

Over the next few years Alan had several hits, some quite big. One or two were picked up offshore, including Australasian chart and club hits from a band called The Chain Gang, that Alan put together in-house.

As we moved into the 1990s I was still heavily involved in clubs, as well as managing a couple of bands and hosting an influential weekly dance-music show, *Beats Per Minute*, on 95bFM. At Cause Célèbre and Box we aimed to provide the most exciting and cutting-edge musical entertainment in Auckland. We were about the music first: this was our major point of difference from the many other clubs. And we consciously took risks. Our bands and DJs pushed boundaries other clubs wouldn't approach. Although this was partially instinctive it was also driven by the venue. The club was in a great location and had a reasonably stylish interior, but it was housed in a dark grotty basement.

Célèbre boasted killer bands: the pop-funksters Supergroove, long before they began their string of New Zealand hits or even boasted a recording deal; the Fuemana family group; the dark and moody late-night band Bluespeak, featuring the smoky, sometime chart popster Greg Johnson doing his jazz thing; some left-field jazz led by a legendary Auckland keyboardist, Murray McNabb; and a big band put together by a bunch of edgy young musicians who called themselves Freebass. This band included two brothers from Auckland's North Shore: Joel Haines, a virtuoso guitarist still in his mid teens and therefore underage for a place licensed to sell alcohol – he relied on us to hide him out the back when the cops arrived – and his elder brother Nathan, a saxophone prodigy.

Freebass pulled increasingly large crowds throughout 1991 and 1992 and recorded an album, *Raw: Live At Cause Célèbre*. In early 1993 it disbanded as members went their separate ways. Nathan had already left a year earlier and headed to New York to spend twelve months studying on a music scholarship. When he returned, Tom and I approached him about putting together a new band to play a short residency at the club. With a couple of breaks, that residency extended through to late 1995 and helped us achieve record Friday night attendances. Nathan and his band were mesmerising; they provided a live experience the like of which I have not seen before or since in Auckland. When they played, often on both Friday and Saturday nights, we would almost always have queues down the street. It was common for them to play until five in the morning or later, holding the crowd until the climatic end. Sweat poured down the walls and mixed with thick cigarette smoke; the atmosphere was everything a jazz club was supposed to be and more.

Next door, Box featured DJs. We had made contact with several overseas promoters and in 1993 we began touring international DJs, most from the UK and US. The DJ scene was a phenomenon that had exploded worldwide in the aftermath of the Acid House movement, when literally millions of kids began dancing to sounds that had started in the underground gay clubs of the US and swept the UK and then the world. A raft of DJs had not only become pop stars in their own right but were now touring the globe and pulling crowds that often numbered in the tens of thousands. We leapt at the chance to tour some of these DJs, although at times it was tough to persuade middle New Zealand blokes they should pay money to 'see a guy put on records'.

In early 1994 we brought out Gilles Peterson. Peterson was and remains a legendary figure in the music industry. Since 1996 his jazz-tinged BBC radio show has been beamed around the world and he has long had the power to make or break acts, often including once obscure acts from the far corners of the planet. At the time he came to New Zealand, he was working for London's former pirate station Kiss 100 FM, and was the high priest of a fashionable new style tagged Acid Jazz, a fusion of traditional jazz styles with contemporary hip-hop and soul sounds.

He also owned a record label, Talking Loud, that was financed and distributed by Phonogram, part of the global Dutch-owned PolyGram conglomerate. Talking Loud was about as close to hip central as it was possible to be. It had a stable of very hot acts and its logo screamed underground cool – highly collectable, it adorned T-shirts, record bags and other paraphernalia – so when we were offered Peterson for two nights we would have been nuts to refuse him despite the financial risk involved. The goodwill and sheer kudos a DJ like him would bring our small business was huge. And just as importantly I really wanted to see him play – and play in our club.

Nathan Haines' music fitted very much into the Talking Loud style: the band leader was increasingly including DJs and rappers in his sets. My sometime business partner Mark Phillips was now working for PolyGram New Zealand, and he and I talked of the possibility of getting Peterson to hear Nathan's band, which would be playing at Célèbre on the night Peterson was performing next door at Box. We decided that since I would be driving Peterson around during the week he was in Auckland and doing a radio show with him on the night before his Friday gig, I would get across how hot Nathan was.

After Peterson arrived, he and I spent much of the week hanging around second-hand record stores and shoe shops, collectable trainers seeming to be a fixation with many UK DJs and New Zealand seen as a mecca for finding them. We also had another legendary UK DJ, Norman Jay, in town; he was to play the club the following weekend. As the three of us rattled around town in my old MGB GT I spent a lot of time chewing my companions' ears off about Nathan, while Peterson, the smaller of the two men, hunched in the back seat, probably wishing I would shut up.

Second-hand stores in Auckland were overflowing with what we were assured were globally rare records and Peterson purchased several hundred, most for resale in places like Japan and Germany. One afternoon we arrived at PolyGram with a car full of 12-inch vinyl, about five hundred records in all, that Peterson wanted to have airfreighted to London and Tokyo.

Although horrified at the expense, PolyGram was obliged to comply: Peterson was the owner of an important label in their roster. After negotiating with the production manager about the nuts and bolts of the shipments, we wandered into the office of the company's managing director, Victor Stent, where Peterson chirpily asked, 'So, who's this Nathan Haines then? Why haven't you signed him?'

Stent was startled by the cockiness of the 5'6" British tastemaker putting him on the spot. If he had heard of Nathan he didn't show it, although I found out later that Mark Phillips had been trying for months to persuade him to sign Nathan, to no effect. This was not surprising. PolyGram, like most of the big record companies in New Zealand, signed and released little local music, apart from a token act here and there. New Zealand music was regarded as a big loss-maker. Radio mostly wouldn't touch it, and recordings were expensive to produce in both time and money.

It was also accepted wisdom that artists signed and recorded in New Zealand had virtually no chance of their records selling in the world's major markets. Australia was tough enough: it steadfastly ignored most talent from across the Tasman. Any idea of trying to sell local acts further afield was seen as verging on insanity. Usually when local acts were recorded it was only to assuage a company's guilt at not doing what record companies were supposed to do – namely make music – rather than just stripping profits out of a territory.

At this time PolyGram had no local acts signed and had not had any for two years. The last had been The Exponents, who had done very well when Adam Holt, label manager of PolyGram subsidiary Polydor Records, had put his all into them. However, Adam had since moved to Polydor's Australian office and direct local signings had been non-existent.

When Victor Stent became PolyGram New Zealand's managing director in 1993 he had vowed to change this. Stent had a long history of support for local music and had been instrumental in setting up a distribution deal for my Propeller label with Festival Records in the early '80s. He and Festival had often supported me well beyond their contractual obligations. The downside to that support had been Stent's continual interference in the artistic process. He had once gone as far as to remix a record at my cost, without my knowledge, forcing me, again at my cost, to revert to the earlier and better mix.

4

ON THE NIGHT OF THE PETERSON GIG, Victor Stent, Mark Phillips and most of the PolyGram staff were at Cause Célèbre. Mark was a club regular and ardently followed Nathan's gigs. Victor was there because this guy who owned a record label he distributed was playing, and had told him the band next door was supposed to be good and signable.

It was a blistering night. Peterson pulled out obscure 7-inch single after 7-inch single, at times stopping the music to lean forward and quietly explain to the completely enthralled crowd, who had seen nothing like this before, exactly what they were hearing. He appeared to feed off the positive energy and enthusiastic feedback radiating from the audience.

After he finished playing around three in the morning, he wandered next door and was clearly impressed by Nathan and his band – newly named The Enforcers by Nathan's flatmate and Célèbre DJ Gerhardt Pierard – who were now in the middle of their second set and soaring. Leaning on the bar, he smiled and told me I should sign the band, record them, and use PolyGram for distribution. Since his Talking Loud label was part of the same worldwide network, he could look at picking them up.

Mark nodded in agreement. It was exactly what he'd been saying to me for some time: sign the band and we'll try and hawk it to Talking Loud.

The big difference was that we now had a verbal nod from the label's boss. Peterson called Victor over and told him the same thing. He agreed.

There were a few details to iron out. First, I didn't have an active label. Apart from Propeller's various successful compilations of older back catalogue and New Zealand archive material, for which I still had a deal with Festival Records, the label was in hiatus. Stimulant was long gone, and anyway not really mine to do what I wanted with it. I would need to form a new label.

Secondly, and more importantly, Nathan was still in the dark. Mark and I sat him down in my living room the next night and explained the idea in general terms. He was thoroughly and unhesitantly keen. His first words were, 'Where do I sign?'

First thing on Monday I received a call from Victor Stent's PA. Victor wanted to meet me that evening in his office. At six o'clock I went to PolyGram's faceless single-storey offices at Mount Eden in the shadow of the mountain. There Victor proposed that I form a label and sign Nathan to a long-term deal. PolyGram would fund this to the tune of $10,000 per album. As a sweetener I would be allowed access to the PolyGram catalogues to make compilations. I would be paid an override[4] for these and could add this to the label's funding pool. The copyrights in the label would be mine but PolyGram would have worldwide distribution rights and release options.

It was a win-win. Victor had worked out a legitimate way to fund the label, which would still allow it to maintain its independence. The budget offered per album wasn't large, especially when I factored in the videos, artwork, remixes and everything else involved in signing an artist and releasing a record, but I had always figured these things were open to renegotiation once a deal was signed. It was also hard to say no when the offer was coupled to a compilation proposal that could, and did, prove lucrative over the next few years. The idea of playing with

---

4   An override is a small percentage of a recording or album's wholesale or retail price.

and combining tracks from the vast PolyGram catalogue, which ranged across almost every major style of the last eighty years from Motown to Marley, was very enticing. In addition, Mark Phillips would be my liaison person at PolyGram, which, given my relationship with Mark, his grasp of the project and his love of Nathan's music, was ideal.

Over the next few nights, Mark, Nathan and I nutted out the details, with some input from Gerhardt Pierard, who came up with a name for the new label. I had tried the toss-a-dart-at-the-dictionary method, which had served me well with Propeller and its subsidiary, Furtive. This time it had failed miserably, offering up only such names as 'Desk'. Musing over one of my CDs, an American modern jazz collection called *Huh?*, Gerhardt suggested using this word without the question mark. I tossed an exclamation mark on the end, James Brown style, and Huh! was born.[5]

I told Victor about the name the following day. He was extremely unhappy and suggested all sorts of alternatives, including Buy My Records, Local Records and worse. I decided to stick with Huh! and Peter Urlich quickly sketched a logo.

We now had an artist, a distributor, a name and a corporate brand. We were missing a catalogue. It was obvious that $10,000 wouldn't buy us a lot of album, so at Nathan's suggestion we decided to record the debut work essentially live. Two weeks later Nathan and his band went into Revolver Studioss in suburban Mount Roskill, next to the famous Sanitarium Factory where the nation's Weet-Bix breakfast cereal was produced, with engineer/producer Steve Garden for two nights and walked out with eleven usable tracks and a few outtakes. Steve quickly mixed these down from the multitrack and I took cassettes to PolyGram for our first serious listen outside the studio.

Victor and I drove around Auckland in his Audi, playing the rough mixes over and over, and eventually ended up in the car park at the summit of Mount Eden, enjoying the breathtaking view of Auckland

---

5   The original plan was to end every release with a recording of Brown grunting loudly, 'Hhhuuuuuhhh!' It was a great idea but never happened.

city and listening to the record one more time. We both agreed that, although it was almost there, it needed something more.

In 1991 Alan Jansson had got himself even further in hock to the bank. He had bought out one of his partners and substantially upgraded his Fairlight and the crucial effects units that went with it. In June 1993 he opened a new recording suite, which he called Uptown Studios, in Drake Street behind Victoria Market. He moved his family into a small purpose-built apartment downstairs, added a raft of other recording gear, and threw himself headlong into this make-or-break project. Setting up the studio was a massive risk both artistically and commercially – unless you were Alan Jansson. Alan operated instinctively and was guided solely by his gut belief in the project and its potential – and his dream of that US number one.

In the early 1990s he worked on a variety of projects, including tracks for iconic New Zealand acts such as Tim Finn and Greg Johnson, and developed an increasingly credible profile as the producer with the best facility and ears in New Zealand. He was constantly being offered attractive deals by offshore companies to work full-time on their projects but repeatedly declined them. He was more motivated by his own grand plans than by the thought of becoming a well-paid cog in a corporate wheel.

He and Tim Mahon, a former member of the early '80s Auckland band Blam Blam Blam, a Propeller Records act, concocted an adventurous plan to record an album of new bands from South Auckland. A massive explosion of talent was happening in the place that, despite being tagged a part of Auckland, was in every possible way a different world to the one we inhabited in the central city, and one largely ignored by the established music industry.

This musical explosion had been building and snowballing for years, and many of the young South Aucklanders coming to our clubs were in bands and making music. In reality there had been an enormously creative musical community for many years within the massive urban sprawl that lay 30 minutes down the Southern Motorway from Auckland's city centre. In suburbs such as Ōtara, Ōtāhuhu, Māngere and Manurewa, where the population mix was tilted heavily towards Pacific Islanders and Māori, there were numerous venues and several thriving music schools. The Manukau City Council had employed Tim Mahon as youth music coordinator and was supporting musical arts in a way the Auckland City Council never had.

Many of the newer bands and creatives centred themselves on the Ōtara Music Arts Centre, a community-based council initiative set up in 1988 with its own practice, performance and recording facilities, and many had a connection with Philip Fuemana, the influential leader of the musical Fuemana family.

Through Tim's connections and liaison with Phil and the Ōtara centre, Alan gained a grant from the council to record several South Auckland acts. He brought on board an independent Australian label, Volition, owned by Andrew Penhallow, an industry pioneer who had been recording and releasing edgy and adventurous records in Australia since 1977. Together Alan and Andrew set up a joint venture to release the collection Alan was wanting to record. They called the label Second Nature Records and worked out distribution deals with EMI in New Zealand and CBS in Australia.

The recording project was appropriately named *Proud* and given its distinctive cover image, a blackbird, by Andrew Penhallow. Charlie Brown, a member of one of the bands, asked Alan what the future held. 'The future is up,' Alan answered, to which Charlie responded, 'Urban Pacific.' Alan grabbed the tag and added it to the title of the forthcoming record, which became *Proud – An Urban Pacific Streetsoul Compilation*. It was an album that would change the face of New Zealand music.

Over the next 15 months, grossly overspending and blowing the Manukau council grants and the contribution from his Australian partner several times over, Alan recorded fourteen tracks from ten different acts, some of which shared members. Five of the acts were suggested by Phil Fuemana; the rest, handpicked by Alan, came via Tim Mahon and the pool at OMAC.

Alan wanted perfection. He worked and reworked basic tracks day and night over many months. He exceeded the budget by more than $70,000 but that seemed to matter little: it was the beginning of his project to record a US number one. Given the costs and the risks involved, the artists and bands agreed that all income from the album would go to Alan and his studio until the costs were covered. As it happened nothing from album sales was ever returned to him. All income was gobbled up by other costs across New Zealand and Australia.

The album was released in May 1994. It sold moderately well and hit number one in the New Zealand compilation chart but didn't achieve the sort of numbers Alan needed. By the end of 2000, total sales of *Proud* would have reached around 3,000, substantially short of the 11,000 needed to break even.

However, the album's impact was resounding. It showed New Zealand that something very musically significant was happening in South Auckland and put a direct spotlight on both the region and the work of people such as Phil Fuemana. With the assistance of an Auckland DJ, Phil Bell (aka Sir Vere), Phil signed a label deal for his Urban Pacific Records with a German-owned multinational record company, BMG. Over the next few years the label would take many of the acts on *Proud*, and people who first recorded for that album, into the charts. It would lay the groundwork for a new label, Dawn Raid, and its commercial and artistic successes, and promote urban styles that became major influences on New Zealand pop music.

Several singles emerged from the *Proud* album. One was 'In The Neighbourhood' by Sisters Underground, two teenage girls from Ōtara, Brenda Makamoeafi and Hassanah Iroegbu. The track brilliantly placed a tough and sassy urban lyric over a classic hip-hop loop taken from a sample disc but based, heavily reworked, on the famous 'Ashley's Roachclip' sample, as also found on Eric B. & Rakim's 1987 hit 'Paid In Full'. The whole song was sweetened by a soft choral effect laid seductively under the verses and then lifted, and driven, by an acoustic guitar played over the beats, in a trademark style that was to go around the world as 'the Uptown sound'. At the time it sounded revolutionary. Two decades later it is just accepted as an established New Zealand urban style.

The video of 'In The Neighbourhood', directed by a young Polynesian director, Greg Semu, and filmed in the streets and markets of Ōtara, was evocative of youth, innocence and South Auckland. It helped propel the song, with little radio airplay beyond the urban stations, into number six in the New Zealand charts, on to the Australian urban charts, and then on to the very white Australian Top 50. It also reached number 19 in Italy.

The Semi MC's 'Trust Me' also became a single, issued by their management via CBS, and was a minor hit in New Zealand.

But another single would be for me the album's standout track. From the Phil Fuemana-led Otara Millionaires Club, it was based on a rhythm built up by Phil in his studio in a South Auckland church, and had been heavily mixed, reworked and overdubbed by Alan at Uptown. Defiantly entitled 'We R The OMC', the song was a strident call to arms from a crew known for brandishing machetes on stage as part of their performances. It featured vocals from Herman Lotto, who would later release several well regarded solo albums, and Phil's brother Pauly Fuemana.

The song was far more accomplished on CD than it was live. In late 1994 I saw OMC on stage at an open-air festival arranged by Tim Mahon outside Manukau City Centre, a shopping mall at the hub of the huge expanse that is Manukau City. The group's DJ Soane Filitonga, who was also a doorman at Cause Célèbre, turned up without any turntables. The audience waited for the best part of an hour as the group fumbled about on stage. After a couple of half-hearted, half-begun beats and raps the gig collapsed into an abuse session with the audience, who seemed more interested in the nearby food stands than the fast disintegrating band.

The recorded single, however, was quite something. To my knowledge, New Zealand has not produced anything since that sounds quite like it. Remixes were arranged in Australia from Boxcar, a techno act signed to Andrew Penhallow's Volition label, and the song, as with 'In The Neighbourhood', picked up extensive airplay on the alternative Australian

Triple J network, with the station's music director Arnold Frolows strongly championing both the single and the *Proud* album. This airplay was to prove massively important in opening doors in Australia for the album, the bands, Alan, and later for me.

'We R The OMC', also known as 'O To The M To The C', was resolutely staunch in a way no other Auckland hip-hop track had been, and it stood out from everything that had come before and everything released around it. And yet it was an odd record. It was hip hop but not at all as we knew it. It mixed, in a fairly radical way, all sorts of elements you would not necessarily find in a classic hip-hop record of the era. It was a rock record. It was a rap record. It had a clearly defined Polynesian core. It even, especially in the intro, had techno elements that could have been lifted from an early Prodigy record.

It was a fairly accurate pointer towards the sort of records that Alan Jansson and Pauly Fuemana would make. Pauly once told me that when he heard Alan lay the acoustic guitar on that OMC track, he knew instinctively and immediately he had found his collaborator and mentor.

Six weeks before *Proud* was to be released, Phil Fuemana and Tim Mahon put together a touring party consisting of eight of the bands on the album. It was a daring but risky plan to take the album to the nation. As foolhardy as it may have seemed, it was vital if *Proud* were to have an impact beyond its core audience.

The tour was ill-starred. The packed bus, grossly overloaded, broke down at the end of the Southern Motorway as it crawled slowly out of Auckland. The crowds the sessions attracted around the country were not nearly large enough to cover the costs of such a big touring party. Many of the performances were at best haphazard. Tragedy struck in the South Island when a dancer with one of the bands drowned after diving into a river despite warning signs. The tour bled money and the Manukau City Council was forced to bail it out to the tune of $40,000.

For all that, the tour was a major step forward for South Auckland's fledgling scene. Like the album, it proclaimed: 'We exist and you can't ignore us any more.' It stopped at all kinds of towns, big and small. It must have been a shock for places such as Invercargill, at the bottom of the South Island, to see around forty South Aucklanders arrive in town. The final sold-out gig at Auckland's Powerstation was a triumph, with the clear stars, Otara Millionaires Club, finally gelling in front of a friendly crowd.

In a weird postscript, Pauly would later tell a journalist from Sydney's *On the Street* that in the South Island 'in front of our motels we had crosses burnt. We've got the Third Reich down there and Ku Klux Klan.'

In June Pauly and Phil appeared together on the cover of *NZ Musician*. They looked confident, but Phil's position towering over Pauly seemed to denote an uneasy relationship between the two. Pauly would often state his desire to prove he was musically his own man and not just Phil's younger brother. By the time the article appeared, he had made the first tentative moves to do just that.

5

FROM THE MIDDLE OF 1994 I found myself spending more and more time hanging out with Alan at Uptown Studios. I had not seen a lot of him while he was recording the *Proud* collection but I'd bought the album on the day it was released and loved it. What made it so phenomenal was that it brought together the disparate threads of the music being made in South Auckland and applied extremely high production values to them. It sounded amazing. I was aware of the input from Phil Fuemana, Tim Mahon and others but the production was very much Alan's. He was a perfectionist, a musical loner who refused to comply with any rules and was eccentric in the way he approached the music he wanted to record.

Music production had always been the Achilles heel preventing locally made songs and records having legs beyond New Zealand. It didn't matter how good the song was – and many New Zealanders had been able to turn out a great song – the end result of the studio process was more often than not thin, tinny or hollow. There were exceptions but many of the recordings over the decades before *Proud* sounded like crap. I understood why radio programmers were so reluctant to add them to their commercial playlists.

A great single, a killer pop record – which is what a musician and producer are invariably trying to create, even if they position it as underground or alternative – almost always needs to be carefully nurtured and slowly matured, sometimes over a long period. Phil Spector, Brian Wilson and Berry Gordy, the three greatest pop magicians of the 1960s, understood this. So did John Lennon and Paul McCartney, who, to quote Oasis's Noel Gallagher, wrote the book the rest of us are just photocopying. Rare is the pop masterpiece or anthem, be it indie, alternative, hip-hop or mainstream, that is written quickly and knocked off in limited studio time, despite myths to the contrary. Woody Guthrie famously took a year to write 'This Land Is Your Land', a song that sounds like something he strummed and casually penned in a moment of easy inspiration.

Alan not only understood this completely, he had a facility that allowed him to slowly develop and record a song. A good example was Sisters Underground's 'In The Neighbourhood', which Alan painstakingly moulded into the version that was eventually released to the world. It's doubtful any of the bands who appeared on *Proud* understood how much work went into the record after they'd done their bit, or how much loving joy Alan took in their song's evolution.

One day over coffee I told Alan that, of all the acts he had recorded, the one I'd be most keen to work with him on was Sisters Underground. Unfortunately, however, Sony in Australia had just offered them a deal I couldn't match. I was also concerned the two singers were too young.

I now told him I wanted the first option on anything he did with Pauly Fuemana. I had heard Pauly only briefly on 'We R The OMC' but I was excited about the direction Alan was taking with such artists. He agreed and we shook hands. Shortly afterwards I gave him five thousand dollars to fund demo recordings with Pauly.

Meanwhile, there was still the problem of what to do with Nathan Haines' album. Recorded at Revolver Studios by Steve Garden, it was very good in itself but a little less concise and contemporary than we had hoped, mostly due to the small budget and the severe recording limitations – the studio had not been finished when we recorded the album. Nathan was one of the most talented musicians I knew and a gifted composer. I was aware that if we released his album the way it was we would garner a few good reviews and reasonable local sales, but the chance of it being picked up internationally by a label such as Talking Loud was about nil.

I suggested to Victor that we get Alan and James Pinker, who was now working with Alan at Uptown and had a thoroughly contemporary ear, to rework the project, taking the tapes and remixing them, adding what might be needed, mostly a loop or two, and generally tightening them. Just as importantly, we needed them to work up a single from the album. This would be a vital promotional tool to release to radio stations and, with a video, to television.

After I finished my lengthy spiel, Victor said he had no idea who Alan and James were. 'What about the guy who produced this record?' he said. He put *Proud* on the car stereo and turned up the volume. I rang Alan and made a time to take Victor to Uptown.

Lack of money remained a barrier. We had completely blown our recording budget on the studio without thinking about artwork or any of the other expenses we would incur getting the project to market. On top of this, at least another ten to fifteen thousand dollars would be needed to fully rework and remodel the album and produce a single.

My philosophy was that you spent the money and then worked out where it would come from. In my experience, record companies usually came grumbling to the party. This time was no different. Victor rang PolyGram's Australasian head office in Sydney and spoke to Sue Cohen, the director of legal and business affairs. An enormously practical and hard-nosed lawyer, Sue had a solution. PolyGram would fund the balance of the required budget but would, in return, ask me to assign the Nathan Haines contract to them. In effect, we would jointly own the album and any subsequent ones.

I was uneasy about this transfer of the rights but was stuck very much between the proverbial rock and hard place. I discussed the matter with Nathan's new manager Campbell Smith, who also happened to be my lawyer.[6] We went back and forth with PolyGram until we worked out a deal that allowed us to maintain some semblance of control over the use of the recordings. They picked up the option on Nathan's album and agreed to fund the Uptown reworking. We limited the amount that could be charged to Nathan's recoupment account[7] and obliged PolyGram to release the album outside New Zealand. If it failed to do so the international rights, territory by territory, would revert to my label, Huh!.

The deal extended beyond the Nathan Haines project to a full-blown joint venture in which I would effectively become an A&R manager under contract to PolyGram. I would offer the company the first option on any act I found. If it declined, I could take the act elsewhere. The releases PolyGram picked up would go out internationally, via the Polydor wing of the company, under the Huh! label with global branding. I would have full say over any and all uses, marketing and presentation of the records. It was almost exactly the sort of arrangement Gilles Peterson and his Talking Loud imprint had with PolyGram. I signed the deal in mid December.

After talking through the proposal to rework Nathan's album with Alan and James, I took Victor Stent to Uptown Studios to meet them and work out the details. Our simple brief was to add an 'edge' to the recordings and work up a single. I then discussed the idea with Nathan and Campbell. Nathan agreed, but then went to Uptown, burst into tears and pleaded with an astonished Alan to 'save' his record. Whatever doubts he may have had at that stage, he would work enthusiastically with Alan and James to mould the unfinished Revolver recordings into the extraordinary album they became.

Pauly Fuemana appeared on one of the album's tracks. In a song called 'Twelve' he several times whispered, 'Please tell me the time' and 'Twelve times an hour I glanced upon her face.' It would be his first released recording outside those of the Fuemana family.

---

6 New Zealand's music industry handles massive conflicts of interest better than just about anywhere else I've worked, and without blinking.

7 A recoupment account is the money an artist owes a label for recording and other costs. It is deducted from royalties paid to the artist.

The track on the Haines album that received the most intense reworking was the chosen single, 'Lady J'. To give this instrumental piece the effect it had when played live Nathan wanted to add a rap.

Alan suggested Pauly try out for the vocal. I wasn't present when the recording took place, but next morning Nathan turned up in my office fuming. Pauly, he said, sounded 'like a mumbling idiot'. Contractually, Nathan had a right of veto and he demanded Pauly's vocals be removed. Having implicit trust in Alan's instincts I wasn't happy but Alan reluctantly agreed. An alternative vocal by a rapper called Sani Sagala was left in. I had to agree that this fitted the song perfectly; it stayed on both the single and the video. In all the confusion I never heard Pauly's version although Alan spoke highly of it and it still lives somewhere in the Uptown archives.

Shift Left, as Nathan's album was named, remains the biggest selling New Zealand-recorded jazz album of all time.

6

ACROSS THE TASMAN, *Proud* had gone pretty well. It may not have been flying off the shelves, Australia being then a notoriously difficult country in which to sell music that wasn't white-skinned, but the critics loved it. That, plus Andrew Penhallow's strong connections and the airplay the key songs were getting on alternative radio, meant Andrew was able to secure a place in the Big Day Out's dance tent the Boiler Room for both Otara Millionaires Club and Sisters Underground. Sony had not only made moves towards signing Sisters Underground directly for an Alan Jansson-produced album, it had advanced substantial tour support and helped arrange club showcases in several Australian cities.

The Big Day Out was a touring live music festival and the pre-eminent rock 'n' roll show in Australasia. Its stages made or broke acts, and places were highly sought after. For Alan, this meant putting a group with Pauly, and an OMC live band was duly strapped together. Ned Roy, a former New Zealand champion DJ, was hired. Sina Saipaia, a young but seasoned South Auckland singer with close links to the Fuemana family, was signed as OMC's other vocalist. Six years earlier, Sina had been a featured vocalist in Sistermatic, a band I had recorded; its 1989 single 'Million Dollar' had been the last new record to appear on my Propeller label.

On January 20, 1995, the eve of the Big Day Out tour, Pauly gave his first major newspaper interview. 'We'll do things with an acoustic hip-hop feel, a real New Zealand feel I think, nothing like the gang vibe,' he told Graham Reid of *The New Zealand Herald*. 'I grew up in that and that's not where it's at. There's a new vibe and that's what I want to get into. And if it doesn't happen by the end of the year, then at least I'd be able to say I gave it a good go and had a good time.'

I didn't see the first OMC performance, which was in Auckland's Mount Smart Stadium, but by all reports it was a mess. The Boiler Room was steaming hot. Pauly appeared in a winter suit and was almost unable to move. According to a disappointed Alan Jansson, the place quickly cleared out.

OMC improved on the Australian part of the tour, but Alan quickly realised it was essentially a studio act and that an ongoing live show was less than desirable. He had his hands full keeping members of the touring party not only in one place but in one mindset as various hangers-on wandered off into places such as Kings Cross in Sydney to score all sorts of things that would have put the band and Pauly's career into a nosedive if they had been caught. Given the commitment, time and money Alan was putting into *Proud* and OMC, he was justifiably furious when a member of the touring party disappeared for two days.

In Melbourne, Alan encountered for the first time the temper explosions that would come to plague Pauly Fuemana's career. James Pinker, who was on the tour playing percussion for Sisters Underground, and Andrew Penhallow were sitting on a sofa in the hotel lounge. Andrew had his arm stretched across the back of the sofa behind James. Spotting the pair, Pauly announced that not only was Andrew gay but he was doing a deal with James that would cut Alan out of the picture. Alan assured him there was nothing to worry about, and furthermore he strongly doubted the firmly heterosexual buddies were having a fling.

Pauly later confronted James in the room they were sharing. Andrew would overhear him violently threatening, assaulting and abusing James. When Alan confronted him about this, Pauly claimed he was just watching

Alan's back and nervously asked if he was trying to cut him out.

The upshot of Pauly's irrational and scary behaviour was Alan deciding his days touring with bands were over. He told Pauly that if he wanted to play live he was on his own – although, having seen him on stage, he didn't recommend it. Live performance was not, he said, what OMC was about and not beneficial to the project.

Pauly agreed without argument. It was an agreement he would not remember a year or two later.

In Australia Clinton Walker, a friend of Andrew Penhallow, was mesmerised by Pauly. He watched OMC and through all the chaos and disarray believed he saw something special. One of the country's most respected and widely published music writers, Walker wrote in the local edition of *Rolling Stone* magazine: 'Fuemana is an absolute natural, a man who sings and moves with the sharp easy grace of a young Marvin Gaye.'

This comment engendered a buzz that went around New Zealand's music industry like a tornado. Alan Jansson was apparently working with potentially the hottest act in the country. Even the craggy rockers who had been dismissive of the *Proud* album and its various singles were less able to dismiss the view of one of Australia's foremost rock music writers, and the phrase about Marvin Gaye quickly found its way into New Zealand's mainstream media.

It's hard for New Zealanders today to understand a time when the country's musical acts meant little beyond our shores. There were a bunch of acts that did fairly well in Australia in the 1960s, and Dragon, Split Enz and Mi-Sex made a big noise there in the 1970s and '80s. These were rock acts. None of the country's Polynesian or Māori artists bothered the foreign charts at all, and hadn't since the late 1960s when John Rowles had had two hits in Britain, both recorded there.

In the late 1980s the situation had worsened as major record companies pulled back from investing in local music. The quality of many of the albums and singles released by major labels fell, and innovative recording was increasingly pushed into the hands of a few brave indies such as

Flying Nun and Pagan. It was these companies that took the substantial financial risk of trying to get a record into stores offshore.

In 1987, the singer Dave Dobbyn and Polynesian band Herbs had topped the Australian charts with a catchy single, 'Slice Of Heaven'. The theme from a hugely successful animated movie, the record was seen as a novelty and it's doubtful many in Australia even picked Herbs as New Zealanders or Polynesians.

Split Enz and Crowded House had done well in many international territories but these bands were solidly Australian-based and produced and had little to do with the New Zealand music industry.

This time it was different. A couple of young Polynesian women from the 'hood were charting in Australia, and the authoritative *Rolling Stone* was touting the key member of a band on an urban compilation from South Auckland that refused to compromise the local sound.

The night before Alan and Pauly had headed off to the first *Big Day Out* gig in Auckland they had sat together in Uptown Studios, guitars and pens in hand, developing themes and writing songs that would become the core of the new act. Years later, both would recall writing eight songs in just four hours.

One of these songs, 'Doof It Up', referenced New Zealand street slang: the term meant having a bit of a scrap or tussle, working things out but not in an overly aggressive or violent way. By the time the band was halfway through its Australian itinerary, the song had entered its set, although it did not yet have the trademark hooks that would come to define it.

Back in New Zealand this song became a focus of Pauly and Alan's writing. The name 'Doof It Up' quickly evolved into 'Big Top' and circus references appeared. Using the five thousand dollars I'd given him, Alan began recording and gave me an early cassette of the song.

In early 1995 Alan and I applied to New Zealand On Air, the government funding agency, for a grant to produce a video of 'Big Top'. We supported the application with a cassette of the song's working version. Grants by the agency were approved by a panel supervised by its head of music, Brendan Smyth, in Wellington, every few months. Alan was a golden boy of the newish New Zealand on Air video scheme as two of his productions – Sisters Underground's 'In The Neighbourhood' and Nathan Haines' 'Lady J' – had been the first and second most played local videos on New Zealand television the previous year, and so approval for 'Big Top' came fairly easily.

Alan and I had agreed in principle that the track that resulted from the OMC project would go out on my label, but I had not yet informed Victor or anyone else at PolyGram of this. It seemed too early to have a major record company messing with such a project. Their job was to market not create, and we were still in genesis mode. When New Zealand On Air's funding list was published in March, nobody at PolyGram seemed to notice a grant given to Huh! Records for an unknown act.

Over the next few weeks 'Big Top' became 'How Bizarre'. The phrase was suggested by Pauly, who would say it had been partly inspired by Alan's wife Bernie, who frequently used it, and by Alan's earlier offhand comment that the line 'Doof It Up' was just 'too bizarre' to use.

The next part to evolve was the chorus. For some time it had been 'Every time I turn around you're not there' but Alan, who had lifted the melody from one of his earlier unrecorded works, changed it to 'Every time I look around it's in my face', which was not only more positive but made more sense in terms of the song's lyrical flow.

The composition was now complete. The recording and final arrangements that developed next across the autumn of 1995 were in every sense a joint effort. Pauly was fascinated by Latin rhythms and suggested using mariachi horns. Inspired by Herb Alpert's '60s records, the horns were arranged by Alan. The infectious guitar was inspired by nothing in particular, although it clearly drew something from the classic street anthem 'Spanish Stroll', written and recorded by New Yorker Willie DeVille with his band Mink DeVille in 1977 – which, in turn, had drawn from the iconic 'Spanish Harlem' penned by Phil Spector and Jerry Leiber for Ben E. King in 1961. However, it was far enough away from both of them to be as original as you can hope for with the few notes writers have at their disposal – or at least so we hoped.

As Alan explained the song to me, it was essentially a melding of everything he and Pauly had grown up with as kids, listening to commercial radio stations that were not, as now, hemmed in by narrow formats but happily played every song that found its way on to the pop charts. As a kid myself, I had listened to Auckland's most popular and arguably switched-on station Radio Hauraki, which in one show would play songs by artists as joyfully diverse as Queen, Kraftwerk, Split Enz, Bob Marley, Stevie Wonder and Wings. Until this revolution of the early '70s, New Zealand had not had youth-targeted commercial pop or rock radio. The advent of such an exceptional range of music on the airwaves meant a generation grew up with numerous sounds mashed together in their heads and were influenced across genres. This brief – it was gone by 1990 – cross-pollination of styles and genres on urban New Zealand radio eventually found a voice and it was called 'How Bizarre'.

Recordings of 'How Bizarre' matured across several iterations, with Alan growing increasingly protective: each cassette I was given was on a for-your-ears-only basis.

The opening and very important guitar hook was added in the middle of 1995 and was played by Alan's friend Lee Baker, a film-maker, under Alan's very precise instructions.

Sina Saipaia, who appeared in the revised lyrics as Sister Sina, sang the backing vocals and was the dominant voice in the chorus's duet. This had proved necessary. Pauly had a brilliant and distinctive, almost nasal, rapping style, and he could talk-sing in an infectious and quite charming way, but his singing voice was not strong enough to stand on its own. In truth, he was never able to sing a lyric in tune. His vocals needed to be carefully placed in the mix to hide their weakness: they were flat unless almost spoken or mixed in with another, stronger voice.

This would remain a serious and vexing problem, which Alan had to repeatedly battle and overcome in the recording and mixing process.

44

For some songs on the album he quietly brought in a session vocalist, whose vocals were mixed into Pauly's to bring them back into pitch. Pauly didn't know and the vocalist was uncredited and sworn to secrecy.

Pauly's overwhelming urge was not to be a rapper. Once he had made the jump from Otara Millionaires Club to OMC, he didn't want to ever see himself as a hip-hop artist again. The clash over his vocals that began as a niggle would grow to become an increasingly major division between Alan and Pauly. As 1995 turned into 1996 Pauly's determination to be seen as a singer rather than a rapper caused problems in the studio that would never really be resolved.

Understandably, Pauly's overwhelming musical urge was to be respected. He decided the way to achieve this was to be recognised as a vocalist, a more than proficient musician, and a studio whizz. Unfortunately he was none of those things, and his failure to deal with this and work within the confines of his substantial talents proved to be a barrier that dogged him. The truth, obvious to all who were close to him musically, was that he was a collaborator, and a superb one.

To finish the single, Alan employed Herschel Herscher, a versatile New York musician who had moved to New Zealand ten years earlier, to play the accordion, and another immigrant, British jazzman George Chisholm, to play the mariachi trumpet line.

In late June he phoned and excitedly asked me to come into the studio. 'I've got something I need to play you,' he buzzed.

'When?'

'Now.'

It was obvious from his animated tone that something big was up. I quickly headed to Uptown.

I have a passion for listening to newly recorded and/or mixed music. I love hanging around recording studios, and have always especially loved the previewing ritual at Uptown. It usually goes like this: you arrive and are given a cup of the best industrial strength coffee you'll find anywhere in New Zealand, and then you talk. I've lost track of the thousands of hours I've sat in Uptown, either at the table downstairs in the old kitchen or in the lounge area outside the recording suite, simply talking to Alan and whomever else he invites in. Sometimes the conversation is short, but other times it can stretch into another coffee and beyond, into the night.

Alan and I, from habit, gossip, praise and bitch about people in the music industry, chatter about movies, songs and mixes, both ours and others, and toss around the odd in-joke. We often spend a moment or two pulling apart random pop clips on the video channels that are always playing on the huge screen TV in the lounge area, analysing the structure of the ones we rate highly.

If you have come to hear something newly recorded or mixed, you are now ushered into the inner sanctum, the studio's booth. Alan asks which speakers you would like. The choice ranges from the huge ear-thumping high-end studio variety that hurl displaced air almost painfully across the room to tinny little baby speakers that blur the audio definition so as to replicate cheap stereos or car radios.

I almost always pick the big ones. And I know from years of experience my best position in the room, the one that allows me to gather the most perfect balance of sounds from these big speakers. I follow that with a second run-through on the smaller JBL studio monitors and, if I hear potential, the mono TV speaker. The combination allows me to work out exactly how people at home or in a car would hear the mix. At times, if the mix is close to finished, it's taken into the outside room and played on the resident ghetto blaster.

I've also spent countless hours simply sitting in the booth listening to takes or mixes, sub-mixes of elements, or remixes. I get a buzz from the process of working up a sound over several hours, and sometimes through the night when the best mixes are almost always done, often to toss it away as unacceptable at the end of the session.

That afternoon we followed the usual coffee ritual, but Alan was keyed up and far more excited than I had ever seen him before. He rushed me, still with the cup of strong coffee from his Faema espresso machine in my hand, into his control booth.

The booth at Uptown is an extraordinary and unique piece of audio engineering and construction. Built to float independently of the building and designed by New Zealand acoustic scientists operating out of a government-funded lab, it is visually gorgeous. Its electric-blue downward light beams reflect off – and soften – the banks of red and green lights that glimmer, sparkle and pulsate up from the wide mixing desk to the stacks of complex effects units banked around walls in racks shaped and placed so as not to disrupt the important sound flows.

Depending on where you are in the room, that sound is remarkably flexible. As you move around the focus on the elements that make up the overall audio mix changes, sometimes subtly, sometimes dramatically. This lets you hear the recorded audio and its various elements in a range of ways.

Alan likes to sit clients two-thirds of the way towards the centre rear of the room. It's here they are likely to find the most warmth and roundness in the mix, and where the music layers its elements in the way you would be most likely to hear on a very high quality car or home audio system – the sort of playback most paying clients will be used to.

I've always preferred a place closer to the centre front, just behind where the producer or engineer hears the output. The sound here is clean and absolutely immediate, with each element beautifully defined and finding its own special space in the air. It's the place where, like the engineer or producer, you can best work out precisely what the sound is doing and what may or may not need to be removed, mixed back, or further worked on, where you can isolate the niggling mistakes, and where – and this is the bit I like – the subsonic bottom end really seems to kick in.

Alan, meanwhile, sits on a large, ergonomically designed chair with silent wheels that allow him to move quickly around the room to judge a mix or a recording in progress.

As always, Alan asked, 'Which speakers?'

'The biggies please – at least for the first run-through,' I said, as always. Alan looked at me, grinned and held up both hands. Two sets of fingers were crossed. And then he hit play. 'How Bizarre', in a version that was pretty much as the world would hear it several months later, came out of the speakers. Alan looked at me and his smile grew.

I asked to hear it on the smaller speakers. Then I asked for a run-through on the TV speaker, in glorious shitty mono. Finally, we took it to the room outside and did the crucial off-cassette, ghetto-blaster check.

Alan assures me I beamed and shook his hand, saying repeatedly, 'It's huge, it's huge.' But if I'm honest I have no memory of saying anything at all, especially nothing that predicted global success. I did know, though, that he had a huge record on his hands. Or, to be more accurate, we had a huge record on our hands.

The five thousand dollars had been well spent.

Alan was immensely proud of what he and Pauly had created. He kept asking me if it needed anything. Should the vocal come up? Or was it too loud? Would more brass be good? These questions would continue right up to the song's release. My answer was always the same: 'Don't touch it.'

I could claim in hindsight that I knew 'How Bizarre' would be an international hit. Such a claim would be simultaneously true and untrue. Did I think the record would be big in New Zealand, and even in Australia? I can honestly say I did: I was telling people this within a few hours of hearing this mix. However, I had absolutely no idea how it would fare beyond this. While Alan was convinced from the outset that the record would be a worldwide smash – it was the record he had talked repeatedly about making all these years – I was more cautious. Worldwide smashes just didn't happen out of distant New Zealand.

At the same time 'How Bizarre' clearly had the elements needed to stand a chance. It was beautifully crafted, full of hooks, perfectly produced, and had a charismatic front man. And perhaps the most crucial factor of all: it was, as far as I knew, nothing like anything that had come from anywhere else.

7

PAULY FUEMANA HAS OFTEN BEEN GIVEN PROPS for opening the door for New Zealand, and in particular South Auckland, hip hop, but strictly speaking his brother Philip and Alan Jansson deserve much of the credit as the originators of *Proud*, and Tim Mahon, as the person who convinced Manukau City Council to support it.

Pauly opened different doors. He had no desire to be a rapper and none of OMC's records after 'We R The OMC' were rap records, although a kind of hip-hop sensibility ran through some of the tracks on the *How Bizarre* album, and in his early interview with *The New Zealand Herald* he said he saw the records he was creating with Alan as a kind of acoustic hip hop.

It's a slender claim though. Unlike much of what came out of South Auckland at the time, 'How Bizarre' was never a try-hard Tupac Shakur or N.W.A. Nor was it a soul record. It did have huge soul and warmth but this drew from the islands of the South Pacific, from the immigrant boats of the 1950s and '60s, from South Auckland and Wellington Central, not from South Central LA.

'How Bizarre' was a pop record. It pulled together Pauly's and Alan's lifetime of listening and absorbing influences and coupled this with a refusal to bow to trends. It was influenced by the pop radio and island rhythms and songs Pauly had heard as a kid and the punky stuff Alan had played in his late teen years – and yet, happily, it wasn't really any of these. The first time you heard the record on the radio, you asked yourself, 'What exactly was that?' It got under your skin, inside your head, and you wanted to hear it again and again, as did radio stations the world over.

After Alan and I had heard about a dozen playbacks on various speakers and machines, Pauly walked into the lounge. He had been downstairs waiting while I listened, and Alan had now signalled for him to come in.

He beamed a huge smile, tinged with a little nervousness.

'What do you think, bro?' he said.

'It's a hit, a big one,' I gushed.

He quizzed me again and again. 'Are you sure? You're not just saying that?'

Neither he nor Alan really needed any confirmation. They both knew they had produced a potentially chart-damaging hit record. We just needed to work out how to make other people hear it. That was my job.

As was the tradition when we had a successful mix, Alan pulled out a bottle of something and we toasted the record – several times, until we were somewhat inebriated.

When I left I took away a cassette, with firm instructions from Alan not to play it to a living soul.

I almost managed to keep my word, but couldn't resist playing the recording in my office the next morning. A few people wandered in and out, with mixed reactions. I didn't tell anyone who the artist and producer were but Tom, my business partner, quickly worked it out. After a lukewarm response, he listened a couple of times, announced he loved it, and began to play it over and over. We had our first fan.

Our office assistant, Lisa, was also initially less than enthusiastic. A determined follower of musical fashion, she asked cynically, 'What's that supposed to be?' Over the next few days, as Tom and I played it repeatedly, she warmed to it.

After an hour I phoned Victor and told him he needed to come to Uptown and hear this new track. We agreed on four o'clock. When he arrived, Alan and I, without saying much, took him into the control room and played him the near-final mix.

While Victor had loved what Alan had done with Nathan Haines' record and the *Proud* compilation, he had been unconvinced when I'd mentioned I was thinking of signing a young guy, Pauly Fuemana, with whom Alan was writing and recording songs. I think he saw my label as stylistically more inclined towards acid jazz, following on from where Nathan had taken us.

PolyGram had the right to turn down anything from me they didn't like. However, if they did so they ran the risk of some other company having a hit with the record. The Dick Rowe effect is always factored into such decisions in the industry, even if only subconsciously.[8]

Victor asked to hear the track again. Then, with a perplexed look, he said, 'I really don't hear a hit.'

Alan and I looked at each other; we felt as if we had been slapped.

I insisted Victor listen again. After one more run-through he shrugged. 'It's okay, but I really can't hear anything special. But,' he said, looking at me, 'if you believe in it, I'm happy to release it.'

I walked Victor to his car, happy that at least we had a guaranteed domestic release, and knowing that Polydor in Australia, where the key ears belonged to my friends Adam Holt and Mark Phillips, who had moved to Sydney to take up a promotions job in the company, would have the option to pick up the record. On the way, Victor told me he would rather I cast my net a little further than South Auckland – towards album artists we could sell offshore.

Back at the studio I told Alan that, in light of Victor's tepid reception, our best option was to try and get PolyGram in Australia as enthused about the record as we could, and use that as a lever to get New Zealand happening.

---

8 Dick Rowe was the A&R man at Decca who famously turned down The Beatles.

It had always been my intention that once I had something I felt we could fly with – a record with the potential to go further – I would take it to Australia first. At the back of my mind was the industry truism that the music world takes some notice of what happens in the Australian charts but doesn't care, or even register, anything that happens in New Zealand. You could sit at number one for weeks in New Zealand but nobody beyond its shores would notice, aside from perhaps a one-liner in the international columns of *Billboard*, the weekly US industry bible. Few people read these columns, which tell any interested reader what's big that month in Iceland and Chile.

I rang Roger Grierson, my music publishing partner at PolyGram Music in Sydney, and carefully explained it might be to his advantage if his office flew both Alan and me over to play him his next big hit as soon as possible. I relayed a verse and a chorus down the phone and Roger, without any other comment, said he'd call back shortly.

He did so an hour later. He could justify the trip if we first flew to Melbourne to see an act he was working with, which he would like Alan to consider producing, and perhaps co-writing with. We would then fly on to Sydney, although I would need to cover the cost of this internal flight. That way the accountants would be happy.

After I agreed, he said he would authorise the New Zealand office to buy the tickets into Melbourne and out of Sydney and charge them back to his office.

8

ROGER GRIERSON IS A FASCINATING but complicated guy. A legend in the Australian music industry, he was born in the town of Nelson, population 46,000, at the top of New Zealand's South Island. In the 1970s he moved to the UK and then to Australia, where he played a pivotal role in the indie and post-punk music scenes as a member of the legendary band The Thought Criminals and part-owner of an influential independent label, Green Records. He toured many New Zealand acts through Australia in the 1980s and later managed Nick Cave and The Bad Seeds, among other bands.

In 1995 he had taken the corporate dollar and now ran the music publishing arm of PolyGram, perhaps its most lucrative operation in Australia. Here he had not only signed many of the acts he had worked with over the earlier independent years, but also a range of quite adventurous young groups, including New Zealand alt-rockers Shihad.

Music publishing tends to be a confusing business, even to some in the music industry. Essentially it is the arm of the industry that revolves around and earns money from the compositions – the written songs – rather than from the people who perform them. These people may or may not be one and the same.

Song publishing is a far older part of the music industry than the recording branch – it began in the early 19th century – but record companies and publishers often share ownership and are closely interrelated, working tightly together in a co-dependent way.

Publishing earns from a quite different and distinct copyright to that created by an artist's performance in a recording. Every time a record is played on a radio station, featured in a movie or an advertisement, or used commercially in any other way, and every time a recording of a composed song is purchased, the song's writer gets paid, regardless of whether he or she is performing the song. The chances are that the work is 'published' – that is, controlled by a music publisher who administers the song and pays a royalty to the writer, who will have licensed the work to the publisher. This is a similar process to book publishing, where an author normally gets a royalty for every copy of his or her book the publisher sells.

In earlier times a song publisher would buy the copyright outright from the writer and own it for the legal duration of the copyright. However, since the 1970s music publishers have mostly leased the rights under what is called an assignment. Depending on the contract – and these vary greatly – the lease will eventually expire and the assigned work revert to the writer.

Publishing is the industry's key money-spinner as it is mostly easy, passive income with no recording costs, tour support, or other expenditure upfront. The overwhelming bulk of the net funds earned by Pauly Fuemana and Alan Jansson from 'How Bizarre' would come from their publishing copyrights.

After forming my publishing imprint and signing up Alan and others, I had entered into a partnership with PolyGram Music Publishing whereby it would collect and administer royalties on our behalf. As part of the company's contractual obligations to me, it would also actively chase opportunities worldwide and pursue monies due through its global networks. I could have reasonably published the songs assigned to my company myself, but I would never have been able to pursue the sorts of deals a multimedia company such as PolyGram could offer us as a result of its international web of companies and other partnerships.

Despite his New Zealand roots, Roger Grierson was that very uniquely Australian thing, an Oz Rocker. The breed tends to be brash, even for a country like Australia, and loud. They wear tight black jeans and cowboy boots. And they really don't get things musical that are not rock 'n' roll.

Looking back, I don't think Roger ever quite got OMC or Alan. I don't think he quite got me either. But he did get hits. That was his job and he was very good at it. Stocky, opinionated and at times wildly funny, Roger was proactive. And he strongly smelled a hit involving Alan Jansson and this new song Alan had written with Pauly Fuemana.

A few days later a PolyGram-billed corporate cab collected Alan and me at four in the morning and we drowsily headed off to the airport for our flight to Melbourne. Shortly after arriving at Tullamarine Airport, we picked up a rental car and headed into the city. This would turn out to be the first of 38 business trips I would make to Australia between 1995 and 2000. Most would be on OMC matters and the routine would become mundane. This first time, though, Alan and I were exhilarated, if jittery. We had a hit record in our hands and we knew it but Victor's response had induced a few nagging doubts.

As he drove along the toll road into the city and I tried to work out the location of our hotel on the map, Alan pushed the cassette of 'How Bizarre' into the car audio and played it, rewinding and playing it again and again. I looked at him and said, 'This is either going to be the biggest record we are ever likely to work on or we're both completely mad.' We knew we weren't mad.

Going around in circles we finally found the hotel near the inner-city suburb of St Kilda. The rest of the day was spent talking about the record and the coming meeting in Sydney. After dinner we went to see what we were supposed to be in Melbourne to see: Vika and Linda, a sisters' duo, at The Continental in Yarra. The young women's mother was Tongan and somebody, perhaps the duo themselves, had decided a back-to-the-roots album might have some potential, and who better to produce it than the man who gave the world *Proud*?

As far as Alan and I were concerned, the pair were atrocious, peddling a middling, mostly faceless Oz rock that seemed oblivious to the passage of musical styles. However, the almost full house seemed to love it.

Standing next to us was Mark Seymour, the leader of the once hip '80s Australian alt rock band Hunters & Collectors and brother of Crowded House's Nick Seymour, who was lounging at the bar. Mark seemed fairly drunk. He swayed in his rock 'n' roll biker's jacket and loudly roared out fanboy stuff. 'It's a hit… beautiful… go girls… Oh yes, what a song! More, babes, more.'

Nick Seymour, drink in hand, wandered across. As Vika and Linda launched into another nondescript tune Mark headed to the bar while Nick wailed, 'Mark, Mark, yer missin' it. Rock on girls, rock on.'

As the evening dragged on the band seemed to announce every second song with, 'Here's another one written by Paul Kelly.' Endless tributes to the highly regarded and hugely talented South Australian songsmith followed. The crowd clapped appreciatively. Not content with this, at a volume way above the PA one of the Seymour brothers yelled back, 'Fuckin' beautiful, girls, just fuckin' beautiful.'

The drunken raptures of the rock 'n' roll icons were starting to get on our nerves. We contemplated leaving but felt obligated to stay. When the gig finally finished we introduced ourselves to the sisters. We quickly worked out they were as uninterested in us as we were in them. Later, I left CDs of *Proud* and Nathan's album at our hotel reception for Vika and Linda's manager to collect. When we returned to the hotel a year later they were still there.

Next morning we flew to Sydney. Mark Phillips was waiting at the airport and drove us straight to PolyGram's premises in a barren industrial estate off South Dowling Street, which the company was occupying temporarily while waiting for work to finish on its new purpose-built downtown offices.

We were ushered into the Polydor suite, where Adam Holt greeted us like long-lost friends. The room had a positive vibe. Without much in the way of niceties, I asked Alan to bang on the cassette. I wanted to let the music speak for itself before we moved on to the complex part: selling it to the Australian office. I was fairly confident the song had the legs to stand on its own and didn't need the pitch from me that a lesser record might.

Despite this I was shaky as hell. If Alan was as well it wasn't showing.

About a minute into the song, the Polydor boss Paul Dickson ran into the room and, grinning broadly, inquired what we were playing. His next words were direct: 'That's fucking huge!'

Adam nodded in agreement and before the record had played all the way through he looked at us and rather courageously said, 'I promise you a Top Five Australian hit with this, if not number one.'

That Adam Holt, a fellow New Zealander and an increasingly important player in PolyGram Australia, was prepared to offer such a commitment really meant something. There would be other pivotal moments in the rise of 'How Bizarre', but those few words from a man I trusted and who had clout in the company took the record up a notch. It would now be a priority release in Australia, and thus also in New Zealand.

Adam – who in 2001 would become managing director of the New Zealand operation of Universal Music, the successor to PolyGram – is that rare beast: a person in a position of power in the recording industry who not only loves music passionately and has good ears, but is honest to a fault. I was aware that if the record didn't have what it took to break through, Adam would unhesitatingly tell me despite our fifteen-year friendship.

I had first met Adam in 1980 when he was one of the swarm of kids from Auckland's sweeping new 'burbs on the North Shore who formed bands and trekked across the harbour bridge to fill the bars and clubs of central Auckland, providing a breath of fresh air after the punk explosion of the late 1970s had grown stale and then decayed into a morass of violence and ennui.

He was in a good but now forgotten power-pop act called The Ainsworths, which I recorded for my *Class Of 81* collection of new bands. The Ainsworths' career didn't go far beyond that track and a later single, but Adam was also part of the extended family that was another band, The Screaming Meemees, with whom I had some success in 1981 and '82. As the group's unofficial fifth member, he often played with it live. Afterwards he worked in music retail and in the early '90s moved into a job at PolyGram, where he rose quickly after his bosses saw his obvious potential.

Adam would be crucial to the success of 'How Bizarre'. We needed allies to make the project work and he and Mark fully understood what the record was and where it came from.

Paul Dickson also played a key role in PolyGram's pursuit of the song. He seemed to grasp the cultural mix and evolution of the single and later the album, or at least he worked hard to do so. A huge man, standing well over six feet, Paul was immensely intelligent, with a wide engaging smile and an even bigger presence. We were lucky to work with him; I would continue to enjoy doing so for years, even after the relationship with PolyGram and then Universal had ground to a halt and most of the people in this story had moved on.

'When can we have it?' Paul said anxiously. Before I could answer he was on the phone to Roger Grierson, enthusing about the hit-to-be. We were quickly ushered across to PolyGram's music publishing office, where Roger shook our hands and asked about Vika and Linda. Before I could work out a way to sidestep the question, Paul said, 'Roger, forget that. Listen to this' and pushed the tape into the office deck.

As the song played, Roger said, 'Not bad' and smiled. His first question was to ask Alan if he were the sole songwriter. When we explained the 50:50 split between Alan and Pauly, who was still an unknown to the Australians, Roger looked at me and said firmly, 'Get the rest of the song signed. And quickly.'

I felt as though I were floating and Alan seemed completely at a loss for words. We could not have asked for more.

After we returned to the Polydor offices, Paul asked if Victor Stent had heard the record yet, and if so what he thought of it.

'He says he can't hear a hit,' I said.

'He's mad. Tell him if he doesn't do it we'll do it without him,' Paul said.

With that he got on the phone to Auckland and raved about the record to the New Zealand boss who had not been able to hear its potential two days earlier – but now, given the enthusiasm coming down the phone line, agreed furiously as to its merits and massive chart prospects.

We had in one momentous hour nailed the record's release on both sides of the Tasman. Victor would have to get behind the record. He would look ridiculous if the drive to make 'How Bizarre' a hit came from his offshore head office and not from him.

Alan and I were ecstatic. We'd achieved what we had wanted to achieve and much more. The Australian connection was our potential ticket to the rest of the world and already put us a long way ahead of the rest of the New Zealand music industry. From that day onwards we thought only outwards.

If I had to name the single most important thing, the critical tipping point, that pushed 'How Bizarre' from a promising domestic release to an international hit record, I would have to point to this trip and the results and promises we managed to extract at Polydor that afternoon.

9

A HIT RECORD IS NOT JUST MADE in the recording studio: this is merely the first part of the song's passage from writer to public consciousness. In reality, success is at least 60 percent politics. Many a hit record wanders up the charts with a far higher percentage of industry politics in the mix than that. However, although you can go a long way on the right connections and playing the right game, the bottom line is that the product – the song and the recording – must shine. If it doesn't, sooner or later you will meet an immovable wall. We knew we had the recorded product to get past that wall, and now the politics were starting to fall into place.

The political game relies on advantage. A record stands a vastly better chance of being a hit if it offers a career lever to someone who has the keys to a door you need to open and offers a way to further their progress up the job ladder.

It is also vital that your record doesn't hurt their personal prospects by interfering with something to which they have already put their name: there are few pluses and some serious negatives for a record company's head office or offshore branch putting effort into breaking an act if the act threatens an artist the company has already put its neck on the block to sign and develop, often at great cost. This is the case around the world, and underscores why the soundalikes that New Zealand major labels love to groom rarely get international traction. It's unlikely Sony USA would want to spend time and money on a singer such as Sony New Zealand's Brooke Fraser when they have already signed a dozen other Brooke Frasers, hence Brooke Fraser needed to go via an independent US label.

I knew that for Polydor in Australia there was serious career leverage to be derived from 'How Bizarre'. Pauly sounded like nothing else in the world, and on top of that Polydor was in the middle of a major dry spot globally. It needed a hit urgently. And 'How Bizarre' was not an expensive project, not yet anyway.

Back in New Zealand, Victor appeared to have done a 180-degree spin on both the record and Pauly. Following Paul Dickson's call, he now not only loved the single without reservation, but was desperate to take full ownership and credit as fast as possible.

I was now faced with urgently resolving two matters with Pauly. He was still not signed to Huh! or PolyGram, and he and Alan had not formalised their profit-splitting agreement in writing. Sorting out both of these was imperative. I needed to move as quickly as I could without overstepping my ethical obligations to all parties.

Over dinner at Ponsonby's Prego Restaurant, Pauly, Alan and I discussed the profit split, and I explained how it would impact on their deal with PolyGram and Huh!. Alan and Pauly's verbal understanding had always been that everything would be split 50:50. This seemed clear until Pauly announced across the table that he saw a future that included touring. He would, he announced, sing and front the show. Alan would do the live sound and run the band.

'No,' Alan said firmly. 'There is no way I want to go with or take OMC on the road.'

He was emphatic. He was happy to create the music in the studio while Pauly fronted with the public, making videos and doing interviews. He didn't see a touring band as either a viable or necessary part of what they were creating.

He then offered Pauly a revised split. Since Pauly was to be the public face of the project he would be happy, once the album had covered its recording costs, including creating artwork and making videos of singles, to take 25 percent of the net income from record sales and other uses of the recording, leaving Pauly with 75 percent. If Pauly wanted to tour or to take a band on the road, the costs incurred would come from his 75 percent.

Meanwhile, all publishing income and songwriting credits would be split 50:50, rather than an attempt being made to sort out each person's contribution into each song. This made sense: arguments over who wrote what in a song have destroyed many a friendship and creative partnership.

Pauly agreed and he and Alan shook hands and hugged to seal the deal.

The next nut to crack was the recording contract. All parties agreed that Pauly would be the one to sign to Huh! and PolyGram, and that Alan and Pauly's freshly negotiated agreement would be attached to the document to make clear the division of monies between the two. Pauly agreed that, subject to the terms of agreement between the two of them, he would issue a letter to the record labels, instructing them to pay Alan his share of the income.

We then hit a roadblock. Pauly was adamant that he should get money upfront before he would sign anything – and not just a token amount but tens of thousands of dollars. This was clearly out of the question. After we had spent a little time on this sticking point, he said quite animatedly, 'You've got a BMW. If I'm part of this we have to be equal. I need a car like that.' Alan and I pointed out that what I drove was neither here nor there: the car had not been paid for with the proceeds of the as-yet-unreleased record.

I understood, of course, that Pauly needed money. For most of the year he had been living with his girlfriend, Kirstine Gee, in a council flat on Greys Avenue, on a low floor of a dreary 1970s block with a mishmash of neighbours. He had been on the dole for a while and had picked up the odd bit of work, but was being largely supported by Kirstine, who worked at a Marbecks record store in Queen Street.

I suggested that since Australia had been so enthused about the single and its possibilities, PolyGram might be willing to provide some sort of advance, perhaps payable weekly, although clearly they wouldn't consider that until he was a signed act.

This seemed to calm the situation and next day I asked Sue Cohen, PolyGram's Sydney-based business affairs lawyer, to fax over a contract. I forwarded this to Noel Agnew, who acted for both Pauly and Alan and was one of the few lawyers in New Zealand with music industry experience. Noel cheerily assured me he would go through it and get back to me in a couple of days. He was not known for processing paperwork with any sense of urgency but I felt fairly relaxed as I tried to progress our various ideas about a video and about how to visually present Pauly to the world.

During the week Pauly and I met with Noel, who had a series of questions and comments on the draft contract, mostly minor. He faxed them to Sue Cohen and with a dialogue underway we seemed to be moving in the right direction, targeting an end-of-year single release for a summer hit.

Two days later another bump appeared in the road. Pauly walked into my office and in an offhand way said we needed to talk straight away. We wandered across the street to Rosini's, a High Street café and hangout owned by Poi Niuloa, a fellow Niuean with whom Pauly liked to spend time, and his wife Frances. Over a coffee Pauly told me he had just come from a meeting with the A&R man at Warner Brothers New Zealand. The company had, he boasted, offered him a car of his choice and cash – lots of it, six figures – to sign a long-term contract.

Was it true? I had no doubt that Warners would be fairly keen to sign up a guy who had come back from Australia in February surrounded by a buzz, but the tiny New Zealand recording industry usually offered no advances or car incentives to unproven acts. And given that only Alan Jansson and I had copies of the rough cut of 'How Bizarre' the story sounded like a fantasy.

It rapidly grew to embrace two free vehicles and even more cash. I was pretty sure it was nonsense, but Pauly touting himself around, trying to start a bidding war between us and Warners, was annoying even though I had no doubt he would sign to us. He was nowhere without Alan Jansson, and Alan was completely committed to a Huh! deal.

I stepped outside the café into High Street, phoned Colin Brown, the financial controller at PolyGram's Mount Eden office, and told him I wanted two return tickets to Sydney leaving the next morning and returning on the last evening flight. I was happy to cover the cost if needed but I thought it best to put a contract, with the terms as negotiated by his lawyer, in front of Pauly within 24 hours. Next, I phoned a slightly incredulous Sue Cohen and told her Pauly and I would be in her office at eleven next morning.

I went back into the café and reiterated to Pauly that once he was signed to PolyGram a weekly cheque would come his way – something I had no authority to promise. Further, I would negotiate a publishing deal that gave him a big cash advance. Given Roger's strict instruction to get the other 50 percent of the writer's share of 'How Bizarre' signed with some urgency, I thought I might be able to pull this off.

The courier arrived at my front door later that evening with two tickets to Sydney, and at an ungodly hour the following morning I drove to Greys Avenue, picked up Pauly and headed to the airport. Pauly appeared increasingly eager to sign to PolyGram, the cars and megabucks from Warners having seemingly evaporated. On the way across the Tasman he told me he had spent some time in Sydney as a contract hitman for the mafia.

By eleven o'clock we were sitting in front of Sue Cohen with copies of phone-book-sized draft recording contracts in front of us. We rang Noel Agnew in Auckland, explained we were in Sydney, and asked if we could work out a few sticking points via phone conferencing. Pauly wandered out of the room and over the next 45 minutes Noel, Sue and I came up with a document we all felt we could live with.

Sue and Noel then faxed drafts back and forth, until around 1.30 Sydney time Sue was able to send a final copy to Auckland. Noel faxed it back with a written approval for Pauly to sign. He followed this with a long call to Pauly, explaining in detail what he was about to sign, what his obligations to PolyGram were, and what theirs and mine were to him.

At about two that afternoon – August 3, 1995 – Pauly Fuemana signed the recording deal in Paul Dickson's office. Pursuant to the arrangement with PolyGram, the contract was assigned to my label deal with PolyGram in a separate covering letter, which Paul Dickson and I then signed.

It was done. The pressure lifted. We had a drink, I called Alan, and a group of about six of us went out for what Alan would later, when told about it, describe as a 'reassuringly expensive' late lunch on Pauly's new record company.

The terms of that recording deal remain confidential, but suffice to say it provided for an album deliverable in early 1996 and included the standard options for PolyGram to record several more. An initial recording budget of NZ$35,000 was allocated to finishing the debut album. However – and this is something I've kept to myself until now – there was a hole in the assignments. According to the terms of the contract, Pauly was assigning the existing recording of 'How Bizarre' to PolyGram. However, as the recording had been commissioned and paid for by Uptown Studios Limited, he was assigning something he had no right to assign.

To add another complication, in 1994, before I signed anything with PolyGram, I had paid Alan to work up several tracks, as yet unwritten. One of those was 'How Bizarre'. Although I have searched the original documents and other related paperwork, I have yet to find an assignment of the original single to PolyGram. This has never been tested in court and probably never will be, but the advice I was given some years back was that PolyGram owns the OMC album except for the track 'How Bizarre'.

10

ON THE NATHAN HAINES FRONT, things were going awry. Nathan and his manager were at loggerheads with Victor Stent, who was trying to manipulate the direction of Nathan's artistic career. Victor wanted Nathan to trim down his band so we could feasibly offer it to Australia without breaking the bank on airfares and accommodation.

There was some logic in this. Polydor Australia was very keen on Nathan's record, especially after the company had signed Pauly, but it had cold feet over the cost of taking an estimated fourteen people across the Tasman. Nathan was, after all, essentially a live act and had no hit single with which to sell his album.

In early August 1995, Nathan, Victor and I had dinner at Kermadec, a pricey seafood restaurant overlooking the America's Cup moorings in Auckland's Viaduct Basin. Victor began by telling Nathan that his latest demo recordings, produced in London, were 'borderline crap'. Things went downhill from there. A few minutes later, although Victor had seen Nathan and his band play only once since the Gilles Peterson date, he told him his current live line-up wasn't cutting it. Nathan stood up, told the label boss to 'get fucked' and stormed out.

I could see both sides of the argument and felt caught in the middle.

Either way, though, I felt Victor's behaviour and the way he treated and talked to Nathan was completely out of order.

The following month Victor reacted badly to a plan by Nathan to play the Powerstation in Mt Eden Road with a group called Joint Force. The hip-hop flavour of the month in Auckland's inner-city indie scene, Joint Force consisted of Mark Williams, better known as Rhythm Slave, his long-time collaborator Otis Frizzell, and DJ Darryl Thomson, who went under the name DLT. Thomson had been a member of the legendary Wellington rap pioneers Upper Hutt Posse, and would later, with singer Che Fu, write 'Chains', a record that became one of the biggest local hits of the decade.

Joint Force had quite some drawing power in the alt hip-hop market so I thought playing with the group was a smart move on the part of Nathan's management, but Victor was dead against it. As he saw it, Joint Force was likely to attract a strongly Polynesian crowd, rather than the predominantly white, middle-class, acid jazz crowd he was targeting with Nathan's music. At an ugly meeting in his office, he told Nathan and his manager, Campbell Smith, he didn't want Nathan playing in front of a 'bunch of sooties'. Nathan and Campbell were aghast and appalled. Nathan once again stormed out. Victor then threatened to punch Campbell's head in.

The relationship between Victor and Nathan was now irreparably broken. Campbell Smith wrote a brutally honest letter to PolyGram, which he first sent to me and then decided to sit on as a document of record. Although Victor never received it, he and Nathan never communicated again.

We would release another record of Nathan's – the live *Soundkilla Sessions Vol. 1* – via PolyGram, but by the end of 1995 Huh! was more or less a one-act label. It was good the roster was sparse. The next twelve months were to be tumultuous, exhausting and insane, not just for Alan, Pauly and me but for many of those around us.

On the flight back from Sydney, Pauly said he wanted to talk video with me. Alan and I had many times discussed the video concept he and Pauly had worked up for 'How Bizarre'. Pauly had enthusiastically tossed in ideas and appeared to be a willing collaborator. As far as I knew, the concept was now fully developed and storyboarded. Lee Baker, a film-maker who had played guitar on the recording of 'How Bizarre', had told Alan he would be happy to direct the clip for a token fee. I knew very little about Lee but I thought the overall concept, especially the pivotal long car shots with a red Chevy convertible that Alan had already lined up, sounded good. As far as I was concerned it was a done deal.

Pauly leaned across and whispered, 'I don't like the video, bro, and I want you to say something to Alan. I want to go with something else. I need you to watch my back on this one and sort it out.'

Pauly had a habit of tossing in unexpected and often dramatic things like this from left field. I would come to see that they were designed to challenge you, to work out whose side you were really on and, even more crucially, to cause divisions among people around him. At this stage, though, I was still figuring this out. Tired and at 30,000 feet over the Tasman Sea, I was thrown by his unexpected attack on the video idea.

Over the next two hours he repeated his objections, growing ever more strident in his demand that I quickly 'sort Alan out'. His eyes flared, a warning sign I would come to know well. By the time I dropped him back at his flat at around one in the morning, he was shaking with anger, demanding I 'sort it' and 'watch his back'.

Across town in my bedroom in Parnell I lay awake all night. In the morning I rang Alan and asked if I could come over. When we met at the studio, I told him Pauly had said he didn't like the video concept and wanted the whole script dropped. 'He says you've forced the video on him,' I said.

Alan was perplexed. 'But many of the ideas were his,' he told me. 'I just developed them and added to them. I've worked with him on the video all the way through.'

As Alan voiced his confusion, Pauly arrived at the door. Alan quizzed him with a puzzled tone. 'You don't like the video? You want to change the storyboard?'

Pauly looked at me and sneered, 'What sort of bullshit are you making up? Why are you trying to get between us? I never said anything of the sort.'

I protested and then realised it was completely pointless. I had been played. It was divide and rule, street-style. In Pauly's mind, I had taken the fall. After he left, Alan and I went to a café. Over lunch, his advice was, 'Get used to it. It's the way his mind runs. I know you had no reason to make this up.' Pauly and I never spoke of the incident again.

Late that afternoon I went to the PolyGram office, taking with me a copy of the signed recording contract for the company's records. As soon as I walked in the door Victor called me into his office. Pauly had just rung him, demanding an outsider be brought in to script and direct the video of the single, and asserting Alan and I were forcing him to make a video he didn't want to make.

Early that evening, smoothed by a beer or two, Victor, Alan and I held a strategy meeting in my office. We needed a way to deal with Pauly's games. Alan said that over the past week Pauly had told him I had been continually badmouthing him, Alan, and trying to cut him out – although out of what we had no idea as Alan was clearly central to the project.

Then Pauly had revealed to me in Sydney that he had decided to record and work with James Pinker and Lee Baker. The three of them were forming a new band and Alan was no longer needed to finish the album. He had followed this by informing Paul Dickson in Sydney that he had written and recorded 'How Bizarre' pretty much on his own, and would, with access to a budget and a studio, be able to deliver a completed album without Alan's input.

That night Victor, Alan and I made a pact. If Pauly rang or spoke to any one of us, or passed on what one of us had allegedly said about one or both of the others, we would consult the other two before reacting. In the years ahead, Alan and I would refer to this seven-day stretch as the week the insanity began. It was to get much worse.

11

PROBLEMS WITH THE VIDEO CONTINUED. Despite Alan and Pauly having agreed to film the idea they'd been developing, and my full approval for this, Victor asked several young directors for their proposals. Without consulting us he settled on two guys: Gideon Keith, an aspiring but struggling young designer, and Marcus Ringrose, an English art and film director with a rising reputation, who had recently settled in New Zealand. The two men owned V-8, a multimedia studio in central Auckland.

We had our first meeting with Gideon and Marcus in PolyGram's expansive boardroom. Victor, who I understood had worked successfully with Gideon before, did his best to sell the pair to Alan and Pauly. Pauly was now flatly denying he had ever demanded a new director, while Alan was quietly fuming.

I was reasonably relaxed. My instincts told me the script with the '69 Chevy that Alan and Pauly had dreamed up was hard to beat, but I was acquainted with Gideon and Marcus and knew their work was impressive. However, the video concept they were offering was, in my view, much weaker.

A compromise was reached. Marcus and Gideon would make a video using their script. If we didn't like it, we would go back to the original concept as storyboarded by Alan and Pauly. Overlying this decision was concern that making a video from beginning to end would distract Alan and Pauly from the pressing work of producing the all-important album. It was still a long way from completion.

The push to finish the album was coming from both sides of the Tasman but there simply wasn't enough material. Alan and I sat down and worked out that, including 'How Bizarre', he and Pauly had about six mostly written tracks and a few tracks recorded in part. At least five more songs were needed.

I was getting increasingly anxious about releasing a single internationally, which Australia was promising would be a huge hit, when we had no album – and, worse, no album likely in the near future. There was talk of holding back the single's release until the album was almost completed but I didn't want to lose the anticipation that had already been generated. If we waited until 1996 it would be almost impossible to capitalise on this in New Zealand, where a buzz on commercial radio would be an important element in a successful release.

PolyGram Australia was less concerned about a local buzz. Release of the record there would not hit a radio wall, as we feared it might in New Zealand: the record would survive on its own merits and the airplay it got. The company therefore decided to delay the Australian release until February 1996 in the hope the album would be ready by then.

With the pressure on, Alan and Pauly began to spend more and more consecutive nights in the studio, writing, playing and occasionally recording. I found myself there two or three nights a week, often staggering out close to dawn, sleep-deprived, to work at my club. Throughout August, September and October I was a wreck, barely coming up for air.

Often nothing would come of these sessions; many times we'd leave and simply drive around, talking over ideas. Pauly was getting harder and harder to motivate. There were nights when we'd end up at three a.m. in the distant eastern suburbs, or checking out the imported car yards of Greenlane. There was camaraderie in this but it wasn't making us an album, and Alan's frustration was causing tension between him and Pauly. The record company in Australia was also asking almost daily where we were up to and I was having to sidestep the question.

In late October I suggested to Alan and Pauly that to alleviate the pressure for an album they concentrate on a follow-up single. They had written a new song they called 'Right On', an infectious ode to growing up in Auckland, the de facto capital city of Polynesia. We agreed that, barring something else turning up, it would be single number two. As it developed Alan played me many versions, some just on acoustic guitar. It seemed a worthy sequel. The Australian office's scheduling of 'How Bizarre' and the creation of a potential follow-up single did briefly lift the demand for an album, but the respite was shortlived.

The finished master of 'How Bizarre' had been given to PolyGram in late September. By then the signature brass had been added. This had prompted a message from Roger Grierson saying the song was great 'apart from that cheesy trumpet, which has to go'.

Other things, too, were starting to fall into place. The shoot with V-8 was scheduled for October, with the video to be delivered at the beginning of November. We had a B-side for the single, a straight instrumental of the A-side. (It would later be used as the backing for a series of popular parodies.) The single also included a dance mix knocked out one evening by Alan, Alan's patient engineer Rick Huntington, and me. It had absolutely nothing to do with 'How Bizarre', apart from a brief snippet of the vocal, placed strategically in a couple of places, so we could tag it the 'How Bizarre Dance Mix'.

Pauly had not been present when this was mixed but ironically, after the success of the single, the track would be picked up for at least a dozen compilations and become a minor club hit in its own right in Europe. The mix was credited, tongue-in-cheek, to Buck Sterling, Bullion Gold & Seymour Diamonds. The same names would be used for a further OMC remix in 1996, although that time just Alan and I were twiddling with the tracks.

In June 1994 Pauly Fuemana and his brother Philip appeared together on this cover of the magazine *NZ Musician*. Pauly would often say he wanted to prove he was musically his own man and not just Philip's younger brother. *NZ Musician*

Top Alan Jansson (left) playing with his punk band the Steroids in 1980. The band had just released a self-financed single 'Mr Average' on its own indie label. The bass guitarist is Andy Craig, aka Andy Drey. *Murray Cammick Collection*

Above Drummer and percussionist James Pinker (left) and producer Alan Jansson in Jansson's Module 8 recording studio in Auckland in 1988, working on 'Jam This Record', a single released on Simon Grigg's Propeller label. *Simon Grigg Collection*

Right Saxophone prodigy Nathan Haines, seen here with Simon Grigg circa 1994, was the first signing to Grigg's Huh! label. *Simon Grigg Collection*

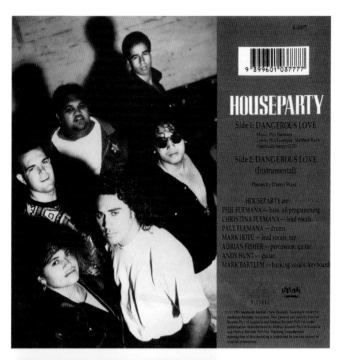

HOUSEPARTY

Side 1: DANGEROUS LOVE
Music: Phil Fuemana.
Lyrics: Phil Fuemana · Matthew Rata
(Southside Songs) (3:53)

Side 2: DANGEROUS LOVE
(Instrumental)

Photos by Darryl Ward

HOUSEPARTY are:
PHIL FUEMANA — bass, all programming.
CHRISTINA FUEMANA — lead vocals.
PAUL FUEMANA — drums.
MARK HOTU — lead vocals, rap.
ADRIAN FISHER — percussion, guitar.
ANDY HUNT — guitar.
MARK BARTLEM — backing vocals, keyboard.

Top This 1991 single 'Dangerous Love'
by the Fuemana family band Houseparty
credited Pauly Fuemana as drummer, but
when the song later appeared on the
Fuemana – New Urban Polynesian album
he was noted only as a backing vocalist.
Southside Records

Left Released in 1994, the landmark album
Proud, produced by Alan Jansson, featured
fourteen tracks from ten South Auckland
groups. It included 'We R The OMC' by
Pauly Fuemana, Philip Fuemana and Paul
Ave, the original Otara Millionaires Club.
Propellor Lamont Ltd.

Right Alan Jansson at his Uptown Studios,
circa 1994. It was the dream of the talented
producer to create a US number one hit
record. *Michelle Hopkinson / Simon Grigg Collection*

Teenagers Brenda Makamoeafi and Hassanah
Iroegbu made up the Sisters Underground,
whose song 'In the Neighbourhood' from the
Proud album became a successful single in
New Zealand and Australia. The duo toured
Australia with OMC and were signed by Sony
but decided against pursuing an international
career. *Greg Semu*

1. seasons
2. seasons
3. rockit love
4. dangerous love
5. last summer
6. deep of the night
7. closer
8. broken hearted
9. cool calm
10. fa a samoa
11. closer

deepgrooves

OTARA MILLIONAIRES CLUB
WE R THE OMC REMIX

Top Christina Fuemana's voice dominated the family album *Fuemana*, released on Kane Massey's Deepgrooves label in July 1994. Christina was pictured on the album's front cover and Pauly on the back. *Deepgrooves*

Above For Simon Grigg 'We R The OMC' was the standout track on the *Proud* album. Based on a rhythm by Phil Fuemana, the song had been heavily mixed, reworked and overdubbed by Alan Jansson and combined elements of hip hop, rap and rock with a strong Polynesian flavour. *Propeller Lamont Ltd.*

Roger Grierson, who ran the music publishing
arm of PolyGram in Australia, immediately
recognised the potential of 'How Bizarre'
when Alan Jansson and Simon Grigg flew to
Sydney and played it to him in July 1995. A
New Zealander, Grierson had managed Nick
Cave and the Bad Seeds in the late 1980s,
and at PolyGram had signed the young New
Zealand group Shihad. *Roger Grierson Collection*

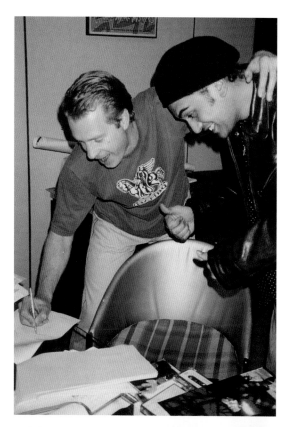

Top Mark Phillips, who set up the record label Stimulant with Peter Urlich and Simon Grigg in 1986, moved on to work at PolyGram in New Zealand and then in Australia. Here he witnesses Pauly Fuemana signing the contract for 'How Bizarre' at PolyGram's Sydney office, August 3, 1995. *Simon Grigg Collection*

Left Pauly Fuemana in Wellington, November 1995. The plan was for him to record drum tracks for several songs, but the studio session was a failure. *Simon Grigg Collection*

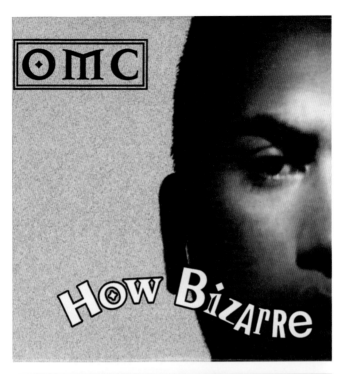

Left The original sleeve of the single 'How Bizarre'. Released to New Zealand record stores in December 1995, the song went gold on its first day and by the end of January had reached number one in the Top 40. *Universal Music NZ / Huh! Records*

Below left After an initial video for 'How Bizarre' was scrapped, a second went into production in November and was released in January. Featuring Pauly Fuemana, Sina Saipaia and a Chevrolet convertible, it was created by Lee Baker, a film-maker who had played guitar on the recording of 'How Bizarre'. Baker had told Alan Jansson he would be happy to direct the video for a token fee. *Universal Music NZ / Huh! Records*

Below One of Pauly Fuemana's first purchases when PolyGram gave him a cash advance in early 1996 was this 1979 Mercedes two-door metallic gold coupé. Pauly, who had a love of classic European cars, paid the full asking price of twelve thousand dollars, although a mechanic advised him it was worth two thousand less. *Stephen Langdon / Universal Music NZ*

Left Victor Stent, managing director of PolyGram New Zealand, at the New Zealand Music Awards, April 1996, where 'How Bizarre' won Single of the Year in a public vote. Stent was originally unenthusiastic about the song but came on board after his Australian colleagues gave it the thumbs-up. *Simon Grigg Collection*

Below DJ Willie Boaza (left) and PolyGram's Mark Phillips during the Australian promotional tour for 'How Bizarre' in March 1996. Pauly Fuemana appeared with Sina Saipaia and Boaza on the hugely popular Channel Nine show *Hey Hey It's Saturday*. *Simon Grigg Collection*

Adam Holt, then marketing manager at Polydor Records, a subsidiary of PolyGram Australia, with Pauly Fuemana, 1996. Holt, who had formerly worked for PolyGram in New Zealand, was a keen supporter of 'How Bizarre' and played a major part in its success. *Adam Holt*

Top Soon after 'How Bizarre' went to number one, PolyGram took Alan Jansson, Simon Grigg and Pauly Fuemana to dinner at Auckland's French Café, where the managing director, Victor Stent, presented them with gold awards. By this time the single had passed the platinum sales mark of 10,000 copies shipped. *Simon Grigg Collection*

Right 'Right On', the follow-up single to 'How Bizarre', was released in New Zealand in May 1996 to a mixed response. The shot of a suited and booted Pauly on the sleeve was taken by Nicole England, a photographer who influenced Fuemana to move from his Latino jazz boho look to a more sophisticated, urbane image.
Huh! Records / Polygram New Zealand

In the video for 'Right On', Sina Saipaia
again played a prominent role, sitting
near Fuemana in the bus that formed the
centrepiece. The upbeat video, made
for only $15,000, used many volunteers,
including Simon Grigg's niece and her
schoolfriends. *Universal Music NZ / Huh! Records*

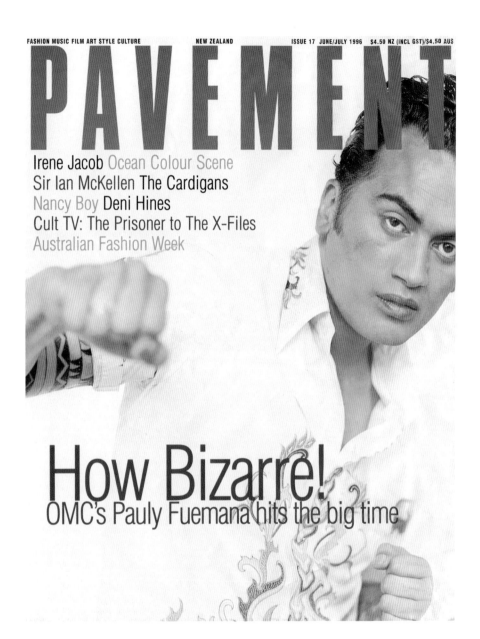

FASHION MUSIC FILM ART STYLE CULTURE   NEW ZEALAND   ISSUE 17 JUNE/JULY 1996 $4.50 NZ (INCL GST)/$4.50 AUS

PAVEMENT

Irene Jacob Ocean Colour Scene
Sir Ian McKellen The Cardigans
Nancy Boy Deni Hines
Cult TV: The Prisoner to The X-Files
Australian Fashion Week

How Bizarre!
OMC's Pauly Fuemana hits the big time

Pauly Fuemana made the front cover of *Pavement*
magazine for June/July 1996. Although the story
portrayed him in a positive light, he was unhappy
with both it and the cover photo, telling Simon
Grigg he was going to 'take out Pervement' and
give both the editor, Barney McDonald, and the
writer, Jock Lawrie, 'the bash'. *Pavement*

Despite the tape of 'How Bizarre' being strictly under wraps, we discovered it had been played to a few outsiders at the V-8 office. Pauly began to get comments from the self-appointed hip-hop massive. An influential DJ approached him in High Street and sneered, 'You can do better, bro. This is not your record.' A well-known Polynesian female vocalist told Sina that Pauly had 'sold out'. This was not altogether surprising. Although it is much harder to make a record that people want to buy than one no one wants, the act of making a popular record is often denigrated by hard-core fans as 'selling out' to 'the man'. The implication was that Alan, by pushing aside predictable hip-hop clichés, had watered down the real Pauly Fuemana. The comments cut Pauly deeply. 'How Bizarre' was his creation as much as it was Alan's.

In November Alan decided he needed to go to Wellington. An old audio buddy of his there owned an expensive microphone and Alan wanted to borrow it to record vocal tracks for the album.

He was also interested in recording some live drum tracks in a Wellington suite. Pauly had insisted to Alan that he was a proficient drummer, and indeed the early Fuemana single 'Dangerous Love' had credited him on drums. However, a quick listen revealed that the gorgeous Pacific soul single used a Funky Drummer loop, with no obvious live drummer in the mix. Nevertheless, we were happy to extend the range of instruments that Pauly could contribute to the album.

We decided to drive to Wellington on a Monday, spend three days there, and drive back on Friday. Alan, Pauly and I duly set off in my 1989 BMW 325i and headed down the western side of Lake Taupo. On the way we loudly played and replayed a newly remastered copy of what may be the greatest live album of all time, *The Who Live At Leeds*, which we'd picked up from PolyGram before we left, followed by a couple of New York dance comps, and finally the completed mixes of 'How Bizarre'.

When I played the dance mix Pauly started telling me where he'd got the idea from. 'But you weren't even there, Pauly,' I protested. 'Alan and Rick put this together and I helped them mix it.'

Pauly answered firmly, 'It's my song.' In the interests of peace, diplomacy and the bigger picture, I let it ride. A few months later Pauly would explain to British journalists where he had got the inspiration for this particular dance mix.

In Wellington next morning we went to see Brendan Smyth, the head of New Zealand On Air's music funding division. Alan handed him a finished copy of the single, burned to CD, so he could add it to Kiwi Hit Disc, a collection of radio-friendly tracks the government-funded agency supplied to radio stations once a month in the unending battle to try and ease local music on to the airwaves. We then visited Alan's friend and booked four hours the next afternoon to record Pauly playing the drum tracks.

That night we took a drive alongside the city's wild southern beaches that face Cook Strait, the turbulent stretch of water that divides the two main islands of New Zealand. The wind was up and conditions were stormy. Sitting in the back, Pauly seemed unhappy: we could feel it from his silence. Alan and I had commented to each other on his moodiness since we'd left Auckland but had shrugged it off. After a ritualistic trip up Mount Victoria to take in the harbour views, and dinner at Café Paradiso in Courtenay Place, we visited some other friends of Alan, who always had funny stories to tell. This night was no exception. In no time everyone was laughing except Pauly, who sat frowning.

Next morning we headed to the top of Cuba Street to have a crack at the drum tracks. The studio was housed in what seemed to be an old warehouse, acoustically divided into a drum-friendly space by huge sound baffles. The drum kit sat on top of a large blue Star of David, surrounded by astrological imagery sprayed on the floor.

After we had set up the recording gear, Pauly sat down and Alan asked him to play.

'Play what?' Pauly said.

'Play whatever you thought you wanted to play.'

Alan was mostly looking for loops, tracks he could cut up and use as breaks behind the recorded work, but he also wanted rhythm tracks for a couple of songs he and Pauly had written and had given Pauly guide tracks to work from.

Over the next couple of hours Alan tried everything. He used the guide tracks, played bass rhythms, introduced a metronome. Nothing helped. All he had at the end was a formless bundle of random drum sounds.

The trip had been largely a waste of time. Pauly could not play a drum kit, keep a rhythm or produce a passable beat. Despite this he looked pleased with himself and seemed to think he'd done well. This was an illusion he would suffer from often. He was simply unable to see something he'd created for what it was, convincing himself of its artistic and commercial worth even if it had little or none.

That afternoon we picked up another old acquaintance of Alan's, an odd character who talked a continuous stream of drivel, and drove to Titahi Bay, north of Wellington. Alan's friend, sitting beside Pauly in the back seat, kept holding forth. After we turned on to the motorway to head back to Wellington, Pauly suddenly lost it. His eyes flaring, he snarled at the man to shut his 'fucking mouth' or he'd physically shut it for him.

As we drove back there was silence inside the car. When we reached the city Pauly broke the uneasy quiet by mentioning, in a completely relaxed tone, the sunglasses Alan's friend was wearing. Nonplussed by the train of events, the friend offered them to him as a gift. After we dropped the man home, Pauly, wearing the sunglasses, smiled and said without a touch of irony, 'What a great guy.'

Next morning as we set off back to Auckland Pauly informed us in a whisper that the studio in Wellington was owned by a devil-worshipper and no good would come of us being there. That, he said, was why he had had trouble drumming.

'Sorry?' I said.

'The pentagon on the floor, bro. The man's a devil-worshipper. And he had a ponytail.'

Alan explained that the studio had been used for a Telecom advertisement the week before. The stars and symbols on the floor had been part of the ad.

Back in Auckland, Alan tried to mix some of the Wellington drum tracks into recordings and brought both Adam Holt, who was in town, and Victor Stent in for a preview. After listening, Adam said, 'The tracks are good, Alan, but the drumming is awful.'

We nodded. Alan removed the offending clatter.

We needed a sleeve for the single. Alan had an idea in which the left half of Pauly's face would be on the right-hand side of the cover over quite a plain background, and a semi-gothic font used for the OMC logo. Victor suggested we get Gideon Keith to do the design as part of the video package so I passed on the idea to him. A few days later Alan, Pauly and I went to his studio to view the preliminary result.

As a reference, Alan had lent Gideon the cover of a single from Babble, a band that had, until it changed its name, been UK-New Zealand 1980s pop stars the Thompson Twins. The cover had the face and the positioning as Alan wanted it, albeit with the head on the left side of the cover.

Gideon had positioned the shot of Pauly well and the actual image, taken from the video shoot, was fine too. However, echoing the Babble original, the colours were garish and overblown. Alan sat with a reluctant Gideon and on the spot tweaked the design, including the typeface and logo, essentially creating the sleeve that was used worldwide. Gideon laid it out and delivered it to PolyGram a few days later.

The video, though, was about to become even more problematic. In early November Marcus and Gideon announced they had finished it and had a rough cut. I had stayed away from the shoot, apart from one long session when Pauly was doing a series of close-up shots. I dislike video shoots and tend to absent myself unless I'm directly involved in the process. As with recording sessions, I also do my best to ban friends, girlfriends, boyfriends, family and record company staff, all of whom usually have opinions that directors and producers don't need to hear.

On this occasion, though, I had been remiss in not being present, given Pauly's emotional fragility and the way he could unpredictably react to situations he found threatening in some way. He had decided he didn't like Marcus and Gideon, nor what he thought they were doing to his song. Alan shared his opinion, so when the two men played us the rough cut at PolyGram the room was tense.

It quickly became clear that no one liked the video, aside from those who had made it. It included toy cars – why we couldn't work out – and shots where the camera seemed to have been rotated around Pauly's head. The lighting gave his face an odd greenish-brown colouration. Worse still, it accentuated Pauly's teeth, the one feature of which he was acutely conscious.

After the video finished playing, Alan exclaimed with his usual brusque honesty, 'It makes Pauly look like a fucking raisin.'

There was an uneasy silence, after which we quickly listed other things we disliked about it. Most of them were minor, but for me the colouration, the rotating camera and the cars added up to an insurmountable difficulty.

Looking very downcast, as anyone would when a client has just rejected a month's work, Gideon and Marcus suggested a re-edit at their cost. Although the video was dead in the water as far as Alan, Pauly and I were concerned, we agreed. After they left, Victor tried to talk it up, not surprisingly as it had been his idea to use V-8. Alan was furious. We quickly departed, taking with us a VHS of the rejected video.

12

WE WERE RUNNING OUT OF TIME. The record was being released to radio on the last week of November and we still had no video. In an age when New Zealand radio stations were utterly cold to almost all New Zealand music, a video was a vital marketing tool.

Victor insisted we wait and see where we found ourselves after the V-8 re-edit. I explained this was pointless unless he wanted an artist and producer on strike or on the warpath. I also felt there was little in the raw footage that could be used to rescue the video.

At issue, too, was the funding. We had been given a grant of $5,000 and PolyGram had kicked in another $7,000. All of this had gone on the V-8 video. The cupboard was now bare.

After, in due course, we rejected V-8's re-edit, Victor somehow found another $7,000. Just happy the money was available I didn't ask where it had come from, although I know he had argued Marcus and Gideon down a few thousand on the firm understanding that their work would never be used.

A new video was shot by Lee Baker and his team. Pre-production began in the third week of November, this time under the strict eye of Alan. In the first two weeks of December we dragged in all the High Street cool kids we could find, plus two professional dancers and a couple of my staff, and shot the indoor scenes on a soundstage in Ponsonby, followed by outdoor shots in the lush subtropical grounds of the Ellerslie Racecourse.

Sina Saipaia featured heavily as Sister Zina. DJ Soane Filitonga – Brother Pele in the lyrics – didn't make the shoot and we substituted a Filipino man named Hill as the guy grinning and grooving in the back seat of the Chevy in the opening shots. Hill had arrived at Alan's door a few days earlier asking for help on some recordings he'd been working on. He then came to the OMC shoot asking if he could assist in any way. Alan took off the Island shirt he was wearing, gave it to him and told him to jump in the car. Some years later, when Hill asked Alan if he could help him with his ultimately successful immigration application for New Zealand, he told him that when he went back to the Philippines he had been interviewed by the local MTV channel and treated like a big star because of the video.

The material was edited at a production suite in Grafton, with the final shot – a policeman tapping his shades in amazement at seeing the Chevy – taking place in January. The Christmas shutdown meant slow progress. Mark Phillips pulled in a favour for a final edit in Australia. The finished clip was finally delivered and approved in the middle of January.

Opinions were mixed, especially at PolyGram, but the rest of us loved it, as did Adam Holt, whose views I respected. The video spoke to the song perfectly, and to me it strongly said Auckland and New Zealand. Most importantly, like the song, it was strikingly different from anything else. I've seen it countless times since and have never tired of its uncomplicated charm. Over the next two years it would get more than 15,000 plays in the US alone.

In a strange postscript, somebody, I suspect in Australia, heavily re-edited the clip without our knowledge or approval – and not once but twice. With hack-like cutting and pasting, shots were moved, removed and added. Record companies, often with the best of intentions, will often feel a need to interfere with a record, artwork or video, usually with disastrous results. We were to suffer from this over and over again as the project progressed. We learned that the re-edited version was being used in Australia and parts of Europe and were given VHS copies. It also made it on to YouTube. Happily, though, when the video aired in America and the UK the original was used.

By late November we had a finished single and were at last heading towards a final video. It was time to take the record to commercial radio. Alan sat up all night with Pauly and me, burning fifty CDs of the record and auditioning each of them all the way through. I dropped Pauly home about nine in the morning just as Kirstine was leaving for work.

We presented the record first to Mai FM, a fledgling urban station owned by an Auckland iwi, Ngāti Whātua. Mai targeted young Māori and Polynesian listeners, especially those in South and West Auckland. Its programme director Ross Goodwin was a successful radio veteran, known as much for his long lunches at the brasseries of Ponsonby as for his radio talents, which were considerable. His history as an innovator and renegade went back to the original New Zealand pirate station Radio Hauraki in the 1960s.

Mai FM was still regarded as an outsider in the Auckland radio hierarchy. Its ratings were slowly nibbling into those of the established big boys but its ability to break records was limited to the hip hop and funk beloved of its listeners, and these listeners were regarded by advertisers as essentially penniless and not worth a big advertising spend, aside from for junk food such as Coca-Cola and McDonalds. These kids were the reason CD stores had started removing even the printed sleeves from cassettes and CDs on the shelves to prevent the cases being nicked.

Mai needed to notch up a huge crossover hit to give the station the extra credibility and kudos that would lift it beyond its urban niche. Victor assumed, correctly as it turned out, that Ross would be keen to jump on a record like this, especially if he wanted to grow the station out of its initial target demographic.

On Tuesday, November 22 we brought Ross into the PolyGram boardroom, and after the normal polite industry chit-chat, followed by a brief well-targeted burst of hype from Victor, we played him the record.

He listened to it and then asked to hear it again. He looked at us and said he liked it. Radio people are given to ecstatic hyperbole and overstatement with everyone except record company people.

We asked the critical question: 'So, will you add it?'

'It needs more bottom end,' Ross replied.

Radio programmers, like some other sectors of the industry, are fond of thinking they are recording artists – or, worse, music producers. Some are very good at their jobs, as Ross was, but none I've met have had the chops to make it as a successful recording artist, aside from with the odd radio jock novelty disc. However, they love to boast about the input they've had into the creation of a local record they are about to add to their playlist. It's one of the few creative things they get to do as their playlists are mainly determined by what is being played on American, British and Australian radio.

Naturally we were happy to play the game. I took the record back to Alan and explained that Ross Goodwin said the bottom end needed boosting. 'Bullshit!' was Alan's response. The next day we took the record, absolutely unchanged, back to Ross and said, 'Here you go, buddy.'

'See,' Ross said, 'now it's perfect.' He added it to the daytime playlist straight away.

The response elsewhere was not encouraging. The people in PolyGram who dealt with radio stations met an almost immovable wall of negativity. Absolutely no one wanted to know about 'How Bizarre'. Perhaps this wasn't surprising. These were, after all, the same stations that had refused to play Crowded House's 'Don't Dream It's Over' because they couldn't find it on their US radio programming sheets. Once the song became a hit in the States it was not only quickly added to local playlists but programmers from Bluff to Kaitaia claimed ownership.

In the years to come, dozens of programme directors from every corner of New Zealand would also loudly claim they had helped break 'How Bizarre'. The truth was that until it was just about to hit number one, courtesy of Mai FM, most commercial radio stations in its homeland ignored it.

At Mai the record was an immediate success, rating extremely well in its phone polling and being ordered by the record stores where the station's listeners shopped. In the 1990s there was a belief in the music industry that the singles chart was created in two large stores in Manukau City Centre on late-night Thursdays, when the kids poured in and bought that now forgotten oddity, the cassingle, in vast numbers. Those two shops, ECM Music and Sounds, were now asking for 'How Bizarre' in large numbers.

In December I was invited to *Rip It Up*'s Christmas party. *Rip It Up*, the most important music magazine in the country, had recently been acquired by a successful publishing entrepreneur, Barry Colman, and his company Liberty Press but was still being edited by Murray Cammick, its founder. Cammick had as his right hand one of New Zealand's best young writers, John Russell. John had given 'How Bizarre' its first press review and it was close to a rave, predicting the record would go 'at least Top 10'. In the context of the times, this was a big prediction for a New Zealand record. And given *Rip It Up*'s huge influence, it was a crucial endorsement that would help attract the potential audience that wasn't anchored by Mai FM.

For Murray, the Liberty Press deal had been a godsend. Not only was *Rip It Up* now financially secure, with suppliers and printers being paid, but he was able to annually entertain hand-picked members of the music industry on Barry's gin palace, MV *Liberty*, which came complete with jet skis and several beautifully appointed suites to which guests would disappear on occasion.

The *Liberty* Christmas party was the hottest in town and tickets were highly prized. Both Murray and John suggested I bring along the rising man around town, Pauly Fuemana. The storm had started to break around Pauly and his song. Everyone, including those who'd been cynical about 'How Bizarre' just a few weeks back, now wanted to know him.

We arrived about eleven in the morning and were ushered upstairs to the sweeping rear deck, where guests were greeting each other and the first of the day's many drinks. By the time we set off there was a mishmash of about forty people – label people, TV people, band members, *Rip It Up* staff and hot alternative radio hosts such as 95bFM's Mikey Havoc. I settled in next to Pagan Record's Sheryl Morris, Flying Nun's Paul McKessar and Big Day Out promoter Doug Hood.

In blisteringly hot sun, we headed out into the Hauraki Gulf. Pauly seemed in good spirits. His record was out and he was about to start his first climb up the charts. People were interested in him, in his music, in his opinions, and in his plans. He seemed to have forgotten, or at least have decided to ignore, the critical comments that had cut him badly just a few weeks back.

Out on the gulf the sun's rays bounced off the water, annihilating any protection a hat or sunshade could offer. I went downstairs and noticed a steady stream of people heading to one of the cabins, where a group of people, led by a well-known radio personality, were carving out lines of white powder.

Pauly was there, smiling. I pulled him aside and said he should leave it alone.

'C'mon, bro, let's get into it,' he said and flashed me a grin.

I grabbed the media jock and whispered very firmly in his ear, 'Please don't give him any more.'

'C'mon mate,' he said. 'Nobody's going to know out here.'

I told him that wasn't my primary concern. I just knew that, given Pauly's emotional fragility and his potential to get aggressive, feeding him drugs was not a good idea. Coupled with free-flowing alcohol and an alien social environment, there was the making of a bad situation. He agreed not to supply him with any more.

As the afternoon wound on, the jet ski was lowered and most of us ended up swimming in the sea. Around six o'clock, as the boat was about to head back to shore, I went downstairs. Pauly was emerging from the room where the drugs were being dispensed. After again pleading with the radio man, I went back up to the deck and sat next to Pauly.

Looking into his eyes I asked him if he was okay. 'Yeah, bro,' he said, 'but this boat is full of wankers. Up themselves, all of them.'

As we sailed towards the mooring he seemed to recover his good spirits and by the time we docked he was laughing again. Sheryl Morris had invited us both to her apartment in Freemans Bay for a coffee. I asked Pauly if he wanted to come. If he didn't we could drop him off at his apartment in Greys Avenue, which was only a short distance from Sheryl's. He was in deep conversation with a couple of guys from television. He assured me he would rather stay. Sheryl and I said goodbye and headed off to find a cab.

I would receive several reports of what happened next. The party had almost finished. There were only some *Rip It Up* staff members and a few hard-core guests remaining. Even Murray Cammick, the host, had left. Pauly was sitting next to the owner of a television channel, who had for some reason decided to make offensive comments to him about his ethnicity and how lucky he was to be there.

Furious, Pauly strode over to John Russell and said, 'You guys don't think I belong here. You don't want a brown face here.' He then said something to a woman from Liberty Press. When she rebuffed him, he pushed her hard. She fell back and hit her head on a door frame.

The boat's captain decided to intervene. He put Pauly in a headlock and punched him in the face several times, cutting his eye. A member of the *Rip It Up* staff and another man then helped him pull Pauly down the stairs and throw him off the boat.

 John Russell tried to calm the situation but Pauly refused to be placated and took off into the night. Later we discovered that the captain was in the middle of an illicit affair with the woman Pauly had pushed, which may have explained his reaction, which was so violent he should probably have been charged with assault.

If the matter had ended there, Pauly could have been seen as just an unlucky victim. Unhappily, though, things were to get much worse.

Sometime after leaving the boat, Pauly arrived home. Apparently he couldn't find his keys and started abusing Kirstine when she let him in. He then appeared to be going to leave. Kirstine asked him where he was going and heard him reply, 'I'm going to get a knife.' He would later claim his actual words were, 'I'm going to get a life.'

Whatever the truth, and Pauly would change his story several times, Kirstine jumped from a third-floor window and broke the bones in both her heels, leading to a long spell in hospital.

The first I heard of this was the next morning when I had a raft of calls from Murray Cammick, John Russell and others who had witnessed the boat incident, as well as from Alan and Victor. When I heard from Pauly later that day he seemed thoroughly distraught. Kirstine, however, had forgiven him.

I was shocked by these events. They seemed to underline how vulnerable Pauly was to excessive consumption of drugs and alcohol. From the middle of the afternoon he had obviously been walking a tightrope. I felt guilty for having left him on the boat.

A week or two later Alan, Pauly and I were having dinner during a break from recording. Pauly was talking happily about the work in progress when he suddenly leaned across the table and accused me of 'setting him up' on the boat. I had, he shouted repeatedly, paid the captain to have him beaten.

Alan and I quickly pointed out this was ludicrous. Why would I have my new recording artist with a coming hit single roughed up? It had been done to teach him his place, Pauly said. But his rage was slowly subsiding. Towards the end of the meal he announced there were only two people in the world he could truly trust: Alan and me.

Aside from this outburst, Pauly was contrite about the episode on the boat, although when Alan, Victor and I tried to talk him into sessions with an anger management counsellor he refused. As 1995 ended and the record took off, we hoped and prayed such incidents were behind us.

13

REVIEWS OF 'HOW BIZARRE' started to appear. John Russell had got the ball rolling when he wrote in *Rip It Up*: 'This is gonna be large.' As November rolled into December the buzz grew. Each day there seemed to be yet another effusive review. Most were appearing in the street and alternative press, driven by a few switched-on journalists, plus of course the kids who were hearing this unusual, incredibly catchy tune that sounded like nothing else on Mai FM, and every now and then on 95bFM, the Auckland student station.

Around the time the record went to radio I had phoned Auckland journalist Graham Reid. Graham was music editor at *The New Zealand Herald*, the nation's biggest morning newspaper with a daily readership of around half a million. He and I had a personal history that went back some fifteen years. I'm not sure how we met. Most likely it had been over the counters of the record shops where I worked.

Around 1980 Graham had begun publishing a cutting-edge music magazine, *Auckland Jazz News*. Later he had added another, *Passages*. He was also a host on Radio Pacific, an independent station. Graham had somehow convinced this conservative station to give him a show late on Sunday evenings, where he played the eclectic and left-field stuff that few other stations, aside from the low-powered student ones, dared to.

On two occasions he asked me on to play tracks from my treasured collection of obscure indie post-punk gems from around the world, bought at a time when you couldn't buy records in New Zealand unless the major labels deemed them releasable. The few imports that did get through were mostly older albums from mainstream jazz and classical acts. There was little room for the independent singles from middle America or Perth in Scotland that I craved, and sourced mainly through swaps with overseas collectors.

Graham and I had stayed friendly over the years, and as one of New Zealand's most important and adventurous music journalists he was usually open to stories I threw his way. When I rang him I talked about Pauly and 'How Bizarre' and how much I believed in both the record and its creators. I asked, hopefully, if he would write a piece for the nationally read entertainment section of which he was editor.

I had already decided to limit press exposure. I wanted one or two major pieces and that was it. When you are trying to create a sense of mythology about an act, there can be value in creating an appearance of unavailability rather than letting the artist talk to all and sundry. I had learned the value of targeting only the most valuable media and so limiting the overexposure that can kill an act's publicity interest. With Pauly we had a huge record in the making and a big story to tell. That story needed to be told with sensitivity, and only by those I thought capable of telling it sympathetically. No hacks allowed.

There was another aspect too. Alan and I knew Pauly had the potential to throw a wild card into an interview and that this could spin it off in an unpredictable direction. He was liberal with the truth and many a later interview would contain stories that bore no relationship to events or fact. On top of this there was a chance Pauly would take a dislike to an interviewer and refuse to communicate.

Graham spoke to Pauly early in December and I crossed my fingers he would give us a decent column or two.

I had also talked to Dylan Taite, an illustrious and at times outrageous television journalist who had engineered the Sex Pistols' record contract signing outside Buckingham Palace in 1977, and two years later scored an interview with Bob Marley after playing soccer with him for several days.

I had known Dylan even longer than I'd known Graham. Always after a story, Dylan would enthusiastically tell me to keep him in the loop with whatever I was doing. When we recorded and released the first Nathan Haines album, he did two generous pieces on the late news, both of which triggered brief sales bursts.

A few weeks out from the release of 'How Bizarre' I rang Dylan. He was intrigued by the OMC story – the fact Pauly had come from South Auckland, and the whole Ōtara movement. There was also the Alan Jansson tie-in. Dylan was an admirer of Alan's 1982 band The Body Electric, and was disappointed when I said Alan wouldn't be part of any interview. He had seen an angle in the mix of South Auckland Pacific soul and Wellington's electronic pioneers. I tried rather clumsily to explain that the record itself spoke to that perhaps illogical mashing of genres. Or perhaps the mix of artists that came together on 'How Bizarre' was not as out-of-the-box as it seemed: it's often forgotten that Kraftwerk and Depeche Mode were as big an influence on early hip hop as James Brown.

I saw Dylan in High Street early in the week 'How Bizarre' was due to hit the shops. After checking what looked to be a full diary, he said he could film a short piece on the Wednesday to air the following day. The day before the shoot was to happen, he called and said he'd have to delay it until the day of release. He promised he would still get the story on the late news that night.

The single hit the stores the second week of December 1995. That morning I woke up and rushed across the road to grab the *Herald*, hoping beyond hope that Graham's interview would be more than token. I rustled hurriedly through the pages to find Pauly's face sprawled across the entire front of the entertainment section, *The Voice*. The story covered most of the back page. It was much more than we could have hoped for. From the colour pages of the nationally circulated newspaper, in homes and workplaces across the country, Pauly Fuemana was now instantly recognisable and on his way to becoming a household name.

Pauly called, buzzing and ecstatic but a little worried. His phone had been ringing all morning with calls from his proud family, but he had also found himself being ribbed by people who thought the record meant instant wealth. He said to me that morning, 'You got me into this bro. You get me out.' The only person who seemed to be completely unfazed was Alan, whose attitude was simple and concise: 'I knew this was going to happen.'

The *Herald* pages set off an immediate avalanche of media requests. Dylan phoned to say TV One's editors now wanted Pauly on the six o'clock news, the most watched show on television. We agreed to meet at eleven in my office. PolyGram's press officer rang to tell me that TV3, the opposition network, also wanted to run a story on that night's news but had a camera crew for the morning only.

We couldn't let either station know the other wanted to cover the story, so I called Dylan back and switched his interview to one o'clock. I then called TV3 and suggested we meet the crew in my office at eleven. Meanwhile, I fended off numerous requests from news radio and other outlets for stories, pleading lack of time.

The TV3 crew arrived early and filmed their three-minute segment in my office and around High Street. They wrapped the shoot within an hour and seemed pleased with the result. After we pushed them out we went across town to Parnell, where Pauly and I had lunch and waited anxiously for Dylan and his crew. When they arrived they wanted to film outdoors. Pauly quickly suggested nearby Garfield Street and then St Georges Bay Road, where he had spent part of the 1970s as a child.

There was a quirk of fate in this for me. When I came of age in the 1970s my close circle of friends had included two who lived at 18 Bath Street, Parnell. I spent hundreds of hours at their house, often in my mate Mark's room, where we listened to music for hours on end. Standing on

Mark's first-floor balcony, we would watch a Polynesian family next door and their loud pre-teen kids. We would often smile and wave at the kids and they would smile and wave back.

Pauly and I had worked out that this had been his family and one of the kids had been him, aged four or five. One day, as we drove to my house on Garfield Street, he had pointed out his childhood home on the corner of Bath and Garfield and described how, when his family had been there a few years, men from the government had arrived and strongly suggested they swap their old villa for a brand new home in Ōtara, the South Auckland suburb the government had opened up for immigrant families. The swap had likely cost the Fuemana family several hundred thousand dollars. In the 1980s the rough Parnell hills had gentrified and house values multiplied many times over – unlike Ōtara, where house values had remained among the lowest in Auckland. For a time the government had used the Fuemanas' Parnell house for student accommodation.

After a couple of shots outside a café, Dylan decided to film in Garfield Street. He and Pauly walked along next to the old Fuemana family home. It was an ironic and incongruous backdrop to the story of gangs and wannabe millionaires in South Auckland.

That night both channels ran their story on the six o'clock news. The stories were previewed the same way: bad boy makes good with a killer song about to take the nation. It was a media grand slam. In the almost two decades I had been making and releasing records in New Zealand I had never seen coverage like this for a debut single, from a relatively unknown act that had not yet entered the charts. The cumulative audience of the two television shows and the *Herald*'s entertainment section was almost two million.

Obviously my history and contacts had eased the way for this coverage but there was much more to it than that. The *Proud* album and Polynesian pop music in general had begun to create and ride a rapidly rising wave of interest. Auckland had finally worked out there was something intriguing happening in the streets, clubs and bedrooms cum recording studios of South Auckland. The media barrage over Pauly Fuemana and 'How Bizarre' was one of the moments when the gaze began to focus on that part of the city. It would change the face of popular music in New Zealand forever. The irony was that by then Pauly was consciously distancing himself from his South Auckland roots.

Next morning PolyGram called me. Retailers had doubled their orders and 'How Bizarre' had gone gold on its first day: more than 5,000 copies had been shipped to stores. The NZ singles chart came out the following Wednesday, effectively counting only two days' sales, Friday and Saturday. The record, available on CD single and the more ghetto-blaster-friendly cassingle, had entered the chart at number 15. PolyGram's production manager was urgently ordering more of both formats, but especially the cassingle, from manufacturing plants. Taken by surprise, the company had run out of stock.

Radio was still problematic, with only Mai FM and 95bFM currently on board, but the following week the record jumped to number four. This meant even stations that had been reluctant to play the disc now had to broadcast it or leave an ugly gap on their charts.

Record industry wisdom is that December is a bad time to release a single: the bluster of Christmas drowns out new releases, and sales and marketing staff are distracted by endless Christmas parties and serial hangovers. My philosophy had always been that it was a great time to release a single by a New Zealand artist. There was little competition in the new release stakes, and if you could find some way to leverage the song on to the charts on the last week of December it would stay there for three weeks because there were no new charts until two weeks after New Year. Radio playlists get stale by the end of December and programmers look hopefully towards things they may have overlooked earlier. On top of that it is summer, and summer needs fresh anthems for those weeks at the beach.

I can't say for certain that these things worked in our favour, but at the end of the year a few radio barriers began to crumble. An important

Wellington pop station, 91ZM, added it and more and more provincial stations started to push it up their playlists. The radio pluggers at PolyGram were starting to see dividends from their work and the pressure Victor was putting them under to get the record on to the summer airwaves.

The first chart of 1996 put 'How Bizarre' at number four. We delivered the video and it was aired that weekend on the video hits shows. A pattern emerged that would be repeated around the world. The single slipped to number 5 the following week. Victor called to say it wasn't a bad run and we should be happy. Two days later PolyGram's sales manager Ian Watson called and said sales had gone through the roof. The record had sold 4,000 copies in two days.

On January 28 'How Bizarre' went to number one, selling four times the number of copies as the number two record. Strangely, while I remember so much of what happened in those years, that day is a complete blur until the evening. What did we do? I don't have the faintest idea. Alan says we congregated in PolyGram's offices and had a toast. Later, Victor took Alan and me to an Italian restaurant in Karangahape Road, where he opened a bottle of Moët et Chandon, which both Alan and I, after a quick taste, declined. He then suggested that since Alan was about to be in the money he should pay for a night for the three of us at a local brothel run by the notorious Flora MacKenzie. We again declined.

Next Friday a spirited and elated posse – Alan, Pauly, Victor, other senior PolyGram staff and I – went to Cin Cin, an expensive restaurant on Auckland's waterfront, where Pauly happily and at PolyGram's expense devoured lobster and drank Dom Pérignon.

That week all radio resistance crumbled. Stations nationwide were now playing the record. You couldn't escape it. It was everywhere – on TV and radio, in shops and malls. All summer 'How Bizarre' was ubiquitous. It remained in the New Zealand Top 50 for five more months, selling almost 40,000 copies.

Pauly, Alan and I floated around Auckland on a cloud of success and anticipation. I knew just how far this record could go and increasingly felt the same niggling sixth sense of inevitability that Alan had touted for months.

There was, predictably, a backlash, like the Auckland musician who stopped Pauly in the street and told him he'd now be free to make the music he wanted to make, not the music a couple of white guys wanted him to make. Fortunately, Pauly didn't give a toss.

The magnitude of the hit piled pressure on all of us. There was the album to deliver, the Australian release to worry about, and the urgent scramble for a sequel. My phone went constantly. Alan and I started playing hide and seek with the endless messages as we tried to work out the best way forward.

Soon after the record went to number one, PolyGram took Alan, Pauly and me to dinner at the French Café on Auckland's Symonds Street where Victor presented us with gold awards for 'How Bizarre', which by that time had probably already passed the platinum sales mark of 10,000 copies shipped. It was a late night.

The next afternoon, with heads still throbbing, Alan and I again flew to Sydney. We had a lot to talk about with the Australian company.

Roger Grierson and I discussed a music publishing deal for Pauly and agreed the terms in principle. This would tie up the other half of the publishing, as he had requested earlier. We then met with Paul Dickson. It was agreed that, as Polydor in Australia was releasing the single in the second week of February, Pauly and a band of sorts would be needed there for media purposes. We especially wanted to target a massively important Saturday night TV show, *Hey Hey It's Saturday* on the Nine Network. Cheesy to a fault, the show targeted the lowest end of the Australian demographic and pulled huge numbers. With the help of its powerful music guru Ian Alexander 'Molly' Meldrum, it could make or break a single.

On the final afternoon Alan and I signed an extended version of the earlier publishing deal with PolyGram Music Publishing and Alan asked if we'd be taken out to celebrate. 'Mate,' Roger Grierson said, 'the days of waking up butt-naked on the shagpile next to a couple of hookers and empty champagne bottles and a mirror covered in coke on the table are gone.'

'Gone?' Alan said. 'I never saw them.'

Roger tried instead to take us to see one of his signings, Tex Perkins, at a venue somewhere in central Sydney, but remembering Vika and Linda the previous year we guiltily snuck off, although not before Roger had presented each of us with a glass of red wine with ice.

Back in Auckland I pushed Alan and Pauly hard on the follow-up. We would need a second single for radio as 'How Bizarre' went down the chart. When the pair had begun working together they had written a raft of songs, but other than 'How Bizarre' none were finished. The prolific co-writing had slowed to a crawl. The only song really taking shape was 'Right On'. In its earliest form this was almost a sibling of 'How Bizarre' but Pauly insisted it was the song he wanted to prioritise. I suggested one of the other songs I was now hearing, in particular 'On the Run', might be better as it was more different stylistically. However, Pauly was unmoved.

As he and Alan worked on 'Right On' it began shaping up quite well, with Alan adding an exuberant kick drum and a Polynesian party vibe. Later in *The New Zealand Herald* Pauly would say he voted against releasing 'Right On' as the second single. 'People said I had the right but that's bullshit. I pushed against it.' This was untrue. Both PolyGram and I would have been happier with 'On the Run' as the second single. 'Right On' was always Pauly's preference.

14

PAULY HAD NO MONEY. With the shower of publicity about his hit record he had had to go off the dole, and he and Kirstine were now surviving on her wages and still living in the council flat. I talked to the accountant at PolyGram and we agreed to pay him an advance and cover the weekly rental for a more desirable address. Pauly found a place near the High Court, just off Parliament Street, and signed a lease. He and Kirstine would move there in the middle of the year.

He decided to buy a car with the balance of the advance he would have left after paying some haunting debts. He adored classic European cars and had a clear idea of what he wanted. Some nights we would find ourselves at vintage car yards, where he swooned over aged Mercs and Beamers.

One morning he called to say he'd found a car he liked. I picked him up and we drove to a yard on Great North Road, where a gorgeous 1979 Mercedes two-door coupé, metallic gold and without a mark on the body, sat demanding his attention. The dealer wanted $12,000, which I guessed would be negotiable. I insisted we bring in my buddy Paul Banks, a mechanic from West Auckland, who had long serviced not only my cars but those of a large number of people in the music industry. I trusted

Paul totally: he had saved me and my staff large amounts of money by warning us away from clunkers.

I drove out to distant Swanson, where I found Paul under a hoist. He returned to the city with me and an hour or so later pronounced the vehicle sound, with the strong stipulation that this was based on a superficial look under the hood and a quick drive around the block and down the motorway. He would be happier if he were given time to check it more thoroughly. Despite this, as soon as we drove back into the car yard Pauly leapt out of the car and said to the salesman, 'I'll take it.'

As the papers were being drawn up I reiterated that he was probably paying too much – Paul had said the car was worth only $10,000 – and urged him to wait until it was checked fully. His curt response was that it was his money and he would spend it exactly as he wished. And besides, he didn't want to look cheap.

Papers signed, he handed over a cheque and drove off with the salesman to cash it and take full possession of what was, admittedly, a stunning car and one that thoroughly suited him. For the next year or two, Pauly cruised the inner city in the Mercedes. It ended up costing him a bomb for repairs, but he and the gold coupé epitomised cool. He looked the man.

The cheque Pauly used to pay for the car came from the new bank account he had asked me to help him open. He explained that a Polynesian guy with tats and a scar on his face walking into a central city bank was going to have issues opening an account unless he was accompanied by someone whom bank staff deemed more acceptable.

He chose the Westpac branch in High Street, next door to my office. As we waited to be attended to, the staff looked at Pauly and worked out he was the guy they were seeing on the video shows. There was an excited murmur.

We were shown upstairs to a bland prefabricated office that sported a potted palm, two mass-produced artworks, and assorted posters trying to sell home loans. The bearded manager in a grey suit and shoes appeared rather uncomfortable. I guessed that people like Pauly didn't normally enter his world.

Looking at me he said, 'What can I do to help?'

Pauly answered confidently, 'I want to open a savings account, a cheque account, and get a credit card.'

The manager asked what assets he had. This was my cue. I went into detail about the number one single and the forthcoming Australian release, adding that PolyGram was about to put him on a weekly retainer as an advance against substantial future earnings.

Bank managers are rarely known for audacious thinking. Nevertheless, the fact Pauly had all this lined up seemed to push a few buttons. The manager paused, thought for a moment, and then slightly reluctantly offered Pauly all three. The card would be gold, as Pauly had asked, but would initially have a low limit. This could rise if and when Pauly's finances improved.

Pauly thanked the man profusely and shook his hand repeatedly on the way out. After this, whenever he was asked to smile for a camera his catchphrase was, 'I only smile for my bank manager.' Given his income, I thought he had got the relationship somewhat the wrong way round.

The credit limit on Pauly's gold card would be increased many times in the years to come.

Around February we began to get requests from retailers for the 'new version' of 'How Bizarre', a parody called 'Stole My Car'. When the requests turned into a flood we tracked down the recording. It was clever and quite hilarious. A provincial radio DJ, Dene Young at The Rock FM, a station in the North Island tourist town of Rotorua, had constructed and recorded a version under the name The Māori Brothers. The lyrics went:

Cruising down Fenton Street in the hot hot sun
We pulled into the KFC, going to get a feed
Pile out of the Holden car 'cos we're feeling the need
Five minutes later, pigging out, full up to my eyes

Going back to the parking lot, and
owww, some bugger's stole my car, stole my car.

After the parody took off in Rotorua it quickly circulated around the country's radio stations and became a smash hit. It was politically incorrect but the nation took to it the way it had done to the irreverent Māori entertainer Billy T. James. I loved it, Alan loved it, PolyGram loved it, everyone loved it – except Pauly. He was furious at what he saw as an insult to his song, and by extension to him as an artist and a person. He informed Alan and me that he wanted us to find the guy who'd made it and 'take him out and give him the bash'.

PolyGram had other ideas. 'How Bizarre' was now slowing sales-wise and somebody – I think the sales manager, Ian Watson – suggested we repackage 'How Bizarre' with a cassette of the parody record, for which we undoubtedly owned the copyright, with the likelihood that putting this combo into stores would force the single back to number one.

It was not to be. Pauly's attitude was that we should sue not only Dene Young but any other DJ or station that played the send-up. This was untenable: it would have been expensive and have meant radio and popular suicide as both the radio programmers and the public who loved the parody would probably have turned on OMC. We quietly let the idea rest and stations kept on playing the parody. We claimed 100 percent of the airplay royalties, money Pauly was happy to accept.

As 'How Bizarre' went around the world so did the parody, becoming an airplay hit almost everywhere although it was never officially released. At some stage the recording was made available by someone as a pirate cassette, and sold several thousand nationwide.

There would be further parodies in New Zealand, Australia and the US. Pauly despised them all.

Pauly hated his teeth and often expressed a desire to have them 'fixed', which essentially meant straightened. At one meeting with PolyGram he put in a formal written request for an advance to pay for this. Victor and the financial controller Colin Brown were agreeable, and I could see no reason to deny Pauly the right to do as he wished with his own body. However, Alan argued convincingly that such a move could destroy Pauly's unique vocal tone – the 'million-dollar delivery' as he called it. Pauly was adamant: even if this happened it wouldn't matter as he wanted to be a singer, not a rapper.

Alan pleaded with Pauly to hold back until the album's vocals were finished, but he was determined to go ahead. While Alan urgently tried to make sure he had recorded the tracks he thought he'd need, Pauly visited a dental surgeon on Auckland's North Shore, with PolyGram footing the bills as advances on his royalties. The procedure took two months. I would pick Pauly up from his flat, deliver him to the dentist, and later return him home as he was usually too anaesthetised to drive safely.

Alan was proved right: when the treatment finished, the tone in Pauly's voice had changed forever. And Alan's strategy of trying to record everything he would need had only partially succeeded. When crucial vocal overdubs were needed later in the year he was at a loss. The perfect white smile Pauly flashed around the world over the next 18 months may have played a part in his success but we had lost the voice.

15

Australia had now released 'How Bizarre'. Mark Phillips was appointed our label manager; he would be our contact point with Polydor, and the person coordinating the day-to-day nuts and bolts of releasing and promoting the record in Australia.

Mark's first task was to pencil in a promotional visit for the last week of March.

It was decided Pauly and I would fly into Melbourne, then the hub of much of Australia's music and media industries, and Pauly would perform on *Hey Hey It's Saturday*. As was the case with much promotional television, he would mime to the recording.

We agreed that Pauly would also do a number of targeted press and radio interviews, and Mark and I fine-tuned the list in the hope of getting maximum value out of Pauly's time. There would also be a photo shoot for press shots. After this we would fly to Sydney for a night, put Pauly in front of more media, and then fly home. It was an intense schedule and the first crammed media blitz Pauly would experience.

While I knew 'How Bizarre' would live or die on radio play, we didn't have the luxury of being able to pick and choose the media we would talk to in Australia as we had in New Zealand. Across the Tasman Pauly would be just another aspiring singer with a good song battling a mass of others with the same. We did, however, have a hell of a story to tell and Pauly was a star the moment he walked through any door. With that in mind I vetoed media I thought were too tacky and journalists who simply wouldn't get it. I knew how unstable Pauly could be under pressure; it was important to minimise opportunities for explosive situations.

We decided to use free street music magazines, a powerful Australian urban phenomenon, to position OMC. We knew the edgier side of Pauly's story would resonate with this branch of the media. Pauly had been interviewed by some of the magazines while on the Big Day Out tour and had talked positively about the experience. Radio and TV play of the song would, we hoped, do the rest.

For Pauly to mime on *Hey Hey It's Saturday* we needed a mock-up band. Sina Saipaia, who had sung the backing vocals on 'How Bizarre', would come with us from Auckland, and we would also take Willie Boaza, a DJ with some of the *Proud* bands. Willie had been on the *Proud* tour, albeit as a dancer. He was a pleasant, unassuming man with some style and everybody liked him. He was, I recall, studying to be a doctor. His role was to make the band look as though it was more than two vocalists singing to a backing track, when in truth that's all it was.

Around four a.m. on Friday I picked up Pauly in Greys Avenue in a taxi-van and we headed through the dark cold morning to Ellerslie to gather up Sina and her boyfriend Peter, who was paying his own way to Melbourne. The pair piled excitedly into the back seats and we moved on to the airport, where Willie was waiting for us.

The first hiccup came when I asked, as we pulled into the airport, if everyone had their passport. 'Passports?' Sina said. 'Do we need one?'

A mild panic ensued. Peter and Sina roared off in the taxi back to Ellerslie to find Sina's passport while I went to the counter and explained the situation. The staff knew who Pauly was and as a favour said they'd be able to check Sina in right up to 15 minutes before the plane left, although they could not hold the plane under any circumstances. None of my pleading and carrying on would change their minds on this.

We stood and waited as the clock ticked. About 18 minutes before departure time, as our names were being broadcast on the intercom in one of those uniquely New Zealand 'all the other passengers are waiting' messages, Peter and Sina arrived and we were hustled on board. I wheedled a post-dawn drink out of the cabin staff before putting the drama behind me.

In Melbourne three hours later I grabbed a rental car and we headed to PolyGram's Victoria office. Two staff members who'd been tasked with coming in early took us to our hotel, a modern place near the MCG. Peter and Sina had a room to themselves, Pauly was sharing with Willie, and I was to share with Mark Phillips, who had just arrived from Sydney.

It was now around 9.30 a.m. and none of us had eaten so we met up in the hotel restaurant. Although we were tired, we all – especially Pauly – had a job to do. PolyGram had lined up media interviews and presented us with a schedule. In the two days before *Hey Hey*, Pauly would have a photo shoot with a style magazine and one carefully selected interview. From Monday on he would do a number of interviews in Melbourne and then Sydney, but most would be conducted by telephone from the comfort of the hotel. The schedule included useful commentary about each interviewer and publication or broadcaster, so we knew who and what we would be dealing with.

Mark and I began to go through the schedule with Pauly. The interviewer that afternoon was Nui Te Koha of the *Herald Sun*. Nui was an old friend of mine from Auckland who had risen quickly after moving to Melbourne and was now the most important daily entertainment writer in Victoria, perhaps in Australia. He had rung me and requested a chat with Pauly.

Pauly picked up the schedule and flicked backwards and forwards through it, clearly not reading much. He looked up and his eyes had that fateful dark reddish glow.

He leaned close to my face and snarled at me, "Why do I have do all this shit? Who do you think you are? Are you the white devil? Fuck you!'

As I reeled back he threatened to 'smash your fucking face'.

An immediate silence descended. Knowing Pauly's potential for violence, I stood up and began walking outside. As I did so Pauly threw the schedule on the floor and stormed off to his room.

Mark came outside and suggested it might be politic if I stood back while he and Willie tried to sort it out. Half an hour later Pauly came down from his room, walked over to me and said quietly, 'Sorry, bro, but sometimes I gotta take a stand.' He gave me a quick tight hug.

Mark was shaken by the incident, but I tried to shrug it off and we headed off to see Nui. The next 48 hours were unnerving. Pauly veered between silence and strange pronouncements. The most worrying of these concerned Molly Meldrum, the frontperson of *Hey Hey It's Saturday*'s music section. As we headed towards the television show's Richmond studios, Pauly declared that Meldrum was a paedophile. He was, he said, going to have it out with him at the studio.

He had been making similar accusations about other people in recent weeks. He had several times informed Alan and me that Neil Finn, the leader of the band Crowded House, was a 'pedo'. He had worked this out, he said, because Neil had recently played a charity gig for the primary school Neil's kids attended. Aghast, we had told him that to call someone a paedophile was slander and could cause substantial legal complications. It was not the sort of thing you said without solid evidence.

Luckily it was all talk. When Meldrum put his head into the dressing room to welcome him, Pauly grinned, put out his hand, and told Meldrum, who was looking as ridiculous as ever in his trademark faux cowboy hat, that it was a huge pleasure to meet him.

The recording, which would be broadcast that evening, went without a hitch. It would be the biggest media audience Pauly had had to date. We crossed our fingers and prayed for a positive reaction from the Australian public, who were just beginning to hear the song on the radio.

Breaking records in Australia required a completely different approach to New Zealand. A programme as lowbrow as *Hey Hey It's Saturday* wouldn't wash in New Zealand: when it screened there briefly a couple of years later audiences were appalled and turned off in droves. New

Zealand had its own televised moments of utter brain dross but Australian commercial television plumbed a whole other level. If you were trying to break a record in that vast market you simply gritted your teeth, submerged your critical faculties, and carried on.

Pauly, with his brown skin and extensive tattoos, would regularly encounter racial slurs in Australia. We quickly worked out that what was deemed offensive in New Zealand was both acceptable and mainstream across the ditch. There were many times we felt as though we had been transported back decades but Pauly almost always refused to be ruffled. Often we wouldn't find out what had been said to him during an interview until later, when he would casually mention it. However, there was one incident that I personally witnessed in Sydney after 'How Bizarre' had reached number one in Australia. A highly rated jock on morning commercial radio asked him in a live interview if he had 'sheep shit' in his hair. 'After all,' he said, 'that's what you people use to keep the curls slicked down, right?' He then laughed loudly, as did station staff watching through the glass.

Pauly silently undid the microphone on his lapel and walked out. The jock quipped, 'Wow, that was an overreaction, wasn't it?' and laughed.

I went to the station manager and asked for an explanation. He said there was nothing to explain. I complained to Polydor, who complained to the station's owners, who complained to the on-air manager. The station offered Pauly a loose and very vague apology. As far as they were concerned, nothing out of the ordinary had happened.

After Pauly's performance on *Hey Hey It's Saturday* we went out to dinner in Chinatown, courtesy of the record company. We felt we had made a big jump towards breaking through to the next level in Australia. I knew, though, that in big countries like this success was not nearly as instant as it was in a small place like New Zealand.

The next day was free. After wandering around record stores Peter, Sina, Pauly and I drove out to the Dandenong Ranges, a hilly bush-clad region with good views just east of Melbourne. While Peter, Sina and I strolled around and went to a café at the lookout with high prices and awful coffee, Pauly remained in the car, chain-smoking and calling Kirstine on my cell phone. On the way back to the city he sat next to me, pouting and grumbling about everything: the city, the park, the record company. When Peter told him to cheer up he turned to him and said, 'You are only here because of me. Remember that.'

At breakfast next morning I had to deal with yet another incident. Pauly strode over to me as I was eating and said angrily that Willie was 'a fag'. He had worked this out because Willie had wandered around wearing underpants and a T-shirt in the room they shared. He was adamant: he would not share a room with him for another night.

'That's fine, Pauly,' I said. 'Whether he is or isn't is neither here nor there; he's going back to Auckland today so you, my friend, are completely safe.'

That day's interviews, both face-to-face and via telephone, went without a hitch. Pauly was cooperative and keen. He explained to me over lunch that these were the sorts of things he had fully expected to be doing now he had 'sorted out' PolyGram. By eight that night we were back at the airport. Sina, Peter and Willie were returning to Auckland, and Pauly, Mark and I heading to Sydney.

A serviced apartment in Surry Hills had been booked for Pauly and me. Jane Fisher, an old friend of mine, had a retro clothing store nearby, and next morning after breakfast we wandered up to say hello and kill an hour before the day's work schedule began. Picking up a pair of sunglasses Pauly said, 'These are you, bro.' They were, but I looked at the price tag and promptly put them back. I went next door to buy a newspaper and returned to find that Pauly had taken the sunglasses and gone back to the apartment, leaving me with the tab. He wore the designer shades that afternoon. I didn't ever see them again.

After being taken around the offices of the weekly street newspapers, most of whom seemed uninterested and self-important, we went to PolyGram's splendidly refurbished premises in Miller's Point near The Rocks to meet the state and national staff of Polydor who were handling the record. Afterwards, as Pauly worked his way through a hefty list of phone interviews, I was pulled into a sales meeting and cajoled into making an instant presentation. I have always had a dread of public speaking, but such was the evident level of belief in 'How Bizarre' that I managed to breeze through it. The people working the song day-to-day assured me it was going to be very, very big. It was hard not to feel the momentum building.

The afternoon's schedule was to end with a live interview on Triple J, an alternative radio network that had been supportive of the *Proud* album a year and a half earlier. As we waited in the foyer of the Australian Broadcasting Corporation's expansive radio building, Pauly took a fancy to the expensive-looking '60s-style sofas and asked if I could arrange to buy one on his behalf. I suggested this wasn't appropriate but later, in the studio, Pauly turned to the interviewer, Angela Catterns, and asked if it were possible to buy the foyer furniture. She looked bemused and laughed uncomfortably. After the interview Pauly asked the same question of the building's doorman and then Gary, the PolyGram promotions person who was accompanying us. Eventually he would find a sofa in Auckland that, if not identical to the one in the ABC foyer, was quite similar.

That night Pauly and I rendezvoused with Mark in a bar just off Oxford Street. Mark had brought along Polydor's club promotions manager, a young woman who worked part-time under contract. Pauly seemed distracted and headed back to the apartment after one drink, while the rest of us stayed another hour. The young woman told me Pauly needed professional styling help if he were to go forward. I was taken aback – Pauly was the most instinctively and uniquely stylish person I knew. I brushed the comment aside but thereafter I had a niggling thought that, while Australians might buy 'How Bizarre' in large numbers, they would never completely understand Pauly or OMC.

Back in Auckland there was no time for a breather. The album was proceeding far too slowly. PolyGram was pushing hard and starting to get annoyed. The New Zealand branch wanted the album in the marketplace by late April so it could cash in on Pauly's next single, which had been confirmed as 'Right On'.

One of the biggest barriers we were facing was Victor 's interference in the recording process. Alan complained that the PolyGram boss was constantly arriving in the studio and attempting to sit in on, and exert control over, the sessions. Alan would have to stop and listen to him: he was, as he regularly reminded us, paying the bills.

He would often ramble for hours, insisting Alan change and edit things, which Alan had to change back again after he left. The next night he would arrive again, and, oblivious to the fact his edits from the night before had been wiped or his suggestions ignored, recommence. One night when he insisted Alan remix a track, Alan realised he had come from the swimming pool and his ears were full of water. All this slowed down production of the urgently needed album.

Unlike Victor, unless I was asked I rarely ventured an opinion, other than on a couple of occasions when I thought something was veering in a slightly askew direction. I was keenly aware the production was a partnership between Alan and Pauly. Victor seemed oblivious to this. Somewhere along the way he'd decided that he too was a producer and a creator. He did have talents that were vital to OMC – he was a superb salesman and retail hustler and could sell records with a passion few others could arouse. However, he could also be overbearing, with a self-belief that exceeded reality.

On a later trip to Australia Paul Dickson would pull me aside and quiz me about something Victor had told him – namely that the forthcoming album was about 20 percent Pauly, 10 percent Alan and 70 percent Victor.

Momentarily taken aback at Victor's gall, I laughed.

'No, I didn't think so,' Paul said.

Victor probably believed what he was saying, unaware few of his ideas had ended up on the album. On Planet Earth his creative input to OMC was almost zero.

16

THE AGREEMENT ALAN AND PAULY had verbalised back in late 1994, which would legally define the profit split between the two of them, had not yet been drawn up and signed. This had been much discussed and I had put pressure on them both to put it in writing as quickly as possible, aware of the minefield that could eventuate otherwise.

My idea was to ask Noel Agnew, Alan's lawyer, who had also acted for Pauly, to draft an agreement which Pauly could take to a third party for approval before signing it. However, in early April 1996 both parties asked me to draft it. I said I was happy to do so, but on the proviso that anything I scribbled down would be subjected to legal scrutiny before any signatures were placed on it.

I spent much of the next day working on the agreement. It was a simple one-page document that I felt formalised, in pretty clear English, the conversations we had had. When I was happy with it I rang Alan and Pauly and suggested they meet me that evening to go over it.

My office was on the first floor of the old Kean's Building at 35 High Street, upstairs from Cause Célèbre and behind the popular musicians' hangout Rakinos Café. Alan arrived first, eager and happy, and then within a few minutes Pauly, who also appeared positive. I suggested we eat at Rakinos first, but both Pauly and Alan wanted to get the paperwork sorted before we did anything else. I clarified as best I could that this was a draft document and it was advisable for them to get independent legal advice before they signed.

The document ran to just eight short paragraphs and stated the terms they had agreed upon. Once the cost of recording had been recovered from all income, Alan would be paid a small producer's fee out of the gross income from album sales. He would also receive 25 percent of the net royalties from sales and exploitation of both the 'How Bizarre' single and the album. Pauly would receive the higher 75 percent share in recognition of the work he would need to do to promote the records in the media and beyond. The deal excluded publishing, where the income split would be 50:50.

I read out the agreement slowly and carefully, explaining each clause and its implications. As I did so Pauly became increasingly fidgety and uneasy. When I finished he leapt at Alan, grabbed at him, pulling his face next to his, and snarled, 'You are going out this window right now!'

It was a three-storey drop on to the concrete courtyard below. I called to him to stop and he looked across my desk and barked back, 'You are fucking next, you fucking white devil!'

Then, just as suddenly, he stopped and stepped back. He burst into tears and sat down. He looked over at us both and sobbed. 'You are the only two people I can trust. I want Alan to have half of everything,' he whispered, barely audible.

'No,' Alan said. 'I'm happy with 25 percent.'

Without another word, Pauly grabbed a pen. I pulled the document back and reiterated that he needed to see a lawyer first.

'No, bro, I want to sign it now,' he said.

After signing the two copies he put down the pen and tearfully hugged Alan, saying, 'I'm sorry, bro. I'm sorry. I'm sorry.' And with that he walked out.

Alan shrugged, signed the agreement, and I witnessed his signature. Pauly had recently appointed a new lawyer, Michael Cronin at Russell

McVeagh. I faxed Cronin the document and also sent it to PolyGram in Auckland and Sue Cohen in Sydney. I had doubts about whether the agreement would stand up if challenged, but both Pauly's lawyer and mine assured me that since Pauly had, in front of witnesses, waived legal advice and signed it after being fully apprised of its contents, it would likely withstand any scrutiny.

With 'Right On' about to be the next New Zealand single, we needed a video. Victor suggested Flying Start, an independent production house in Auckland's Freemans Bay, whose director, Rob McLaughlin, I knew fairly well. Given the fiasco of the last video, Alan and Pauly were fine with that. I was too, provided we had absolute control over the video from first concept to final delivery.

'Right On' had developed rather nicely, with pedal steel guitar having been added as an intentional homage to the Polynesian dance bands that had filled the ballrooms and halls of Auckland and the South Pacific in the 1950s and '60s, and an affectionate tribute to musicians and bandleaders such as the legendary Bill Wolfgramm and Bill Sevesi. This connection was underscored by a rhythm Alan had constructed by laying an insistent 4/4 beat under an acoustic guitar strum that referred back to the many recordings of the era's big bands.

Like 'Land of Plenty', another song on the album, 'Right On' openly and emotionally expressed Pauly's pride in his upbringing and his family. The lyrics were moving and joyous and it was important that the video accurately reflected this. Pauly sketched his ideas on a storyboard and we took it to a meeting with Flying Start, where Rob McLaughlin and the producer, Tony Vernal, pointed out some practical limitations.

Pauly and I spent a couple of nights fine-tuning the storyboard, then returned and presented the revised idea. There was some dispute over the inclusion of an Elvis character but Pauly argued that Elvis – or Elivisi as he was called in the song – was such an overpowering musical figure in Polynesian culture he needed to stay as in the lyrics:

Pedal to the metal / Shine until the steel
Sitting up front / Elivisi by the wheel

Dean Martin, whom Pauly loved, had just died so he too was added to the lyric as Deano Valentino.

We filmed the following weekend, with Sina again playing a prominent role, sitting beside Pauly in the bus that would form the video's centrepiece. As with 'How Bizarre', we pulled in as many volunteers as possible, including my niece Libby and her school friends. Even I was in a shot, as a brick-cellphone-toting businessman at a bus stop. The result was a wonderfully upbeat video, celebrating much of what Pauly was and what he wanted to say about being a young Polynesian man growing up in Auckland. The budget was $15,000.

In March 1996 'How Bizarre' entered the Australian singles chart. Over the next few months Pauly, Alan, Victor and I, in various combinations, seemed to be in Sydney or Melbourne almost every second week. This was becoming more and more exhausting for all of us but especially for Pauly, who was getting demands from both sides of the Tasman. A second appearance, this time of just Pauly and Sina, on *Hey Hey It's Saturday* was filmed in Melbourne but I was saying no to almost every request in New Zealand. This appeared to confuse the promotional team at PolyGram but I had my reasons, not least of them the need to provide Pauly with a space where he was not subject to constant pressure.

Late in March, Victor and I flew over for a meeting with PolyGram management. Those attending included Tim Read, boss of PolyGram Australia and New Zealand and Victor's immediate superior. We were lodged at Sebel Townhouse, a hotel that had once been the unofficial home of the Australian music industry, with a huge and glittering lineage of guests from Liberace to Bob Dylan and Elton John, but had now seen better days. We spent a pleasant two days before the meeting spending PolyGram New Zealand's expense account money, hanging out with Mark Phillips and an old friend of Victor's and drinking cocktails at the hotel bar as various Sydney notables wandered in and out. It was the first real break I'd had since 'How Bizarre' had been released to the media four months earlier and it felt good to temporarily forget about the maelstrom, and not have to worry about my club in Auckland or my marriage, which was fast disintegrating.

It would be my last break before the storm hit.

There were several important topics on the agenda of our meetings at PolyGram. The first concerned an adjustment to how the OMC project was being handled by the company internally. A meeting about this was held behind closed doors and attended by only Paul Dickson, Tim Read, Victor and me.

The various national divisions of PolyGram were called Operating Companies, usually referred to as Op-Cos. Each Op-Co had its own budgets and profits and losses, and worked in a semi-independent way, reporting upwards via a corporate structure that resembled a complex pyramid. Each Op-Co had to find the funding to support its own signings and internal operations, and had to make a profit. But it also benefited from what was called the All In Fee, usually tagged the AIF. The AIF was a percentage of wholesale set by PolyGram's head office in The Netherlands. It was paid to an Op-Co by other Op-Cos around the world when they sold copies of recording masters owned by the originating Op-Co.

Although this sounds complicated it was in practice quite simple and encouraged companies to sign acts that might have the commercial legs to make the originating Op-Co a profit externally as well as internally. The downside was that regional companies could be unwilling to prioritise artists signed to another Op-Co when it would be of more benefit to prioritise their own signed acts in their home market.

The system meant that, as things stood, PolyGram Australia would pay a fee to PolyGram New Zealand on Australian sales of OMC records. New Zealand's bottom line would benefit greatly from this and all other offshore income: it would receive the AIF from all sales beyond Australasia.

What changed the ball game in March 1996 was the first significant interest in the record from European Op-Cos, in particular from Polydor's hugely important UK office. This interest, still only slight but perceptibly growing daily, raised a problem: PolyGram New Zealand simply did not have the deep pockets that would be needed to bankroll an international run of the sort that PolyGram in Australia and New Zealand and I thought, or at least fervently hoped, might be achieved. Conversely, if such a run was unsuccessful, New Zealand's Op-Co would be strained by the costs.

A solution was offered by PolyGram boss Tim Read, with the clear if unspoken implication that it was not up for discussion. PolyGram New Zealand would transfer a substantial percentage of the ownership of the project to PolyGram Australia. In return, the Australian company would underwrite the whole international dash. Sue DeBenedette, PolyGram Australia's international artist manager, would work full-time as OMC's international liaison.

The deal meant PolyGram New Zealand would gain a lot if the record worked internationally but lose less if it didn't. The record would remain on the Huh! label and I would be A&Ring it. From Alan, Pauly and my point of view, and from Pauly's, the deal was hugely beneficial – it gave us a chance.

This paper transfer of a percentage of ownership of the OMC project was confidential and remained hidden from almost everyone who worked the project, including Sue DeBenedette, who continued to refer to PolyGram New Zealand as repertoire owner.[9] The copyright note on the record did the same, and indeed still does.

This camouflaged what was in effect a takeover by PolyGram Australia. Any international success would greatly benefit the Australian company. It could now claim, at least internally, ownership in a project that had originated from another territory, as could some senior managers in both Australia and New Zealand who had had absolutely nothing to do

---

9   The repertoire owner is the country division that is regarded as the 'home territory' in record company terms.

with discovering, nurturing or developing 'How Bizarre' or OMC. That said, it had been Australian-based Adam Holt and Paul Dickson who had first seen the potential in the record we offered them back in mid 1995 and they deserved to share in its success.

While the ownership situation didn't affect me contractually, it did very much affect whom I talked to and dealt with on a day-to-day basis. In retrospect, the change was also the moment we began to lose control and the wheels began to slowly come off.

17

SUE DEBENEDETTE WAS A VETERAN of the American record industry. She had come into the PolyGram system when her employer, Herb Alpert and Jerry Moss's legendary US indie A&M Records, had been bought in 1989. She now lived in Sydney, working in an international liaison role at PolyGram Australia, tasked with handling all the acts they were trying to sell to the world. Since Australian acts with international potential were thin on the ground, after March 1996 she worked almost exclusively on OMC in all territories outside Australia and New Zealand.

I liked Sue a lot; she was honest, funny and hard-working. But despite her best efforts, she didn't quite get Pauly or that OMC's music came from a unique New Zealand mix of cultures and histories. I left meetings convinced she thought she was dealing with a rocking balladeer like Bryan Adams, with whom she had worked at A&M, or a commercially mainstream singer-songwriter like Sheryl Crow, another A&M signee whom Sue had played an active role in developing as an artist.

Pauly was fast becoming a celebrity. As we strolled through downtown Melbourne after he had recorded his second stint on *Hey Hey It's Saturday*, we passed the Hard Rock Café in Bourke Street. A group of young girls came out and one screamed, 'It's Mister Bizarre!' This led to yells from the others and a mad dash towards us. Pauly looked at me with a touch of panic in his eyes and said, 'Let's get the fuck out of here.'

The girls chased him for a couple of blocks until I managed to hail a cab and throw him in, leaving his pursuers standing on the footpath. It felt like a crazy out-take from a Keystone Cops movie. In the cab Pauly grinned and said, 'Man, I hope that doesn't happen again.' I didn't believe he meant that for a moment.

We flew to Sydney next day and Alan flew from Auckland to meet us. Polydor was convinced we were likely to have the Australian number one single that week. After pausing for a week to catch breath, sales in Australia had gone ballistic. Retailers were telling Polydor 'How Bizarre' had sold at least twice what the number two record had that week.

We sat waiting in the Polydor offices, surrounded by anxious staffers. Finally the call came. 'How Bizarre' was not only number one on the ARIA Australian singles chart of April 14, it had sold almost four times as many as the number two record. It would stay at number one for five weeks, and at number two for a couple more, eventually selling in excess of double platinum and spending a total of five months on the chart.

As was the custom when a local record went number one, there was a bottle or two of champagne and a promise of bigger things to come. We were taken to a new restaurant in East Sydney with Mark, Adam, Sue DeBenedette and Paul Dickson. Pauly seemed most impressed by the fact that Peter Garrett, the lead singer of Oz rockers Midnight Oil, was at the next table.

After dinner, Mark dropped Pauly and Alan back at the hotel and he and I headed to his Rushcutters Bay house for a nightcap. Next day Alan told me that he and Pauly had gone for a walk in the early hours of the morning along the 'Golden Mile' in Sydney's red light district, Kings Cross. Pauly had tried in vain to persuade him to go into one of the countless strip clubs to celebrate.

The 1996 New Zealand Music Awards, organised by RIANZ, the Recording Industry Association of New Zealand, were scheduled for April 23. They were being held for the first time at the 2,000-seat Aotea Centre in the centre of Auckland. Pauly, with far and away the biggest New Zealand hit single in a decade – the last having been 'Sailing Away', a dire singalong record released in 1986 to coincide with New Zealand's America's Cup Challenge – was likely to pick up an award or two.

OMC, which included the reluctant star Alan Jansson but was perceived by the industry and the public as just Pauly Fuemana, was nominated for Most Promising New Male Vocalist and Most Promising Group. Alan was nominated for Producer of the Year and, with Rick Huntington, Engineer of the Year. 'How Bizarre' was also up for Song of the Year, the premier award, voted for by the public. OMC had been asked to perform 'How Bizarre'. It would be a mime of sorts but with live vocals from Pauly and Sina. Alan had spent a day constructing a special mix that included all chorus vocals. The verses were Pauly's to perform.

For me there was an extra frisson to the evening. Nathan Haines' debut album *Shift Left* on my Huh! label had been nominated for Best Jazz Album. Given it was the biggest selling jazz album ever recorded in New Zealand, I was confident it would win.

My first experience of New Zealand music awards went back to 1980 and a dank conference room in a rundown hotel called Logan Park, far out in Auckland suburbia. It was the sort of place where farming families, up from the sticks for their daughter's wedding, would stay, and where plumbing industry conferences were held.

Over the next few years, as new young blood moved into management at its member companies, RIANZ became aware that if the local recording industry were to be taken seriously it would need to dramatically polish its public face. The awards moved to downtown hotel ballrooms and the shows were enhanced with live performances and a wider invitation list that included politicians and tastemakers from outside the industry.

For all that, the awards remained essentially a self-congratulatory piss-up, where the biggest stories to come out of the night were inevitably about pop stars who got drunk and did something embarrassing or, as in

1992, a brawl took place. That year The Exponents and Herbs exchanged punches after onstage comments by Herbs' Charlie Tumahai about a promoter The Exponents worked with. The day after the awards was commonly spent by industry people trying to fix up the messes and ensure they didn't leak into the mainstream media.

By 1996 it had become obvious that the only way to raise the profile of the awards, and thus the artists themselves, was to have them on television. A sponsor was needed. Clear Communications, a large telecommunications company, was assiduously courted and finally signed up. The awards moved to the prestigious but cavernous Aotea Centre, complete with a red carpet lined with enthusiastic fans given free passes on the condition they stood outside wailing and shrieking loudly at the arriving pop stars as the cameras rolled.

Early in the afternoon we went to the hall to rehearse. This was a straightforward affair that should have taken about an hour. However, as this was the first show the recording industry had staged in such a huge venue, the first to be partially open to the public and the first to be televised, albeit via a delayed broadcast, RIANZ had hired an outside production house.

An hour after we were to do our sound and stage check we were still waiting backstage. The production manager, a surly type who clearly cared little for oddly dressed and self-important pop stars, was being rude to just about everyone, issuing orders without a please or thank you and managing to thoroughly annoy everyone, including the artists, their management and his own crew.

After an hour and a half, Pauly wandered outside to have a cigarette. At that point the production manager came backstage and announced that Pauly was wanted immediately. I sent Sina and Willie, who had agreed to one last performance, to the side of the stage and went to fetch him. Pauly was not happy. The guy had made him wait an hour and a half. He could wait five minutes.

He finished his smoke and joined the band inside. The production manager was livid. He curtly asked Pauly where the hell he'd been. Pauly looked him in the eye and told him to get stuffed. The manager fronted up to Pauly and, an inch from his face, announced, 'If you want to get anywhere in this game, sonny, you'd better pick up your act.'

For a moment I thought Pauly was going to take a swing at him but Sina, her boyfriend Peter, Willie, a sound guy from Oceania Audio and I managed to calm the situation and the group performed a cursory run-through of 'How Bizarre'.

'One more time please,' the sound tech in the TV booth asked politely.

'Fuck off,' Pauly said and stormed out.

As I drove him home he said he wasn't going to do the show. Expecting something of the sort, I tried to explain he wasn't doing it for that prick but for the 40,000 people who had bought his single and might want to buy his album. However, he was resolute. There was no way he was going to perform.

Alan, Pauly, a couple of the young women who were in the video and I were to arrive in a limousine around six o'clock that evening and walk down the red carpet, where screaming fans and what passed for paparazzi in 1990s New Zealand would be primed and ready. Around four-thirty I nervously rang Pauly. To my relief he seemed fine. I assumed Kirstine had talked him through it as she often did, winding back his anger with a few well-placed words.

Three-quarters of an hour later I collected Alan and Pauly from Uptown Studios in the stretched Ford Fairlane and we cruised across the Auckland Harbour Bridge and then back to the city, drinking Dom Pérignon and talking the inevitable nonsense about this being the style we intended getting used to.

When we pulled up outside the Aotea Centre, Pauly was more nervous than I had ever seen him. It occurred to me that the crowd he was about to perform to was probably his biggest yet. He had done very few live performances.

The awards handed out were all over the place. Alan was awarded Engineer of the Year with Rick Huntington for 'How Bizarre' but passed over for best producer in favour of Eddie Rayner for 'World Stand Still', a largely unknown record. OMC took out Most Promising Group and Pauly also picked up the gong for Most Promising Male Vocalist. In his acceptance speech he commented that having a trans-Tasman number one record possibly meant he had gone beyond promising.

Meanwhile, 'How Bizarre' won Single of the Year by a massive margin: it had received more votes from the public than all the other nominees combined. Pauly thanked half the known universe – and since his recording contract said that was his signed territory, why not? – but forgot to mention his South Auckland siblings or me. As he came down from the stage he hugged me and said, 'Man I'm sorry.' He made amends by dedicating his performance of 'How Bizarre' not only to Kirstine but to Alan and me. His performance was hurried and perfunctory. He forgot many of the words and got ahead of the backing CD but few noticed and the kids in the gallery loved it.

The large unofficial after-party was hosted jointly by PolyGram and Huh! at Cause Célèbre. Pauly stayed until the end, standing at the bar grinning widely as people bought him drinks and he held court. He really was the man. However, the failure of the awards committee to give Alan the award for best producer would mark the beginning of a cold shoulder from the New Zealand music industry that both Alan and Pauly would feel pretty much until the day Pauly died. Perhaps it was jealousy, bitterness that both men were fiercely non-conformist, tall poppy syndrome, or a mix of all three, but the New Zealand recording industry repeatedly snubbed them.[10]

'Right On' was released to New Zealand radio in early May. There was a mixed response. While urban stations such as Mai FM understood the

---

10 In 2000 and 2001 Neil Finn's single 'Don't Dream It's Over' took the award for Most Performed Work Overseas at the APRA Silver Scroll Awards after 'How Bizarre' had won it for the previous four years. Before the 2002 awards APRA staff told me 'How Bizarre' was again a clear winner. However, on the night no mention was made of the award. Next day I was told the organisers had decided the top spot was of 'little interest' as 'How Bizarre' was an old record. As time had been tight, the award had been dropped. Alan was furious; he has not attended the Silver Scrolls since.

single and its celebration of growing up Polynesian in New Zealand and added it to their playlists straight away, the reaction from other stations was bemusement. Some tagged it a 'How Bizarre' sound-alike even though the structure, rhythm, speed and content were all markedly different.

There was a bigger problem for radio stations and us to deal with: 'How Bizarre' simply wouldn't go away. It was still rating highly on radio, as was the parody 'Stole My Car'. Understandably, programmers were uneasy about dropping from their playlists a song people obviously still wanted to hear. This in effect blocked the daytime addition of 'Right On' because there was a limited number of slots most commercial radio stations would allocate to any one act at one time. And, even more decisively, they didn't want to drop a popular song that their rivals might keep on playing and therefore gain an edge, no matter how small.

PolyGram's radio pluggers were frustrated by the failure of mainstream commercial stations such as the crucial nationwide ZM network to budge. One important Wellington programmer had even advised us OMC was a one-hit wonder and, given his experience in the industry, he was convinced its run was over.

Meanwhile, the sleeve of 'Right On' was causing something of a stir. Pauly had been hanging around with a young photographer called Nicole England. The relationship, as far as I knew, was purely platonic, but the two of them would often be found in the late afternoon having coffee in cafés in Vulcan Lane and High Street.

Nicole was obviously having an influence on Pauly's clothes and image. Instead of the almost Latino jazz boho look he had cultivated since late 1994, his style was now more sophisticated and urbane. The lounge jackets and cravats were gone. He was wearing tailored suits and polished black boots with Cuban heels. His hair was combed forward in a Roman cut. He looked extremely sharp – and like nobody else in New Zealand or beyond I could name.

The 'Right On' sleeve carried a tasteful Nicole England shot of Pauly in a brown pinstriped suit. It had been laid out by designer Andrew B. White, who worked on almost all Huh! releases. Victor hated the design and had argued that we should go with something akin to the last one but I had refused to budge.

To his new look Pauly had added a new name. In April he had announced that from then on he would be using the stage name Pauly Fuemana-Lawrence, taking his middle name and posting it after his surname. It was, he told me, the only name he would hereafter be known by: he would no longer answer to Pauly Fuemana. I passed this on to PolyGram and we used the new name on the sleeve of 'Right On', adding at Pauly's insistence: 'OMC is Pauly Fuemana-Lawrence.' However, this seemingly important name change was quickly forgotten, and never mentioned again by either Pauly or PolyGram.

'Right On' charted at number eleven in the New Zealand singles chart of June 2. This was to be its highest placing, although it hovered around the teens for almost two months, then spent another five weeks in the lower realms of the Top 40, driven mostly by sales in places such as South Auckland and Rotorua, where large Polynesian populations bought it in such numbers it was certified platinum in August. Eventual New Zealand sales were around 12,000, making it a substantial hit in those pre-digital days.

In mid June Alan, Pauly and I were taken by corporate cab to the national PolyGram conference at Hotel du Vin, an upmarket winery and conference centre an hour south of Auckland, where we were toasted and presented with gold discs for 'Right On'.

The PolyGram staff seemed to take immense pride in the success of 'How Bizarre', a record over which they rightly felt some ownership. Over the past weeks I had gone out of my way to get to know and get input from everyone in the company; they were the ones who had to hustle and sell our records. Our trek to the conference was to tell these two dozen staffers how grateful we were for their work and the effort that had gone into making 'How Bizarre' the biggest selling New Zealand record in a decade, and probably the fastest selling one since the 1960s.

Such successes are always group efforts. It's easy to forget just how much an artist owes to the people, often averagely paid, who believe in him or her. Their support is more important than any amount of media coverage.

For the Australian release of 'Right On' in late August, the catchy and exuberant New Zealand video was re-edited to add in parts of an Australian hit movie, *Sleeping With The Enemy*, which featured the song. Unhappily, the re-worked video made little sense, being just a confusing series of images with no logical sequence. The Australian television networks hardly played it and this, together with the fact 'Right On' was up against the same airplay issue in Australia, with radio stations not wanting to drop 'How Bizarre', meant the song didn't bother the charts at all.

This failure after the huge success of 'How Bizarre' caused panic in PolyGram Australia, which now owned a large slab of the project, and an immediate search for another single with which to launch the album there. The album's release was postponed until a second hit could be pushed into the Australian charts.

In 1997 the peculiar Australian video was used for the European release of 'Right On'. Alan and I protested but by then almost nobody was listening. They were too busy scrambling to hop on board with Pauly and his snowballing international success.

I continued to be extremely careful whom I let talk to Pauly and had a select list of journalists with whom I was comfortable. It included Russell Bailey and Graham Reid of *The New Zealand Herald*, freelancer Colin Hogg, Dylan Taite of Television New Zealand and John Russell of *Rip It Up*. However, I now felt that a longer story in a magazine such as *Pavement* could work if we got the right writer involved and had discussed this with the editor, Barney McDonald, and his business partner Glenn Hunt.

Pavement was a street magazine and the most stylish publication in the country. Large parts of its demographic may have been rather frivolous, but it had a much wider readership than the music press, and carried more cred with the sort of inner-city influence-makers who mattered than did any newspaper. 'How Bizarre' and its journey were also turning into a hell of a story, one that deserved to be recorded. Glenn and Barney needed a little persuasion over several coffees in Rakinos but once they decided to go with it they were very enthusiastic.

Barney suggested a writer called Jock Lawrie. I had known Jock most of his life through a family connection. He had talent and integrity and was passionate about music so I was happy with the suggestion. We were clearly not going to get the right to any editorial control but I felt I could trust Jock. When we met he agreed not to press Pauly on his past gang involvement or other similarly dark parts of his life; I was concerned Pauly might embellish and expand on the truth, as he was prone to doing. Jock said he would document these things only if Pauly raised them himself.

A harder sell than *Pavement* were Pauly and Alan. Pauly's initial reaction was a firm no to an interview with a magazine he called 'Pervement' because of the images of very young-looking models who had notoriously appeared in some of its fashion shoots. I carefully explained the terms of the interview and exactly who Jock was, and pointed out the magazine was well regarded for its writing. I cautioned that he was not, however, to say anything he didn't want to appear in print. Alan also agreed to talk but reluctantly: he was far more comfortable staying outside the spotlight.

Jock and Pauly eventually spent the best part of a week hanging out and talking. Pauly would often ring me or turn up in my office afterwards, telling me how well it was going and how much of a good mate Jock was becoming.

The photo session took place in late May and the magazine appeared in the first week of June. I was pleased with the result. Pauly had been extraordinarily open with Jock and came across well. The story portrayed him as both sensitive and creative, and largely sidestepped the grim stories of his past I knew he had told Jock. Pauly, though, was less than happy. When he read the story he rang and bellowed down the phone, telling me he was going to 'take out Pervement' and give both Jock and the magazine's editor 'the bash'. The images, he said, made him look like a small-time hustler. After a day or so he calmed down but the anger simmered on, as did so much anger over the years about imagined slights. As late as 2006 he would tell me he was still working out a way to 'get' Barney McDonald, despite the fact *Pavement* was no longer being published.

There was an interesting postscript to the *Pavement* affair. In a huge departure for the magazine, which had never before featured a New Zealand musician in this way, it had put Pauly on the front cover and plastered his image on posters across walls and shopfront displays. In the cover shot, taken by Stephen Langdon, Pauly, wearing one of the Chinese dragon shirts he loved and collected, was standing with fists raised, glowering at the camera and confronting the viewer with the fuck-you look I knew well.

Barney McDonald later told me the issue with Pauly on the cover was Pavement's lowest selling to that date and for years afterwards. This didn't surprise me. The image was challenging and uncomfortable, especially next to the beautifully photographed shots of models and starlets that were the magazine's stock-in-trade.

At Pauly's insistence, PolyGram bought the negatives from *Pavement* later that year: he wanted them buried forever. As it turned out he wouldn't succeed. In 1997, when PolyGram's Mercury Records was releasing 'How Bizarre' in the US, it found the photos in PolyGram's files and offered them to a few select magazines. Both *Rolling Stone* and *The Village Voice* opted to run with them.

18

THE FIVE-WEEK RUN of 'How Bizarre' at the top of the Australian singles chart, plus keen communications from PolyGram Australia to PolyGram's international head office in St James Square, London, had raised considerable interest in that part of the world. The UK branch of Polydor confirmed in May it had picked up the option for the territory and would release the record in early July, after taking it to British radio in late June.

I had heard murmurings of this from Sue DeBenedette via the endless email stream between us but nothing firm. In the last week of May 1996 Victor asked me to come into his office for an important talk with the Australian office. On the conference call, Sue, Victor and I went through the progress in the talks with the UK. The gist was that the UK office, having sampled the record to a few crucial radio programme directors and received a good reaction, was now convinced it looked like a hit in the making.

Pauly and I needed to be available over the next few weeks to fly to the UK at short notice and cover the promotional requirements of a British release – and hopefully, if the record were climbing the charts, have Pauly to perform on *Top of the Pops*. This leading BBC

TV music show aired each week, two days after the latest singles chart came out.

As happy and eager as I was to head off to the other side of the world in a business-class seat and leap into what would be a massive jump industry-wise, the UK being one of the world's most important music markets, there were some immediate things I needed to sort out. My home situation had improved. My wife had overcome some health problems, and our nearly two-year-old daughter was bouncy and happy. Pauly had taken to pampering her, regularly dropping off small gifts at my office and arriving at our house to see her unannounced. However, by now Tom and I had several businesses to run – a nightclub, a record store and a fast food outlet – and some 30 employees. I needed to make sure he would be okay with my flitting off to the other side of the world at a day's notice.

Luckily he was completely supportive – his words were something like, 'Whatever it takes and however long it takes.' He realised how much this meant, not just for OMC but for the New Zealand music industry as a whole. In the 70 or so years that music had been recorded in New Zealand, not a single locally produced record had made it on to *Top of the Pops*, let alone the UK charts.

The number of New Zealand acts that had even had a substantial UK release – with a record company that thought they stood a shot at the UK charts – could be counted on the fingers of one hand. In the early 1980s Split Enz had secured a Top 20 hit with 'I Got You' but the song had been recorded in Australia and signed directly to an Australian label. The same could be said of the band's offshoot Crowded House, which, as much as New Zealand liked to claim it, was a band with one New Zealander and two Australians, and was signed directly to a US record label.

In the 1960s, New Zealander John Rowles had reached number three in the UK with his Engelbert Humperdinck soundalike 'If I Only Had Time' and had followed it up with 'Hush, Not A Word To Mary', which scraped into the Top 20. But he, too, had been signed to an offshore label and both songs had been recorded in England. Rowles did have the distinction of being one of only two Māori to have ever graced the UK singles charts, the other being Dame Kiri Te Kanawa, who had had a minor hit with 'World In Union', a Rugby World Cup theme song, in 1991.

We hoped to change that, but this time with an artist signed to a New Zealand label, recorded in New Zealand and based in New Zealand, and with Ngai Tūhoe Māori and Niuean heritage.

My next-door neighbour at Garfield Street in Parnell, where I lived until early that year, was Anita McNaught. Anita was a television journalist for the *60 Minutes* current affairs programme. She and I would regularly chat over the fence. We agreed one day that Pauly and OMC could make a good *60 Minutes* piece. When she talked to her bosses, they said they'd like to wait and see how the story developed: a New Zealander breaking into the Australian music market wasn't considered novel enough for the ratings-driven show, which was up against similar shows on its opposition channel, TV3. As the UK breakthrough was now looking likely I rang her. Anita went back to her bosses and pitched the story again.

After our conference call in May, I had emailed Sue DeBenedette and suggested we try to talk PolyGram UK into dance remixes of 'How Bizarre'. What I thought might take the record into clubs around the world, and especially in Europe, were not the sort of mixes Alan, Rick and I had knocked together in 1995 but contemporary club mixes by a big name remixer.

The UK office agreed and asked if we had any preferences. I optimistically threw up a couple of names: Masters At Work and Roger Sanchez. I had been a fan of both in the mid 1990s and knew they had the sort of name that sold records and ensured global dance-floor penetration.

Both came back with quotes far beyond our budget. Indeed the Masters At Work figure exceeded our entire album budget. The UK office then suggested the Sharp Boys. George Mitchell and Steven Doherty, the duo who worked under that name, were not only hot but willing to do the mix for a reasonable price. The British office also tagged Flexifinger, a duo comprising Ian Masterson and David Green, for a second mix. I was told they had worked with Dannii Minogue and had offered to do a mix at almost no cost, simply because they liked the record. I agreed provided the result was subject to our final approval, and arranged to courier the necessary elements of the song to the UK office.

A digital audio tape arrived in Auckland a few weeks later. The Flexifinger remix was workmanlike, but it had enough of 'How Bizarre' in it to make it an acceptable mainstream remix. However, the Sharp remix was hot. It had been built around a punching and percussive loop that, like the one Alan, Rick and I had created for the New Zealand dance mix, seemed to have almost nothing to do with 'How Bizarre' aside from an occasional vocal snippet. The Sharp Boys swore the original bass line was somewhere in the mix, but in the track's almost eight minutes I couldn't hear it at all. However, the remix was very contemporary and had the potential to work on underground dance floors, opening the record to a whole new audience.

We approved both and the UK office sent them off to be pressed on a 12-inch vinyl single for servicing to DJs.

The single of 'How Bizarre' went out in the UK on the Polydor label, without a mention anywhere of Huh!, even though the contract stated that my branding was to appear on all OMC releases worldwide. When I complained I was assured it would be changed on the next pressing. It was less an ego thing for me – although I certainly enjoyed seeing my label tagged on UK releases and in the British media – than a way of making it clear that the record had come from a little country at the bottom of the world, rather than being just another release on an impersonal multinational label.

The change was duly done but unfortunately most copies sold in the UK had already left stores with only the red and black Polydor logo emblazoned on them. In Europe, the US and everywhere else, however, the Huh! logo appeared, which probably makes Huh! the biggest selling New Zealand-branded record label worldwide by quite a margin.

As in New Zealand, we initially faced a brick wall trying to get UK radio stations to play the song. There was, after all, no story to tell, beyond the slender fact that the record had been a huge hit in Australia and, less importantly, in obscure little New Zealand. We soon had to face the truth that beyond New Zealand, Australia and the Pacific Islands, where it had been lapped up and become virtually a Pacific anthem, 'How Bizarre' would have to stand on its merits as a song. There was no Polynesian market of any substance in the UK, and the swarms of New Zealand expatriates on their fabled OE might fill bars and clubs when New Zealand singers and bands toured but they had not proved a force of any note when it came to moving a New Zealand record on to the British charts.

The British pop market can be impenetrable, fickle and unpredictable. While its hip tastemakers have a symbiotic relationship with the US underground, and the most obscure US record or style may do well, you could sell millions of copies of a record anywhere else in the world and still remain unknown to most UK mainstream music punters and record industry minions.

That said, the UK was notorious for having an annual left-field summer hit or two, often promoted by travellers returning from the sometimes drug-fuelled discos of Mediterranean island resorts and the packed beaches of Spain. In 1996 this hit was 'Macarena'. By the time 'How Bizarre' arrived in the UK, the Spanish dance song was traipsing around the world's Top 10s.

'How Bizarre' had managed to get airplay on a couple of small regional stations but seemed to be going nowhere fast. We were told by both the UK office and Sue DeBenedette that the song was dead in the water. Pauly and I accepted we were not going to the UK.

A week or two later Sue called urgently. Chris Evans, the host of BBC Radio 1's prime-time breakfast show and perhaps the most powerful radio DJ in the country, had discovered 'How Bizarre' while on holiday in Australia. He not only liked it but had added it to his playlist as record of the week, and was playing it repeatedly on his nationwide show. This had led to radio stations across the country playing it, and a flood of inquiries to record stores, which were now placing urgent orders with a bemused Polydor. The momentum had begun.

We were told we should be ready to leave for the UK within the week. We would need to stay there for a certain period, and this could be extended at short notice.

Pauly was still in the process of recording the slowly evolving album. Alan was finding his intransigence on some matters, especially his desire to insert gang-styled lyrics in a couple of songs, a hindrance. Phrases such as 'I'd rather be payin' to the grim reaper / than the law keeper' in 'On The Run' were causing Alan a lot of angst, especially as the song was being considered as a single. Despite strongly and fervently disavowing such sentiments to the media, Pauly was insisting on adding them to the lyrics. Fortunately, though, he had largely concluded his vocals and was not as essential to the recording process as he would have been a few weeks earlier.

19

WE STILL HAD NO FINISHED ALBUM. Not only were Australia and New Zealand demanding masters but the UK office was now also crying out for a full-length release to back its quickly breaking hit single.

In desperation, as Pauly and I awaited the summons to London, Roger Grierson flew over from Sydney to push the process along. Pauly was effectively exiled from the studio and Roger sat down and timelined the rest of the album with almost military precision, working out exactly what parts were needed for the recording and overseeing the schedule's implementation. The album shot ahead rapidly. By the time Pauly and I headed to Auckland Airport bound for Heathrow Alan had reached first mix-down phase for at least half of it.

Adam Holt, Polydor's label manager in Australia, had returned to Poly-Gram New Zealand early in 1996, having decided he would rather raise his kids in Auckland than Sydney. Given his experience he had been appointed local project manager, responsible for liaising with Sue DeBenedette and me, and with handling all other OMC-related matters.

Since I would be on the other side of the world for a while, he was also named point person for the album's sleeve design and coordination.

My first choice of designer was my trusted in-house designer Andrew B. White, but as he was in the US we had to look further afield. I was initially keen on Glenn Hunt, who did the graphic design at *Pavement*, but given Pauly's antagonism towards the magazine, Glenn was quickly deemed to be a non-starter. Somebody, Adam I think, suggested Richard Kingsford, a graphic designer who had recently given Auckland's city magazine *Metro* an impressive visual overhaul. We approached Richard and he agreed.

The photographer would be Aucklander Deborah Smith, whose music-related work had included shots of Crowded House. Deborah was to spend several days with Pauly after we returned from the UK.

On Saturday, July 20, 1996, 'How Bizarre' entered the UK singles chart at number 22. PolyGram UK called to say they thought it would stall there. We wouldn't need to fly to London. I was disappointed not only that the journey was off but that the single seemed to have plateaued. A flop in the UK would impact an American release very negatively.

In the middle of June, Victor and I had returned to Sydney for an update and strategy meeting. At dinner at the famous Bayswater Brasserie, PolyGram's management had quietly but excitedly explained to me just how big this thing could become. At an international conference in Hong Kong, Victor and Paul Dickson had pushed 'How Bizarre' to PolyGram's non-European offices, offering to cut Op-Co deals and reduce the AIF where necessary to make these deals more attractive. All the Asian offices had committed to an end-of-year release.

PolyGram was still working on the grand prize – the US. Polydor, the branch of PolyGram that was releasing the record internationally, had first option rights nation-by-nation but its American office had shown little interest. However, in Hong Kong Danny Goldberg, the CEO of Mercury Records, another side of PolyGram's US operations, and a man with a 20-year history as a supreme talent spotter, had put up his hand and said he would release the record in the new year since Polydor had passed on it.

For us the result couldn't have been better. Goldberg knew his stuff and Mercury had a dominant market share in the US, whereas Polydor was almost moribund. PolyGram hadn't yet officially passed on OMC, but in Sydney we had made the decision to commit to Mercury and so force the issue.

Paul Dickson had also secured a commitment from PolyGram's Canadian office to release the single and the album in November 1996. This was valuable: a hit in Canada would hopefully push the Americans, with the added bonus of airplay drift across the border.

Two days after PolyGram UK told us we wouldn't be needed, Sue DeBenedette called. We were now booked to fly out the next day business class on Air France via Tahiti and Los Angeles, and then through to London on British Airways. It would be a gruelling journey of more than 30 hours, with an eight-hour break in LA. We would arrive on the morning of July 25 and be met at Heathrow by someone from Polydor, who would drive us directly to a rehearsal facility. Pauly would rehearse, with whom we had no idea, and then perform on *Top of the Pops* next day.

What had caused the change of heart were the so called 'mid weeks' – the interim charts that UK record companies receive halfway through a sales week, and that indicate the week's sales trends. They had showed a substantial jump in sales of 'How Bizarre', so much so that a Top 20 place was likely on the coming chart. *Top of the Pops* had agreed that one of its coveted live spots, in front of what PolyGram UK told us would be three million fans, was OMC's.

In the short time before we left I needed to push the go buttons on my domestic and business arrangements and arrange for Alan to create two DATs – digital audio tapes – for me to take. They would contain an instrumental with Sina's vocals intact. One would be a backup for the other on the assumption that what could go wrong would be bound to go wrong.

I furiously threw clothes into a suitcase and tried to compile all the biographical material, articles, images and everything else I could find in my disorganised office. I extracted a wad of notes out of PolyGram's petty cash and a promise that any extra expenses I incurred offshore would be covered as quickly as possible. I also won an assurance that Polydor UK would pay the normal per diems. Unlike other costs, these could not be recouped against Pauly's income.

I also needed to organise Pauly. After checking that his passport had the required time before expiry, I arranged for him to spend the evening in the studio ensuring Alan had all he needed to carry on with the vital album.

The next morning, slightly stunned, we drove to the airport, where Pauly was swooped on by a group of girls wanting not only his autograph but a chorus or two of 'How Bizarre'. We politely declined, and when that didn't work I got a little more forceful.

Pauly seemed flustered by the incident, pleading, 'You got me into this, bro. Now you need to watch my back – it's your job.' I nodded that I would do my best and hustled him into the business class check-in zone.

Upstairs in the lounge a staff member came past and offered us a drink.

'What can I have?' Pauly said.

'Anything, sir,' he replied.

'Anything?'

'Yes, sir, anything at all.'

'Champagne please,' he said, and smiled at me. 'Bro,' he said, 'this is the life.'

I got the feeling that this sortie into luxury meant as much to Pauly as the four awards he had received two months earlier.

We arrived at Los Angeles airport at six in the morning to face a massive queue for Immigration and Customs. When we finally reached the top of the line Pauly found himself being hassled by the immigration officer, who kept insisting he was Mexican and his documents were fake. We were made to sit in a small room for half an hour as I nervously explained to bored men in uniform the racial mix found in New Zealand.

Finally we headed into Hollywood in a cab. Pauly looked stunned. Not only had he not travelled beyond Australia before, he knew little about the rest of the world. I don't think I ever saw him with a book of any sort, aside from his ever present notebook. He wasn't keen on reading. On the first flight out of Auckland I watched him with a newspaper the steward had given him. He was attempting to read every article one by one. I suggested to him that a newspaper was best read by scanning a page and finding stories of interest. He nodded. It had never occurred to me that reading a newspaper was not something that came instinctively but was learned from your parents or school.

More surprises of this sort were to come in the next few weeks. None reflected on Pauly as a person or on his intellect but on the public education system that appeared to have failed him, as it failed many Māori and Polynesian children.

We directed our cab to 7555 Melrose Avenue and Bleecker Bob's. This Los Angeles branch of a famous New York record store was being managed by Kirk Gee. Kirk was not only an old friend of mine but the elder brother of Pauly's girlfriend Kirstine. Smart and with a dry quirky sense of humour, Kirk had worked at various Auckland record stores, not least the legendary Real Groovy, where, with another Auckland rock 'n' roll figure Kerry Buchanan, he had supplied the city's DJs and collectors with the highly desired and hard-to-get records they craved.

In LA he was doing something similar. Bob's was known for things you thought you might never see again. I walked out with a handful of British and American 7-inch vinyls of Elvis Costello I didn't think I'd ever own, and at a price I had trouble complaining about.

Later, Kirk drove us out to San Fernando Valley to meet his wife and child. Pauly's jaw dropped as we drove through Laurel Canyon in the Hollywood Hills. This, we told him, was where Joni Mitchell, Jackson Browne, Neil Young, The Eagles and many other legendary musicians had made music and hung out in the '70s. It's hard to overstate how big a thing this was to Pauly, a place he had seen only on television and at the movies and heard about on records. I was just as amazed about how far we'd come – and how fast. 'How Bizarre' had been released in New Zealand only seven months earlier.

20

IN THE RUSH TO LEAVE NEW ZEALAND we had not had time to get sorted with UK work permits. This was no real problem for me: I would not be working in any way visible on the Home Office's radar. But Pauly was different. He was about to appear on one of Britain's highest rating television shows, where it was likely he'd be announced as coming from New Zealand. This could set off alarm bells if anyone from Immigration were watching.

Since Pauly was 27, we had thought about having him apply for the two-year work visa for which all New Zealanders under the age of twenty-eight were eligible, but this hadn't been practical. First, you needed to show you had enough money to get by for a reasonable period of time and a return ticket, which he didn't yet have. Second, appearing on *Top of the Pops* didn't fall under any employment category allowed under the visa.

Not having much choice, we'd decided to bluff it. We would go in as tourists and hope that if the worst happened and Pauly was spotted on TV, we would probably have left the country again by the time the authorities tried to catch up with us.

At Heathrow, Pauly, carrying an acoustic guitar, and I wandered up to the guy at the Immigration desk. The officer stamped my passport without comment. He then asked Pauly if he played guitar.

'Yes,' Pauly said. 'And I'm here to play my new record on *Top of the Pops.*'

He began to elaborate but the officer, who was now perusing the arrival documents, hadn't clicked.

I leaned over to Pauly and mouthed, 'Shut up.'

Pauly looked puzzled. It occurred to me this was the first time he'd encountered a situation where a work permit was required. He was simply not aware of the rules and regulations. His passport was stamped and I hustled him away.

A woman from Polydor's London office found us as we walked into the mayhem of Heathrow's concourse and introduced herself as Wendy. As we were rushed towards the car Pauly spoke to her for the first time.

'When do we get paid?' he said.

After he repeated the question twice, she looked at him and snapped, 'You haven't done any work yet.'

I forced myself to ask about the schedule, assuming we would go to the hotel to check in and then, after a wind-down and a snack, head off to the rehearsal. How wrong I was. There was to be no hotel and no shower. Although utterly exhausted, we were going straight to the rehearsal rooms. We would have to stay there about seven hours. We would eat on the way.

Outside Heathrow we stopped at a café, where I became reacquainted with the horrors of English fast food and coffee, and then headed north for what seemed an interminable journey to the suburbs. Eventually we pulled up outside a semi-detached in Barnet, North London. Here we met the stand-in English OMC. Who were these musicians and what did they know of the song? Wendy explained to us that this didn't really matter: the guys were supposed to perform only as a make-believe backing band.

Some years earlier the Musicians' Union had stomped on the way songs were mimed on *Top of the Pops.* They'd apparently had enough of singers with hits or wannabe hits miming over backing tracks, instead of British musicians being paid to perform these live. The BBC and the union had met head-on but neither would budge. This led to a boycott of the show for a brief period in the 1980s, during which the BBC featured only non-union artists, thus cutting out many acts who were in the charts. It had been a lose-lose situation: musicians were not getting any work, even mime work; acts were not getting the important hit-making television exposure; and the BBC was missing out on many of the big names it relied on to pull in viewers.

A compromise was reached. The BBC was not technically allowed to have acts with backing tracks, but the union would turn a blind eye as long as all acts on the show were registered union members. When the acts did perform to a backing track, union members had to be on camera pretending they were playing the songs when everyone knew and could see they were not.

This insane pretence went as far as rehearsals. The UK union had rushed through Pauly's membership as part of a standing reciprocal arrangement with the New Zealand Musicians Union – which, like many New Zealand musicians, Pauly had never joined. He was to turn up at the rehearsal space with his membership card, and he and the band were to pretend to practise for the show the next day. We never saw this card but were assured it existed.

The four British musicians were sitting around drinking coffee and smoking spliffs. The group comprised a drummer, a guitarist who would double as a horn player on the live show despite the fact he didn't play the horn, a bassist and a female backing vocalist. Apart from the drummer, none had heard Pauly's record until Polydor had couriered them a copy the day before.

After brief introductions it was decided a quick run-through was appropriate. Using the backing CD Alan Jansson had given me, the four plus Pauly mimed a rough version of 'How Bizarre'. The rest of the day was spent eating the McDonalds' fare supplied and talking until we ran out of things to say to people with whom we had little in common. Around four o'clock our minders decided the union representative seemed unlikely to arrive, given the distance and the traffic to get out from central London, and we should go to our hotel.

As we were departing Pauly told us to stop and went back into the studio. After a couple of minutes I returned to find him inviting the musicians to join his new touring band. I grabbed him, pulled him outside, and asked him what he was thinking: we were there to mime on a TV show, do some media and go home.

'Bro, don't you think we should look at that band for the tour.'

'What tour?'

'We should be getting Alan over and putting together a band to tour the UK. Bro, one even plays trumpet so we wouldn't need George Chisholm.'

They were not the last musicians Pauly would ask to join the 'band' while we were in the UK.

After checking in at the Metropole Hotel on Edgware Road, we were informed we were to have dinner that evening with the management of Polydor UK and a crew from its London-based European head office. The hotel, which billed itself as part of the Hilton group and five-star, was a bit of a dump and sported several laughably expensive restaurants and bars. We had two adjoining rooms and were shown up by a surly porter who wouldn't leave until we proffered a gratuity. He was less than impressed by a New Zealand five-dollar note.

The room looked as though it had last been renovated in the 1970s. The carpet had holes, the plant in the corner looked dead or dying, and the wall was decorated with a photo of Edgware Road taken from the hotel roof; it featured the fortress-like Paddington Green Police Station up the road, infamous as the place where IRA suspects were incarcerated. The most modern piece of furniture was an old television set, complete with the usual pay movies and porn. I rang Pauly and firmly told him he wasn't to watch any of these unless he had the cash to pay for them.

My bed had one pillow and it was rock hard. I rang Pauly again to see if his was the same. It was, so I called downstairs, asked for two more pillows, and was told they were five pounds each. I also asked for an ironing board and was told they were all out but they could arrange to have a shirt pressed for another ten pounds. That pushed me over the edge. I snapped back that we were not just any guests but here to perform on *Top of the Pops*. This seemed to work. An iron was sent up. Thereafter, whenever I left the room I put it in my suitcase and locked the lid.

We had been told we would have full-time use of a car and driver for our time in London. At 7.30 the driver arrived, introduced himself as Om, and told us he'd rather be called Ommie. Suitably showered and polished but still complete wrecks, we were driven to Soho for dinner.

At what looked to be a rather pricey joint we were shown upstairs to a private room, where about twenty Polydor personnel were seated around a long table. The man at the head introduced himself as David Munns, who I knew was in charge of Polydor's pop marketing across Europe. Various others introduced themselves although names were a blur.

In an industry where politics is 60 percent of breaking a successful record, Pauly had to impress these people, and I had to convince them that putting their substantial resources behind us was to their advantage. I was acutely aware we faced an uphill battle: we were a novelty from a faraway land that these people knew little about and cared for even less, our single was just touching the Top 20, and we had no album yet to speak of.

David Munns leaned over and asked Pauly if he had any questions. 'Yes,' Pauly said. 'When do we get out our first per diems?' Fortunately the table laughed, and as the wine flowed Pauly seemed to find it easy to talk to these executives, who spent much of their time working on the careers of global household names who sold millions of records, and were working out if Pauly had the legs to be added to that élite list.

Munns announced that Polydor had selected 'How Bizarre' for release across all European territories in September. This meant that Pauly could be needed in Europe in late September or early October.

Almost delirious with tiredness, we finally got back to our hotel. We were to be at Elstree Studioss, some distance north of London, at 7.30 in the morning for the live rehearsals that would lead to the early evening filming of *Top of the Pops*.

At 6.30 a.m. the phone rang. Pauly had been up for the best part of an hour, had taken a walk and was hungry. I met him in the lobby. He looked like a million bucks. In the dining room we looked at the reconstituted eggs swimming in watery yellow liquid, the reconstituted bacon and the cold white toast and decided we'd ask Ommie to stop at a McDonalds' drive-through on the way to Elstree.

The trip north consisted of a long tedious crawl in rush-hour traffic through suburbia and around endless ring roads. Eventually we pulled up at the green iron gates that marked the entrance to the BBC studios. Even at this early hour a swarm of girls were jumping excitedly up and down. As we drove in they banged on the car windows. We soon worked out that these girls – or variations of them – were in residence day and evening. They would scream at virtually anyone, just in case they were famous. Later in the day, whenever we were bored and had nothing to do, we'd wander out to the gates and get screamed at for a moment or two. It was a cheap thrill.

21

THE ELSTREE STUDIOSS have an impressive history going back much further than their purchase by the BBC in 1982. As we were escorted down the corridor to our dressing room we walked past stills from *Star Wars*, Bond movies, 1950s epics, classic TV shows, and photos of iconic and long dead stars. It quickly hit me that this was now the gilded pop music zone. Almost every act I had idolised over the years had appeared on *Top of the Pops* and many had walked this corridor. The show was one of the holy grails of pop culture: its four stages were named John, Paul, George and Ringo.

I half expected to wake up in Auckland and find that it had all been a dream. I racked up a couple of hundred dollars calling people at home and saying, 'Guess where I am?' Most seemed nonplussed. I didn't care. We were at *Top of the Pops*!

In the canteen, Bernard Butler, formerly of Suede, and a German girl who, we were told, was going to be the next big thing, were eating a traditional English breakfast of overcooked eggs, beans and chips in a sea of warm animal fat. Starving, we sat down with our 'band' and ordered the same.

After the food break we were called in for the first run-through. We discovered that without talking to us Polydor had hired two Hawai'ian dancing girls to sway alongside Pauly. Pauly told me furiously that he didn't want them. I agreed that the whole idea was tacky and talked to the Polydor people. Used to new pop stars who had to do exactly what they were told or go home, they said the dancing girls would stay.

After about ten minutes we were still in a stand-off. It was only after the intervention of a floor manager who clearly didn't care who or what you were, he wanted you on that stage for your allotted three minutes exactly when he said, that they agreed to pull them. As they walked over to the young women to break the news that their gig wasn't going to happen Pauly approached me. He was having second thoughts and now wanted the girls to add a 'Pacific vibe'. I ran across the soundstage to try and stop the impending sacking. Wendy shrugged her shoulders and walked away with a seen-it-all-before look.

There were four ways of getting on *Top of the Pops*. The first was to be an established star with a recognised fan base whose new single was expected to chart in the next week. The second was to be a band or singer whose new record had debuted in the Top 40, or preferably the Top 20, and was expected to rise in the next chart. The third was to have a record that had jumped up in the chart over the past week. The final way was to have a number one record, which meant automatic placement.

There were five acts on the show each week, which meant fierce record company hustling and pressure on the show's producer, who, with a small committee, made the final decisions. Slots were allocated in the middle of the week, and a rise in sales or chart placings didn't always mean a place if there were a large number of hot new releases. The considerable power of the show to sell records in a market where a hundred or more singles were released each week meant the few minutes acts and labels begged for were probably the most sought-after property in UK pop.

After the rehearsal Wendy took me aside and quietly asked if Pauly would agree to appear on camera in a short-sleeved shirt to show off his tattoos. I put it to him and he refused immediately. He had decided to play in a long-sleeved suit jacket.

He retired to the garden outside the café, where he sat with the 'band' and wrote in the notebooks he always carried with him. Meanwhile, I took a call from Anita McNaught. TV3 wanted to do the story. I would be contacted shortly by the network's UK crew to talk about the nuts and bolts of the filming.

I headed off to explore the studio precinct. Walking around a corner I found myself standing in the middle of the set for the BBC soap *Eastenders*. I was in Albert Square, ringed by the famous council houses and shops, or at least their facades. A classic red London Routemaster Bus sat in one corner. I walked over to Queen Vic, the pub used in countless scenes in the show, but any urge I felt to go in and sit in a booth was squashed: it too was a facade. A security guard, alerted by the surveillance cameras, arrived and politely asked me to leave. Only cast and crew were allowed.

Back in the canteen we waited. Wendy bought us lunch: grey hamburgers with chips. Around four we were ushered back into the dressing room. I gaped: Neneh Cherry was standing in the doorway. Just inside there were a bunch of guys who looked like Spanish waiters looking for a table to serve. Their record company minder smiled and said hello. I realised with a jolt that I knew her. Vicky Blood was a New Zealander who had done well in the UK music industry. She was marketing manager for BMG Records, which had released the smash-hit *Macarena*. The waiter lookalikes went under the name Los del Río and would sell several million copies of their single that year. They were never heard of again.

I introduced the increasingly nervous Pauly, who quickly excused himself to change and mentally prepare himself for what would be easily the most important performance of his career to date.

Just before he was to go on, we were ushered into a small room. Sitting opposite us were five young women. They looked like the sort you'd see in any small-town High Street, hanging out in the mall or McDonalds. They stared at Pauly, a couple of them drooling with their mouths open.

The producer walked in and breezily said, 'Guys, have you met The Spice Girls?' We were aware of the growing hype around this group but 'Wannabe', their debut smash, was still on the rise. It would hit number one the following week and remain there for close to two months, but for now they were just another band with a hit to plug.

After a moment Pauly looked across and said with a wink, 'You're spicy.' One of the girls immediately bounced back, 'You're bizarre' and they all giggled.

The stage manager called for OMC and we went out on to the soundstage. The room was a mass of screaming kids, with assistant stage managers shouting commands at them and at the performers as cameras on large cranes and rails swooped over different parts of the vast room. It was dark, and the massive spinning disco lights, mirror balls, smoke and strobes made it look like New York's Studios 54.

OMC was to be first on since our record had been the last to find a slot that week. The allocated stage was empty aside from the band's gear.

'Smile at the camera,' I said to Pauly.

'I only smile for the bank manager,' he replied.

'This will make the bank manager happy,' I said.

The host introduced 'How Bizarre' as 'the biggest song in the history of New Zealand music'. The cameras swung across to Pauly and the hula girls and the show began. Pauly's performance was perfunctory. He appeared unsure of himself and even fluffed a few words. The outgoing charismatic Pauly Fuemana of videos and a thousand photographs was nowhere to be seen. It had hit him walking into the room with all the lights and screaming kids just how massive all this was and he was terrified.

As he came off the stage he put his arm around my shoulders and said, 'Okay, bro?'

'Yes, Pauly,' I said. 'You're the first person ever to make a record in New Zealand and take it all the way to *Top of the Pops*.'

He beamed. We both knew it was an impressive achievement.

We stayed and watched the rest of the show: Neneh Cherry; Los del Río; The Spice Girls on their first ever *Top of the Pops* gig – Pauly wished them luck as they walked past and Baby Spice blew him a kiss – and that week's number one, former Take That teen heart-throb Gary Barlow.

We had been in London only 35 hours. Given our long trip and everything that'd happened since we left home we should have been ready to collapse, but a second wave of adrenaline kicked in. When Wendy suggested Polydor buy us dinner we accepted and headed to Soho, where we were treated to an amazing meal at The Red Fort, a place we were assured was the best Indian eatery in the area.

About 10.30 both of us finally hit the wall. Fortunately, the next two days were to be free: the full-on publicity schedule wouldn't start until Monday. As a bonus we were given five days of per diems. This amounted to ten pounds a day, enough to pay for a one-way cab to somewhere interesting.

Next morning Pauly said he wanted to hang around the hotel until the afternoon. After breakfast in a greasy spoon on Edgware Road, I came back to a raft of messages from industry people, all of whom seemed to think they could offer us something. Deciding to follow them up later, I asked Ommie to take me to Mill Lane in West Hampstead, where I had lived for a couple of years in the 1980s.

As we drove he explained that his family had come to England from South Asia when he was a kid. What struck me was the same thing that had struck me when I looked at the members of our *Top of the Pops* band, who were West Indian: a generation out from his homeland Ommie had lost almost all trace of his roots. The contrast with Pauly was extreme. Pauly knew his culture and had massive pride in what he was and where the blood that ran in his veins came from, as did most Pacific Islanders and Māori in New Zealand.

We turned into Abbey Road, drove over the famous pedestrian crossing, and continued on to West End Lane and into the street where I'd lived. We stopped and I sent a postcard from the post office under my old flat. On the way back via Kilburn I photographed a wall: it was covered in posters advertising our single.

Back at the hotel Pauly was buzzing. 'Bro, have you seen the women who have their photos in those phone boxes?' he said. 'Man, they are gorgeous. We should ring a couple.'

It took a minute before I released he was talking about the hookers who have their cards, with contact numbers, plastered over the walls of London's phone booths. 'Pauly,' I said, 'those pictures are not the women who will answer those phone numbers. They're photos cut from magazines like *Penthouse* and *Playboy*. You really don't want to go there.'

At the time he noticed the cards Pauly had been phoning an old friend of his who had moved to London. His friend was now on his way over. I left and spent a few hours joyfully trawling through the bins of dance music specialist stores, and arrived back at the hotel with an armful of vinyl to find Pauly had company – more company than he expected or really wanted. His buddy was there, squirming. Also present was a middle-aged woman with few teeth and a tight leopard-skin dress. Despite my advice, Pauly had called one of the phone numbers and this hooker from hell had turned up. What had started out as a bit of a joke – Pauly never had any intention of having sex with her – had gone terribly wrong.

His mate wanted no part of it and hurriedly left the hotel. Telling me to get rid of the woman, Pauly disappeared off to his room. I told the woman she would have to go but she was adamant she wanted payment first. When I said the hotel was going to have her physically tossed out, she spat a stream of four-lettered vitriol at me. I gave her a few pounds for a cab fare and she left, but before she did she wandered across to a potted plant in the foyer, pulled down her knickers, and in full view of everyone in the foyer urinated on the plant.

I went up to Pauly's room in a rage. He was adamant it hadn't been his doing but his mate's. This was bullshit, but over the next few weeks he countless times told me and others back in New Zealand that his friend was 'a dirty bastard'. I think he eventually came to believe it. I had no choice but to put the hooker and the hotel pot plant down to experience. I figured that, unlike some of the awful events of the previous months, at least there had been no violence.

Next day, with Ommie off duty, we caught a cab back to Soho, had coffee at the famous Bar Italia, and wandered through the streets to Covent Garden, where I lent Pauly some cash for a pair of shoes. He seemed to have spent all the money Polydor had advanced him. As we walked back to the hotel via The Strand, Trafalgar Square, The Mall, Buckingham Palace and Hyde Park he was the most relaxed I had seen him since the rollercoaster ride had begun. He could, he said, see himself living in London.

Back at the hotel I followed up a few of the messages I'd received. There were at least half a dozen offers to provide UK management from people I'd never heard of, and one from a former New Zealand booking agent called Mike Corless, who now provided insurance to Commonwealth visitors on two-year work permits. I called him and we agreed to meet.

There were all sorts of opportunistic offers from people who wanted Pauly to appear on their show or in their club. One message intrigued me. It was from a man with a fairly substantial reputation as a booking agent and artist manager in the UK. Among others, Steve Hedges handled Oasis. I called him and left a message.

The other message of importance was from Wendy. Our start next morning would be at 7.30. Pauly, who had showered and changed, joined me in the bar and we ordered overpriced beers. In the corner a man was playing a white baby grand, knocking out the sort of songs you hear in hotel bars the world over: the repertoire included Billy Joel's 'Piano Man', Elton John's 'Daniel' and Carole King's 'You've Got A Friend'.

Pauly turned to me and said, 'This guy is brilliant. We should ask him to join the band.' After getting another drink, I returned to find him talking to the piano player. He returned and handed me a scrap of paper with a number on it. 'He's in,' he said. I sighed and put the piece of paper in my pocket. Pauly never mentioned the man again.

Pauly's solicitation of all kinds of people for his band would continue back home. A few weeks after our return I received a call from Paul, the motor mechanic who had checked Pauly's Merc. Pauly had asked him to be his manager and to put together a band with his son, who played guitar.

Next morning the traffic in London was horrendous. The city's entire public transport system had decided to go on strike and roads were gridlocked. To add to the misery it looked like being a filthy hot day, the sort London gets once or twice a year, and the car had no air conditioning. Our schedule included more than three days of press appointments. We were also waiting to find out if our record had gone up the charts. If it had we might be back on *Top of the Pops*.

By mid-morning we were sitting in the BBC studios in Great Portland Street and Pauly was being interviewed live on Radio One, beaming nationwide to millions of listeners. Asked about his success in New Zealand he responded that his manager, meaning me, was one of the most feared people in Auckland. If people messed with me, they apparently disappeared. Wendy and another woman from Polydor, sitting with me on the sofa outside the studio, looked across and slowly edged away.

It took up to three hours in our oppressively hot car to crawl from interview to interview. After Radio One came morning shows on Virgin Radio and Radio London; over the next few days Pauly would also appear on Capital FM, Kiss FM UK and a couple of other stations. This was followed by over a dozen newspaper and magazine interviews, almost all with the same inane questions, asked by people who really didn't care about the answers. It was a job and most were hacks. The exceptions were journalists for *New Zealand News UK* and *TNT*, a weekly magazine published in the UK, Australia and New Zealand. Both seemed genuinely interested in Pauly's story, and quite proud that someone from Auckland had made it into the UK charts – and with a solid hit.

An interviewer from *The Sun*'s 'Bizarre' section, which covered pop music and showbiz gossip, asked Pauly about his tattoos over a beer at a pub in Southwark. For the first time since I'd been working with him, Pauly talked openly about them, carefully explaining the meaning of each.

The man had trouble with the idea that Pauly, whose father came from a tiny island in the Pacific with a population of less than 1500, wasn't some of sort of cannibal and knew how to drive a car. Pauly explained that the large black fish tattooed on one of his arms referred to a family legend that they were descended from black sharks. That, he said, was what the word Fuemana meant.

The journalist laughed. Was Pauly having him on? Did he really think his family was descended from black sharks? 'Yes,' Pauly said.

As the man sneered into his beer, Wendy and I decided we'd better wrestle the interview to an end.

The journalist was Andy Coulson. He would later become editor of *News of the World* and in June 2014 be convicted of phone-hacking conspiracy in Britain's biggest ever media scandal. He never printed the shark story.

On Wednesday, sitting in Polydor's office in Hammersmith, we were told that 'How Bizarre' had not moved on the charts, staying at number 19, and so OMC was not eligible for *Top of the Pops* that week. We would be sent home on Thursday.

I was also given a message to ring Sydney as soon as possible. We were wanted in Melbourne, where Pauly was booked on *Hey Hey It's Saturday* to perform his new Australian single, 'Right On'. This meant we would have to transit through Auckland, do the show in Melbourne, and fly back to New Zealand on Sunday.

I requested and got from Polydor detailed UK airplay and sales data and spent some time studying it. A clear repeat of the New Zealand and Australian patterns was emerging. Despite the record's stalled placing on the charts, its airplay was growing steadily. More importantly, reorders had rocketed in the previous two days.

I took this to Polydor head David Munns down the corridor. Given what was in front of me, I suggested that 'How Bizarre' was probably going to climb in the charts next week but both he and Wendy were adamant the UK didn't work like that. Sales came fast and early and there were few steady risers, let alone spectacular ones. Our chart run was probably over.

On Wednesday afternoon I met with Steve Hedges. I was loosely interested in Steve's offer of representation in Europe as an agent for the sorts of opportunities that always come the way of a successful act. The final decision, though, had to be Pauly's. In spite of my repeated urging he was still without a manager, and kept telling people I was doing the job. This was untrue: I had no desire to manage him and to do so would have been a clear conflict of interest.

Much as I liked Steve Hedges and his fantastic and very funny stories, I felt he was too rock 'n' roll and English to manage Pauly. I had little doubt he would attempt to angle him on to the live circuit since this was how he earned money as a booking agent. Touring and performing was something I had no intention of encouraging Pauly to do, despite his continually wanting to form a band.

On Wednesday night we were offered VIP tickets to a club off Leicester Square, where we had a thoroughly boring time despite the complimentary drinks and keen attention from a bunch of young women who had seen Pauly on television. Pauly, who had been happy to call up hookers from a phone booth, seemed completely uninterested in these three attractive fans. In the whole time we worked together I didn't once see him follow through on a flirtation. He could easily have done so and nobody would have said a thing: as the saying goes, what happens on the road stays on the road.

On the other hand, checking out of the hotel next day I was presented with a colossal account from his room that included a couple of dozen charges for porn movies. I pulled him aside and pointed out that his room charges were destined to be paid by Polydor, whom he would not want to annoy as they were selling his records.

'Bro,' he said, 'I thought if you didn't watch the whole thing you didn't get charged.'

Rather than irritate Polydor I handed over my personal credit card and paid for the porn. Despite my best efforts, I never managed to recover the money from Pauly or PolyGram New Zealand. From then on I made a point of telling every hotel I was not liable for video charges.

At Heathrow we checked in on a British Airways flight to Auckland. Sitting in the business-class departure lounge, Pauly looked at me and

Pauly Fuemana was proud of his Polynesian tattoos, but wary of showing ones on his hands that dated from his gang days. In 1996 he spent some time trying unsuccessfully to remove them. In these images for the cover of the *How Bizarre* album, photographer Deborah Smith carefully avoided the offending tattoos. *Universal Music New Zealand*

Top Pauly Fuemana at Auckland Airport in July 1996, on his way to London to appear on top-rated television show *Top of the Pops*. *Simon Grigg Collection*

Left Peter Urlich, Simon Grigg and Pauly Fuemana in London. Fuemana wowed the crowd at the opening of a new bar with an a-capella version of 'How Bizarre'. *Simon Grigg Collection*

Right top Waiting for hours to appear on *Top of the Pops* at BBC's Elstree Studios, Fuemana sat outside writing in the notebooks he always carried with him. On the show he appeared with Neneh Cherry, Los del Río, the Spice Girls and Gary Barlow of Take That. *Simon Grigg Collection*

Right Pauly Fuemana on the banks of the Seine in Paris, August 1996. The singer's second appearance on *Top of the Pops* was almost scuppered by lack of a work permit. The problem was solved by an emergency dash to Paris, with a visa collected on his return. *Simon Grigg Collection*

Alan Jansson and Pauly Fuemana at the
1996 APRA Silver Scroll Awards, where
they won awards for Most Performed Work
in New Zealand and Most Performed Work
Overseas for 'How Bizarre'. They continued
to win the latter award for the next three
years. *Simon Grigg Collection*

The US release of the *How Bizarre* album took
place in February 1997. Later in the year the
album had a cover of the Randy Newman
song 'I Love L.A.' added, although the single
was a flop. *Huh! Records / Polygram New Zealand*

Top Pauly Fuemana poses next to a Ferrari convertible during his
1996 tour of Europe accompanied by Mark Cathro. *Universal Music NZ /
Huh! Records*

Above Shooting the video for 'Land of Plenty' on New Zealand's
volcanic plateau. Despite a difficult day in which Fuemana was
uncooperative, the editing and colour-grading by cinematographer
Greg Semu and director Kerry Brown produced a minor
masterpiece. *Simon Grigg Collection*

Top Sleeve of an OMC 'I Love L.A.' EP. Alan Jansson worked to produce an arrangement of the song that would be sympathetic to Fuemana but PolyGram decided to record the track in the US with a local producer. *Universal Music NZ / Huh! Records*

Above Pauly Fuemana in 2007, wearing a classic OMC T-shirt. He was visibly unwell with what would later be diagnosed as a rare and serious neurological illness. *Alan Jansson and Simon Grigg*

Pauly Fuemana recording the song '4 All Of Us' with actor
Lucy Lawless for the Human Rights Commission's Race Relations
Day, March 21, 2007. Produced by Alan Jansson, the beautiful
song was lilting and optimistic but the track was limited by Pauly's
nervous vocals. In the accompanying video he appeared unsteady
and unable to lip sync, a shadow of his former confident self.
He would die less than three years later. *Alan Jansson and Simon Grigg*

announced he wasn't leaving the UK. He was forming a band with the guys from *Top of the Pops*. I nodded and said, 'If you want, Pauly.'

Not getting a reaction, he stormed off. When the flight was called I went looking for him. He was on a payphone, deep in conversation with Kirstine. After a minute he said goodbye, hung up the phone, and said, 'Sorry about that, bro, but you know how it is sometimes.' I was indeed aware of how it sometimes was, and equally aware a deep conversation with Kirstine usually brought him back.

Some thirty hours later we landed in Auckland. Since we were booked through to Australia we were forced to sit in transit for a couple of hours. Jetlagged and tired, we passed the time phoning family and friends. I also called Anita McNaught. She had assumed we were going to be in London longer and was pushing ahead with plans to film *60 Minutes* there.

'How does Melbourne sound instead?' I asked before my battery died.

22

THIS WAS PAULY'S THIRD APPEARANCE on *Hey Hey It's Saturday*. Sina had been flown over to appear with him and the filming was straightforward. Molly Meldrum was profuse in his congratulations about the UK success of 'How Bizarre' but Pauly and I agreed he still made our skins crawl. The next morning we flew back to Auckland.

I walked through the door of my home around eleven. Less than an hour later, as I dozed in front of television, the phone rang. It was Sue DeBenedette. London had just called. The sales of the single on Friday and Saturday were such that it looked as though we were going to have to go back to the UK – and within 24 hours. I pleaded for a day or two's rest, if only for Pauly's sake. She said rather unconvincingly she would do what she could. Half an hour later she called back. We were to leave that night, to arrive in London on Monday evening.

I called Pauly and arranged to pick him up on the way to the airport. I rang Tom and told him I was off once again. I rang Alan, and we agreed to catch up early that evening before I left.

Finally I rang Anita McNaught and asked if the *60 Minutes* filming was still on. Not surprisingly it was: this was turning into a more interesting story by the minute.

Alan and I met around five. He gave me two CDs containing rough mixes of the almost finished album tracks; both Pauly and I were to audition and comment on them when we got to London. In the cab to the airport I gave one to Pauly so he could listen to it on the Sony Discman he carried everywhere.

Half an hour after we took off, Pauly looked across at me and snarled, 'Fuck you. I'm not going to live in London. I'm not going to let you make me. What the fuck are you doing here anyway? Alan warned me to watch you, you white demon.'

I reeled back, shocked. There was obviously no point trying to resolve what was essentially an anger issue at 40,000 feet up in the air. I told him that if he wanted I would be happy to get off in Honolulu and fly back to New Zealand. He could carry on alone to London. With that I put on my headphones and began to read.

Ten minutes later I looked over. Pauly had tears streaming down his face. As I took off my headphones he shook his head. 'I'm sorry, bro. I know how much you've done for me. It's all cool.' We never spoke of it again.

At Heathrow, Ommie was waiting for us and we were soon back in the grotty old Metropole, where Pauly agreed not to call any more numbers in phone booths or 'preview' adult movies. This time the extra pillows were free.

Next day the media run began again. Mid-morning we discovered the record had bounced up to number eleven in the charts and *Top of the Pops* was pretty likely to happen. The chart jump meant that a few more people wanted to talk to Pauly. *Time Out* magazine wanted a shot for a potential cover and MTV, courtesy of New Zealander Brent Hansen, the boss of the European operation, approached me for an interview and a performance, to which we happily agreed.

The pressure increased. My phone rang non-stop with requests for Pauly to promote this or that, all of which I declined. When he was invited to open a shopping centre, I rang Polydor and angrily demanded they stop giving out my number to anyone who asked.

Top of the Pops said yes late that evening. The following day Pauly was recorded for MTV singing 'How Bizarre'. He insisted on singing the verses and all the chorus parts, while playing his acoustic guitar. His performance was at best uneven: his vocal was, to be generous, flat.

He also performed a new song he had played for me in the hotel the week before. Called 'Friend', it was absolutely lovely. I told him it was potentially another hit single and should be recorded as soon as possible. The MTV crew seemed smitten with the song and I was told they aired the video several times, although the 'How Bizarre' take was, to the best of my knowledge, broadcast only once.

Late on Wednesday we hit a snag with *Top of the Pops*. The producers at the BBC had asked to see Pauly's work permit. The bluff was not going to work a second time and Pauly's live gig was cancelled. After Polydor kicked up a fuss, the show agreed to run a video of his previous week's performance.

With the single roaring out of the stores, reorders were stronger than ever. And radio airplay was still growing. It was likely Pauly would be asked to perform on the show the following week, and as an added bonus he would be in town for more promotional work. It was decided that on Thursday we would both go to France via the Chunnel on an early train and return later that night. When we got back to Waterloo Station we would pick up prearranged work permits.

Pauly had never been in a non-English-speaking country before. In Paris he was bemused by the fact that nobody spoke English, or at least admitted to it. When he went off to buy a packet of cigarettes he came back frustrated that he had not been able to make himself understood. Using my fractured French, I bought him a pack of Camel Filters and we wandered off, only to find ourselves in Rue Saint-Denis, a street notorious for hookers. It was an eye-opener to see women sitting in windows half naked, their breasts exposed.

At the markets near Saint Germain-des-Prés, Pauly bought a beret and some gifts. I took photos of him negotiating prices but he refused to smile for the camera. We then walked the short distance to Notre-

Dame Cathedral, where Pauly seemed genuinely moved. Needing to be back at Gare du Nord by six, we managed to land the one taxi driver in Paris who had never heard of the Eurostar or the channel tunnel, and only just made it.

At Waterloo we managed to get the visas, and returned to a raft of new messages at the hotel. The callers included Nathan Haines. After I'd released his last album, Nathan had moved to London and was working there, making quite a name for himself. He invited us to the Notting Hill Arts Club, where he was guesting. He would soon start a weekly residency at the club that would stretch over four years and play a major role in establishing him as one of the most innovative and important young musicians in the city.

On Friday we took the day off. This time our driver was Tony, an Eastender who insisted we began the day at his local greasy spoon in Brick Lane. Tony was full of fascinating stories about his time as a driver for the notorious London gangsters the Krays and Richardsons in the 1960s to '80s. We were happy to take his recommended gangland tour along the route of the 1982 funeral procession for Violet, the mother of Ronnie and Reggie Kray, and to the cemetery in Chingford where just a year before Ronnie Kray had been buried next to her.

We were shown the Kray family home in Bethnal Green, the pubs where crimes had been committed, and a heavily armoured jewellery shop, which Tony assured us was still owned and operated by Kray family interests. Pauly said he wanted to buy something from the store, but when he tried to do so he was given a frosty reception by the equally heavily tattooed men inside, and Tony had to negotiate his way out. Next day he ordered a black Kray-style pinstriped suit from a store near Covent Garden.

Over the next few days we filmed extensively with the UK film crew hired to shoot the *60 Minutes* footage. A pattern emerged. Every morning Pauly would resist the idea of filming and demand a day off. I would talk him around and we would head off. We recreated our arrival at Heathrow and were filmed strolling across Trafalgar Square and through Soho, shopping in Camden, walking backwards and forwards across the famous Abbey Road crossing and standing, peering hopefully, outside the studio itself. All this seemed to take an inordinate amount of time because of the number of kids wanting Pauly's autograph and the hordes of Japanese and American tourists on the crossing at any given moment. Eventually a couple of policemen stopped the traffic while we got our shot.

We wanted to film on the roof of New Zealand House on Haymarket near Pall Mall but were turned down by the high commission, whose staff were particularly unhelpful. We finally got the green light after the television company in New Zealand pressured their bosses in Wellington.

Television New Zealand also filmed us for its news shows. We had several nights out on the network's expense account with Mark Sainsbury, the London reporter, and his two fellow expatriate flatmates, dining pleasantly and expensively at a Conran-owned joint in Soho and another high-end restaurant.

We finished filming on Thursday, or at least I thought we had until Anita rang me at dinner, saying that she needed just a few more shots.

'Anita, no,' I stopped her. 'No more.'

She was silent and then said, 'Okay, no more.'

The filming in London was over.

Top of the Pops was scheduled for the next morning. We made it to Elstree around ten o'clock for the stage rehearsal. With Pauly now further up the pecking order after the Britpop band Suede, the changeover between acts was intense but the stagehands, having done it a thousand times, simply forced it through.

After the run-throughs I wandered around the back corridor and realised at one stage I was standing next to Cher. On the lawn outside the café a bunch of people were hovering around smoking and complaining about the previous week's transport disruptions and the still sticky weather. Among them was one of my idols, Paul Weller, whose new single 'Peacock Suit' was on the show that week. He asked me about New Zealand and said he liked the OMC single.

That reminded me I'd lost Pauly. I found him inside the soundstage area, talking to a skinny guy with bad skin.

'Bro, do you know Bryan?' he said.

Bryan Adams had introduced himself to Pauly, asked where he was from, and in the process made himself a quick friend.

'We should work together, maybe write and record,' Pauly informed a bemused Adams.

I had a call from Nathan: he and my old friend Peter Urlich were at the main gate. We managed to talk the two men into the studio lot and then, by swapping passes back and forth, into our dressing room. The art of hustling backstage access is universal. Both stayed in the dressing room until almost showtime, when they went out to join the throngs of hysterical kids who had been allowed through to yell on live TV.

Pauly had decided to wear a gorgeous short-sleeved Polynesian shirt that bared his tattoos to the British viewing public. As we went out to the side stage he radiated confidence, strength and style. His performance was light years ahead of the one two weeks earlier. He was magnetic, absolutely in control of himself and the stage. Two-thirds of the way through, after the pivotal line 'If you wanna know the rest / Buy the rights', he looked straight at the camera and threw a huge and genuine grin to the millions watching. Wendy looked at me. 'You have just sold 20,000 singles,' she said.

It was a phenomenal performance and I was quietly ecstatic. Pauly, too, knew he had pulled it off. At an Italian restaurant in Soho that night, he was stopped several times and asked to sign all sorts of things. Happy to oblige, he drew the line at one girl's bra – she was still wearing it.

There was a message at the hotel from Mike Corless inviting us to the opening of a new bar in London's Chinatown. I remembered the place. It had once been known as the Polar Bear and in the early '80s there was a rumour that someone had lost a python there: legend had it disappearing down a toilet into the plumbing. It had been reinvented as an Antipodean pub, catering for the squadrons of New Zealanders and Australians who filled any bar that flew their flag, played their music and served their beer.

Mike Corless had offered the bar the services of Mike King, a New Zealand comedian who was in London for a festival, as MC and he was keen to have Pauly, the charting New Zealand pop star, as a guest. I thought this was fairly harmless and told Mike I would also bring along a New Zealand rock 'n' roll icon and former member of Th' Dudes, Peter Urlich. Any lingering reservations Pauly may have had were squashed by Peter's rampant enthusiasm: Peter is perhaps the least microphone-shy person I've ever known.

Thus, with Wendy and a couple of others from Polydor, we arrived about one o'clock on Saturday afternoon to find the party in full swing, tumbling out on to the streets of Chinatown and getting messier by the moment. We were given a small dressing room and a free-flow bar tab. Pauly was less interested in the alcohol than the adulatory attention he was receiving from his compatriots.

A band upstairs was turning out the sort of clichéd Kiwi classics heard in every pub in the provinces. On the spot, we worked out that Peter would perform with the band first, then Pauly would sing 'How Bizarre' to the backing CD I had in my pocket. Really he could have stood up and crooned 'God Defend New Zealand' and the inebriated crowd would have gone crazy.

Peter sang 'Bliss', a bogan drinking anthem he had first recorded with Th' Dudes in 1979, with a verse inviting the listener to 'drink yourself more bliss' and 'forget about the last one, get yourself another'. This whipped the crowd into a frenzy and the chorus 'Yaaaaaaa ya ya ya ya' drifted on as Peter left the stage.

Pauly was announced. The crowd, by this time almost crawling, began to chant 'How Bizarre, How Bizarre, How Bizarre'. Pauly, who had been visibly shaking from nerves a minute earlier, walked confidently on to the small stage. Four hundred New Zealanders hollered. The Polydor staff looked stunned. People passing in the street stopped, trying to work out what was going on.

Pauly stood and smiled widely – and the CD player refused to play. The tech prodded and bashed at it but it was completely dead.

The chanting continued. Pauly walked up the mike and hollered at it: 'Brother Pele's in the back.'

The crowd roared back:

'Sweet Sina's in the front.'

And then, all together, they chanted:

'Cruisin' down the freeway in the hot, hot sun.

'Cruisin' down the freeway in the hot, hot sun.'

The bar erupted as Pauly led an a-cappella version of the biggest New Zealand record of all time.

Wendy looked as if she were close to tears and I felt a huge swell of emotion, not only because of the reaction to the song we had recorded and released just a few months before but because of Pauly. For him, this was topping off a triumphant two days.

He left the stage beaming, came over to me and said, 'How did I do?'

I hugged him, but the crowd was screaming for more. Pauly looked at Peter and shrugged. Peter grabbed Pauly by the shoulders and pulled him back up. Then he leaned over the microphone and slowly sang:

'I have a band of men and all they do is play for me.'

Wendy whispered to me, 'This isn't such a good idea. Pauly should leave it at "How Bizarre".'

I looked at her and smiled. 'This is pure genius. Trust them.'

Some things go beyond the boundaries of taste and cool, and for New Zealanders the cheesy Engelbert Humperdinck B-side to his 1967 hit 'Please Release Me' is one of those things. 'Ten Guitars' was a hit nowhere else in the world, but its casual strum hit a nerve from the first moment a provincial New Zealand DJ decided to flip the UK hit 45 and play the other side.

That day in the Polar Bear everyone in the room, notwithstanding Wendy and the gathering police presence in the street outside, understood this perfectly and the endless choruses bought the house down. After later ending up in a West End club's VIP room, we staggered back to the Metropole in huge spirits about three in the morning.

Next day Polydor rang. We were not going to be sent back to New Zealand that week, even if we didn't get on *Top of the Pops* again. Going by sales, the single seemed likely to rise again in the charts. It made financial sense to keep us in London until at least the middle of the following week. We would, however, be moved to a cheaper hotel, The Hilton Kensington at the distant Shepherd's Bush end of Holland Park Avenue. In an effort to compensate, the young woman who called eagerly told me Small Faces and The Who had often played in a nearby theatre.

Pauly had decided Nathan Haines was getting 'too close' and wanted something. I was to cut him off and take no more calls. I did my best to dispel what I saw as paranoia. As far as I could work out, Nathan was merely keen to hang out with us and was being generous with his time and connections. The situation was tricky and I sidestepped it as best I could: Nathan was a signed artist on my label and I was his publisher.

Pauly and I met with Steve Hedges. Steve was still keen to represent Pauly in the UK. We talked about this, and about the urgent need for Pauly to find a manager and work on his future options. He could live wherever he wanted to further his career but I believed it would be wise for him to continue working with Alan: theirs was the magic partnership. Pauly, however, made it clear he wanted to be his own man. He had decided to make his own music, in his own studio, without Alan. I didn't think this was a good idea. In my view he wasn't ready to go it alone.

I tried diplomatically to work through this conundrum but Pauly was increasingly adamant: he was going to write, record and produce his own music. He talked of buying a Fairlight synthesiser and a recording desk the same as those at Uptown. In effect he wanted to create an exact replica of Alan's studio. Aside from watching his brother Phil at work in his production suite in Manukau Christian City Church, this was where his only real recording experiences had been.

As well as his artistic limitations, Pauly lacked the necessary technical expertise. Alan had worked with digital recording equipment all his adult life and his studio proficiency had grown with it. Pauly, on the other hand, had not operated any part of the complex digital and analogue machinery that Alan used so expertly and instinctively. I advised him there were better things for him to spend his money on than a million-dollar replica of a studio to which he already had almost unfettered access.

One day, walking back to the hotel, I again raised the urgent need for a manager.

'Why don't you do it, bro?' Pauly said.

I explained I would have a conflict of interest as part of the manager's job would be to negotiate with the others, including me as the owner of his label, on his behalf. This, not to mention the work involved in owning several businesses, ruled me out. Although I didn't say it, I also had zero desire to manage someone so volatile and violently unpredictable. I was happy to work with Pauly on a recording level and offer guidance but that was all.

One evening we were invited to a party at the famous Roof Gardens in Kensington High Street, where faux Moroccan and Tudor buildings surrounded a rambling pavilion filled with live pink flamingos. The party was hosted by an insurance company that specialised in the music industry. Superstar DJ Paul Oakenfold was spinning old soul and hip-hop records for a crowd that included Richard Branson and Oasis's Noel Gallagher.

Pauly, though, was not in the mood. He was feeling angry about money. In the UK this was always tight and wasn't helped by his desire to buy shoes, music and trinkets. As well as the pinstriped suit, he had ordered a second suit from a tailor in Soho who was thrilled to be making a suit for a pop star, although Pauly never went back to pick it up and pay for it.

I was continually subbing him cash, and the longer we were there the harder it was to extract per diems from Polydor. These would usually came in a lump sum of several days' worth but nothing arrived in the week following *Top of the Pops*. I rang every day. Twice I was told the money was with a one-hour courier but it didn't arrive. On Friday I finally got through to Wendy's assistant, who nonchalantly informed me that the accounts person, the only staff member with the combination to the petty cash safe, had gone to Spain that day on holiday. It was inconceivable that a multinational corporation turning over millions of pounds a year would have only one person able to open a safe. I took a cab to Polydor's Hammersmith offices and said I'd wait until someone who knew the combination turned up. Magically, I got the cash within half an hour.

At Polydor's regional office in St. James's Square I met with the European team to timeline the European roll-out. Alan had couriered me almost final mixes of the album and I had passed them on. The release was scheduled for October 4. It seemed Pauly would be needed back in London and Europe for the first two weeks of October.

On the next UK chart 'How Bizarre' rose to number five, its highest placing, but *Top of the Pops* decided there was no available slot so we were booked to fly back to Auckland on Monday, August 27.

On the Sunday morning I caught a train to Burnham, a small town north-west of London, to visit my friend Dave Daniels, who had supplied us with Gilles Peterson as a DJ in 1994 and so got this whole ball rolling. During the few hours Dave and I spent at the local pub the patrons insisted on playing 'How Bizarre' over and over on the jukebox and repeatedly asked me how rich I was.

I caught the last train back to Paddington. My carriage was nearly empty until half a dozen young guys staggered through, clearly under the weather and in a joyful mood. After singing an Oasis tune, they burst into 'How Bizarre', repeating the chorus over and over again.

One looked across at me and said with a cheerful smile, 'Do you like this song, mate?'

'Indeed I do,' I said, 'very much.'

Next morning we were picked up by a Virgin Atlantic Range Rover and driven in style to the airport. On board the plane the crew treated Pauly like a superstar and all asked for his autograph. In Los Angeles our Air New Zealand flight to Auckland was cancelled because of a mechanical issue and we were stuck in a transit lounge for five hours. Paul Holmes, the highest rating personality on New Zealand television, was also marooned. At first he seemed surprised by the attention being paid to Pauly, and then visibly annoyed.

We arrived back in Auckland late on August 28. We had been away for nearly five weeks. The fun and games were about to begin.

23

MONEY CONTINUED TO BE AN ISSUE. PolyGram was having to transfer weekly advances to Pauly for his rent and I was having to hand over cash on a daily basis. I put pressure on Pauly to sort out the publishing deal I had devised for him with PolyGram Music Publishing.

I was fairly pleased with where we had got to on this. I wasn't signing Pauly via my company and was acting only as a financial adviser; I would receive no financial benefit from his publishing contract with PolyGram, only from Alan's half of the songs. Pauly felt he didn't want to be signed to the same publishing company as Alan, whom he now seemed convinced was working against him. However, using my lawyer and dealing directly with Roger, I had negotiated what at the time was probably the best deal that any artist with one hit, no matter how large, had ever got from New Zealand.

Earlier in the year Pauly had decided to employ new lawyers. He was now represented by Russell McVeagh, a costly corporate law firm which he said had been recommended by Kirstine's father. I was happy that Pauly had finally done what I had repeatedly asked him to – namely find himself a lawyer at arm's length from both mine and Alan's – and Russell McVeagh was a reputable firm, albeit one that didn't seem to have a history with the music industry. An understanding of copyright law is never a substitute for an up-close appreciation of the unique nuances of the industry; to this day I am baffled by the contracts I receive from non-industry law firms and the very odd advice they give clients on music industry matters.

In the publishing deal I had drafted with PolyGram Music's Roger Grierson, to which Pauly had verbally agreed, Pauly had a very advantageous contract almost ready to go. Russell McVeagh's lawyers rejected it and decided to renegotiate. Roger was baffled: it was the first time he had encountered an artist's legal counsel wanting to negotiate into a less beneficial position than the one offered.

At issue was the initial advance on royalties. It was important to Pauly that on signing the contract he received a larger advance than Alan. To get this his lawyers, at his instruction, agreed to a lower overall percentage of income. The irony was that all the song publishing advances were recovered by PolyGram from sales shortly after the agreement was signed. Thereafter Pauly was paid quite a bit less than Alan on all his songwriting.

Anita McNaught filmed a little more footage at the Fuemana family home in Ōtara, and this was edited to make it seem as though Pauly was returning there from his grand adventure. The finished *60 Minutes* story was broadcast on TV3 in early September.

In the middle of that month Alan delivered the completed album. The sleeve design, too, was finished. Deborah Smith had seemed to develop a rapport with Pauly; he had relaxed sufficiently to allow her, in evocative black and white images, to highlight his various tattoos. He was extraordinarily proud of those that had Polynesian designs, but wary of showing tattoos that dated back to his gang days. Earlier in the year he had spent some time trying unsuccessfully to remove these tattoos, which included Rastafarian chants and, on his left hand, SS symbols. As he travelled around the world he would consciously pull his jacket sleeve over his left hand in any media situation. Even more dramatically, he would sometimes wear a bandage covering the hand and tell journalists he had cut himself or sprained his wrist.

Deborah's images carefully avoided those tattoos and instead captured a proud and thoughtful Pauly drawing strength from his Polynesian masculinity. In the shot we used on the front – taken in the Auckland Domain – he was looking directly at the camera with calm penetrating eyes and a look that spoke of quiet confidence in what was inside the CD's plastic case.

One of my favourite photographs appeared in the enclosed booklet. Pauly, with some of his tattoos bared – although the offending left hand was still carefully hidden – was wearing a black T-shirt and the thick-rimmed black glasses that were his trademark for a few weeks, although they had no optical use. He was looking down in a composed, self-assured way in front of a backdrop of Polynesian motifs.

I also loved another beautiful image of Pauly standing in a leather jacket that he had bought during a Los Angeles stopover on our first trip to the UK: he appeared deep in thought, seemingly unconscious of the camera.

Today, these photos remind me of Bruce Mason's play *The End of the Golden Weather*, about a boy's journey out of naiveté and innocence. There is little hint in them of the turmoil that was building in Pauly's mind and the chaos that would erupt around him as the pressures of fame snowballed.

Pauly would later turn on Deborah, claiming she had talked him into a series of nude shots that he now regretted. He demanded we extract these shots from her and there was talk of legal action. In the end nothing came of it and I never saw any nude shots. Did they even exist?

We delayed the New Zealand release of the album until November in the vain hope of first getting another single into the charts. When it did come out the response was mixed. Locally, it received excellent reviews in *The New Zealand Herald* and Wellington newspapers *The Dominion* and *The Evening Post* but almost nowhere else. Outside the country, however, reviews were almost all good. The influential UK music magazine *Q* gave it four stars out of five. *The New York Times*, *The Village Voice* and *Spin* all delivered glowing reports. It was named album of the year in the Philippines and got an A+ review in Japan's biggest music paper.

There was no doubt the album had moments of absolute brilliance. The major let-downs were the vocals on lesser tracks such as 'Angel In Disguise' and 'Never Coming Back'. Alan had struggled with these. After the initial rush of writing and ideas, he had been left to create the album largely on his own with little more than snippets of melody, chorus and ideas from which to construct something coherent.

He had brought in artists as required and used sampling and other wizardry to meld the bits and pieces together. Various session musicians and vocalists could be heard on most tracks. Lee Baker, a guitarist long before he became a film-maker, appeared on two tracks playing guitar. Pauly's own acoustic guitar appeared on a few tracks but Alan provided much of the rest himself. The sleeve credited Pauly with 'all vocals and instruments except…' and went on to list almost every instrument played.

One day when the pressure to deliver was mounting, Pauly had arrived at the studio with a 12-inch Daft Punk single, saying he wanted to use the instrumental as the backing track for 'On The Run'. Alan explained this would be a little too obvious. Pauly quickly dropped the idea, although many years later he was still using other people's tunes as uncredited backing tracks on his own recordings.

For me the standout track on the album was the immigration ballad 'Land Of Plenty', in which Pauly reflected: 'And my father used to say / Oh, we came to this land of plenty / and we came to this land of hope / we came to this land of good times / and we came to this land of love.'

It was the most profoundly moving and beautiful song he and Alan would ever create. Although the words were mostly Pauly's, Alan had reworked and edited them, adding a few lines and dropping others. The vocal from Pauly, backed by his sister Christina, was emotionally powerful. It was perfectly underscored by a warm French horn melody that Alan had added.

Pauly was needed in Europe. The single had been released there and begun to hit the charts. It would eventually reach the Top 10 in a dozen countries, and climb to number one in at least five, including Austria, Sweden and Switzerland. Pauly was in hot demand from the media.

I was resigned to having to go with him, although I didn't enjoy the stress levels, the demands, the growing ego issues, and the uncomfortable reality that Pauly was always potentially on the edge of an explosion. However, it was my job: I owned the label.

A week before we were due to leave, Alan called to say Pauly wasn't keen for me to accompany him. He felt I was trying to get between the two of them and take him over by manoeuvring him out of the country. We both knew this was an attempt to play us off against each other but I was happy to step back and send him with someone else. The core business in the UK had been done. We just needed a minder as Pauly went from one interview and appearance to the next. What could possibly go wrong?

Alan and I came up with Mark Cathro, a friend and long-time business associate of Alan's whom Pauly seemed to like and trust. Mark was wary at first but he warmed to the idea of a free trip around Europe, even if it was going to involve flying, driving and crisscrossing Western Europe on a gruelling ten-day schedule.

He came back from the trip completely wrecked. Pauly had treated him more or less as an unpaid servant who had to do what he wanted, when he wanted, without question. There had been threats of violence. At one point Pauly had threatened to cut off Mark's thumbs if he didn't carry contraband across national borders for him.

Across Europe Pauly had spent wildly. Among his purchases had been a huge range of weaponry, including knuckledusters, flick knives and tasers, all of them illegal to own in New Zealand and import into the country. The bag he had packed with this armoury didn't arrive with his other luggage and he furiously accused Mark of having 'narked' to Customs. A week later there was a knock on his door. A courier from Qantas presented him with his bag, which was still locked. It had not made the plane in Europe. Pauly presented Alan with a flick knife, which

Alan rapidly disposed of, and over the next few months proudly showed off his newly acquired weaponry to all comers. For our part, we were horrified at the thought of Pauly loose with weapons.

A few days after Pauly's return, he and I took a plane back to Sydney for a quick photo shoot. We needed to replenish the fast-depleting stock of images being asked for daily from around the world. Identical shots were beginning to turn up everywhere. This was frustrating our publicity people and damaging our ability to offer exclusives.

We had been booked into my favourite boutique hotel, Regents Court, in Potts Point just off Kings Cross. In the morning Mark Phillips drove us to a studio near Darling Harbour, where a French stylist named Jean Claude had assembled a myriad of designer items. Pauly looked sharp, seemed in really good spirits, and happily cooperated in the long day's filming. At the end he approached Jean Claude and asked if there were any items of clothing he could keep. Jean Claude apologised profusely – the clothes had been borrowed from fashion houses, many were expensive, and he was personally responsible for ensuring they were returned.

Pauly said he would be keen to buy a few items. Was that possible?

'Sure,' Jean Claude said, happy to do a favour for the rising star. 'Which items?'

Pauly went through the rack and pulled out half a dozen pieces, including a jacket and a beautiful dark suit. Jean Claude said he would find out the prices and get back to me.

As we drove away Pauly turned to Mark and me. 'Did you see that fag,' he said, 'trying to force me to buy those shitty clothes? He was lucky I didn't smack him.'

The next day Jean Claude called with the prices. Mark gently told him the bad news. Pauly then asked me to complain to Paul Dickson about both Jean Claude and Mark Phillips. They had, he said, been trying to scam him.

The evening before we were to fly home Pauly called me. I went to his room to find him fuming. He had rented out a bunch of porn videos from a shop just off Kings Cross and now wanted his money back. The videos, he stormed, were 'censored': the really naughty bits were edited out or blurred. I raised my hands and tried to walk away but he shouted after me. As his 'manager' it was apparently my job to get his money back. I took the videos, returned them without a word, and gave him thirty dollars from my own pocket.

24

PAULY'S LACK OF A MANAGER was coming to a head. Michael Cronin, Pauly's lawyer at Russell McVeagh, rang and asked if I would put in an application. When I declined, Pauly phoned and insisted I do so. It was, he said, 'just a formality'. I wondered if having his lawyer sort through management applications from people who had no desire to be his manager and would turn down the job if asked was a wise way to spend the sort of money the law firm would be charging him.

I sent through a cursory document with a cover note explaining that I didn't need or want the job. A few days later I received a ludicrous call from his lawyer telling me that, after some consideration, I wasn't being offered it.

I knew Steve Hedges was still sniffing around but as much as I liked him he was clearly wrong for the job. His business partner was Daniel Keighley, the promoter of the huge outdoors Sweetwaters festivals. Daniel had been quite successful as the UK manager of a New Zealand band, The Mutton Birds, but he too would have been an uncomfortable fit as he was not used to working with South Auckland bands.

I thought long and hard about who could manage Pauly and in late October I called Grant Thomas. Grant was a New Zealander based in Sydney. He managed not only the successful New Zealand singer-songwriter Dave Dobbyn but also Neil Finn and Crowded House. This meant not only might he understand Pauly's background, at least far more than an Englishman would, he had the international experience and contacts we would need if we were to take 'How Bizarre' into the US.

When Grant called back I gave him a brief rundown and he agreed to consider managing Pauly. I then rang Michael Cronin and suggested he contact Grant. Two days later Pauly came to see me and proudly announced his lawyers had hunted down a guy called Grant Thomas to be his manager. Grant was, he informed me, also Neil Finn's manager.

I felt I had done the right thing forcing the issue. It wasn't feasible or practical to have an artist who hoped to break into the US not being represented by a professional manager who knew his stuff. I hoped that Grant would be the best person for the job.

Grant brought in a young assistant, Bill Cullen, to handle Pauly on a day-to-day basis. Early in 1997 Bill would become co-manager: he and Grant would represent Pauly jointly for the next three years, and Grant off and on after that.

Both men would work extremely hard for their difficult client, but there were times I wondered if I had made a mistake. Within a few weeks of Grant taking on the role, Alan, Victor and I became nervous about the touring schedules being planned for Europe and the way the record was to be sold into the US. Grant and Bill seemed to think Pauly was a traditional artist/songwriter/musician whose career would be best served by the extended touring that a band such as Crowded House or a singer-songwriter such as Dave Dobbyn would undertake to break a record.

Nothing could have been further from the truth. When Pauly headed off on his 1997 tours he had never successfully performed as the leader of a band, beyond an occasional mime or vocal performance for TV or a showcase. He was not musically proficient and the closest thing he had done to a live tour, the 1995 Big Day Out shows as OMC, had been mostly shambolic room-clearers.

Luckily, these shows had not cost him any money or damaged his career. In 1997 that would not be the case.

While Pauly was in Europe terrorising Mark Cathro, Asia had come calling. To capitalise on Pauly's fast-rising hit record PolyGram's Asia office, based in Hong Kong, wanted him in the region in late November for the normal round of media publicity and appearances on television and radio. The single had been released in Asia just after its European release and was now in the Top 20 in half a dozen Asian countries, including Thailand and Hong Kong. The label was looking at a potential number one.

Mark Cathro was adamant he was never leaving New Zealand with Pauly again so we had the problem we had faced a couple of months before: who could we send? Pauly suggested Alan but he was not vaguely interested. He then asked if I would go with him again but I demurred: I had done my tour of duty in the firing line.

Needing someone I could trust, I suggested Tom Sampson, my business partner and friend of twenty years. Tom was diplomatic and hard to ruffle. He was also absolutely reliable and Pauly liked him a lot.

Tom and Pauly set off in late November and were met at Hong Kong Airport by PolyGram's Far East international marketing manager, Eric Leddel. Unfortunately Pauly took an instant dislike to Leddel, whom Tom would later tell me was a nice guy doing his job well. Not only that, he was crucial to Pauly's future prospects in that part of the world.

From the start Pauly was rude, demanding and hostile towards Leddel, and this got even worse as the trip went on. After a couple of days of media appointments in Hong Kong the three men flew to Manila, where arrangements struck chaos, with extensive delays at a television station. From there they travelled to Bangkok, where the head of the local PolyGram licensee fed Pauly full of booze and took the group on a wild drunken high-speed car ride through central Bangkok's traffic morass, swerving down Sukhumvit Road with a pocket full of notes to bribe any cops they encountered.

On the flight to Singapore, tired and hungover from the riotous night, Pauly physically threatened Leddel, and a confrontation was wound back only when Tom intervened. Met at Changi International Airport by the local label bosses, Pauly's first question in this most conservative of countries was to ask if they could get him some marijuana. At a meeting convened for PolyGram regional heads to meet their new star, Pauly made a comment about dealing to people in prison before they dealt to you. The executives were reportedly aghast.

Pauly was booked to do a live interview on Singapore's high-rating Channel V. I took an urgent call from Tom. Pauly was refusing to cooperate. Tom had tried everything he could think of to persuade him but without success. In desperation I called Sue DeBenedette in Sydney. Pauly had come to see Sue as an important power broker. She phoned him and managed to talk him around.

The trip had been a disaster. From the label's point of view, the album was dead in the water in Asia. That it sold at all was despite Pauly. After his visit PolyGram Asia did little to support the album. It was not placed in racks at the front of stores or added to the company's promotional campaigns. Having a great record is simply not enough when your label no longer believes in you. Fortunately, Asian radio stations loved the single and played it to death. I still hear it everywhere when I visit Asia.

Tom said he was not keen to do any more tours with Pauly.

At my dogged insistence the next single for release in New Zealand was to be 'Land Of Plenty'. It was the killer track on the album and spoke strongly to and about so many New Zealanders it was bound to be a domestic hit. PolyGram Australia was firmly against it being released as a single there – perhaps mistakenly, given the numbers of New Zealanders in that country who have always been fiercely patriotic and more than a little homesick.

Alan wanted to rework the song as he felt he still hadn't done it justice, so while Pauly was in Europe he went into the studio and rebuilt it from the ground up. He recorded several brand new parts, not least a vocal by

Taisha Khutze that allowed the song to soar at the end. He also added extra horn parts and spent days mixing it to the version on the video.

I had wanted a video that allowed the lyrics full scope. The song was so emotive and Pauly's poignant vocal perhaps his best that the video had to be of equal beauty. My idea was to film Pauly across the country to reinforce the power of the lyrics, which celebrated the emotions many immigrants feel the world over.

I talked to Kerry Brown, who I felt was New Zealand's finest music video director. Kerry came back with a revised concept. It would be far too expensive to fly across the country filming with Pauly. Instead, using cinematographer Greg Semu who had made the stunning 'In The Neighbourhood' video, he would take a small crew around New Zealand and film on the road for two weeks. At the end, I would drive Pauly south to the arid volcanic plateau known as the Desert Road, where we would spend a day filming inserts to fill out the video.

I loved the treatment and Alan was equally sold on it but the budget was still tricky. Even with the reduced concept, the production would be very expensive in New Zealand terms. With money from PolyGram and a NZ On Air grant of $5,000, we had a total of $20,000. No matter how hard we screwed down and trimmed, the video would still work out at about $60,000 – and that was assuming both Kerry and Greg worked for almost nothing.

Someone – I think it was Kerry – convinced the New Zealand Wool Board that a video featuring the country in all its spectacular glory would be a good thing to back and the board contributed $20,000 on the proviso that Pauly wore a wool-lined jacket in the video.

Kerry thought he might be able to talk Television New Zealand into contributing via its ad agency Saatchi & Saatchi. He spoke to an account manager who came up with an offer: TVNZ would put $20,000 into the video if, at some stage in the New Year, Pauly would appear in a station promo. I had to run this past Pauly and he agreed without hesitation. I ran the news back to Kerry and we pushed the green light on the video.

In the middle of November I drove Pauly and Taisha to the Desert Road. We set out on the five-hour journey at dawn with Pauly in a bad mood. The whole way south he chain-smoked and looked out the window. When he spoke it was to question why we were releasing this song as a single. He claimed to have new ones, although they were unheard and unrecorded.

We met Kerry and his crew at a truck stop in the small town of Turangi and headed south into wildlands dominated by three large active volcanoes. Although it was late spring, the air was bitterly cold and the wind was sweeping volcanic dust everywhere.

For a while Pauly refused to acknowledge the camera crew and we had to carry on as if he weren't there. In the first shots he was to walk across the barren plain towards the camera. As he shuffled morosely down a line of scrubby desert foliage he refused to come back or respond to our calls and the shot was scrapped. He was then filmed from the back of a truck that had been fitted with a camera dolly, allowing the cameraman to pull back and forth as the vehicle edged slowly forward.

While the truck driver tried to keep the vehicle steady on the rough terrain, Pauly was supposed to lip-sync to the audio. By now he was almost totally uncommunicative. Asked to smile at the camera and look enthused, he used his oft-repeated line, 'I only smile for my bank manager.'

As the day grew to an end we had only a couple of shots left to do. At this point Pauly announced he was cold and wouldn't do any more; Kerry would have to work around what he had. Luckily the crew were able to capture many brilliant shots of Taisha, who was uncomplaining despite the extended hours and the worsening wind.

By a miracle, editing and colour-grading by Kerry and Greg would turn weeks of work into a three-minute masterpiece in which Pauly's surliness came across as deep thoughtfulness. There was probably not a New Zealander away from home who could watch the video without having to hold back tears.

Later that year, Kerry approached Pauly to film the Television New Zealand piece to which he had agreed as part of the funding package. He refused point-blank. Grant Thomas backed him and PolyGram seemed to have lost Pauly's signed agreement. This was to cause problems both for PolyGram and for Kerry Brown, who had given his word in good faith. As late as February 1998, TVNZ was still asking and Pauly and Grant were still refusing. The promo was never made.

I would sometimes reflect that Grant Thomas had walked into a management contract with an artist who had already sold most of the singles he was going to sell, and with release commitments in place for the territories where he was going to sell most albums. All he needed to do was sit back and take his percentage of the royalties as they arrived.

But for all Grant's failings, he was masterful at getting a good deal. Soon after he became Pauly's manager Alan and Pauly were approached by an advertising agency for permission to use 'Land Of Plenty' in an advertising campaign for the Bank of New Zealand. As publishers of the song Alan and I were offered what seemed a huge sum for the bank to use it in radio and television ads for a year. After managing to push the figure up a little, we happily agreed.

Grant phoned me and said it wasn't nearly enough. He thought he could get almost double the amount. He had had years of negotiating rights for acts like Crowded House, including a deal with the New Zealand Tourism Board for use of 'Don't Dream It's Over' that would lead to the song receiving the APRA Award for Most Performed Work Overseas in 1995, 2000, 2001 and every year from 2003 to 2012. He knew agencies always came in at around 60 percent of what they were willing to pay.

I was nervous but Grant told me to trust him. He managed to push up the fee by about 40 percent. The ad campaign ran for two years. The downside was that because of the steep fee the bank decided not to renew its option after that.

For their second single, rather than go with 'Right On', which they saw as too similar to 'How Bizarre', PolyGram in the UK and Europe decided to go with another album track, 'On The Run'. Later PolyGram Australia, too, would pick this track for a single after 'Right On' failed in their market, and would delay the album's release until early 1997 in the hope that 'On The Run' would be a hit. The company decided to make the video for the song in Australia, an odd decision since its re-edit of the New Zealand 'Right On' video had been a failure. Ownership of the OMC project was slipping further and further away from its roots.

The video was filmed in Melbourne with a director, Mark Hartley, who was known for his work with Peter Andre, among many others. He was chosen by the Sydney office and we had almost no input into what was essentially a video for the Australian and European markets. It would turn out not to be one of Hartley's better efforts, excessively glitzy, and devoid of anything resembling personality – Pauly's or anyone else's. It completely missed what it was that made Pauly stand out from the international mire.

25

ONE NIGHT IN LATE NOVEMBER 1996 Alan and I sat down in his studio and, inspired by a record by a Detroit producer, Carl Craig, turned out an extended and heavily reworked dance remix of 'On The Run', which we named the 'Movin' and Groovin' Mix'. Over the next few years this would make its way on to the B-side of some releases of the single and on to a bunch of international dance compilations.

Meanwhile, PolyGram's UK office sent us its own remix of 'On The Run', which had been done by a well-known remixer, Phil Bodger. Both Alan and Pauly hated it with a vengeance, tagging it the 'Butcher remix'. While I didn't think it was so terrible, it was disjointed and inferior to the original Jansson-created radio edit used in New Zealand. PolyGram's Australian office had allowed it to be released in the UK without our approval and after a period it was withdrawn and replaced with the original New Zealand version. The whole wasteful process cost $8,000; this was billed back to Pauly by PolyGram and deducted from his royalties.

The Bodger mix was indicative of someone in Australia trying to claim ownership of a part of the creative process. I had always resisted this and my contract explicitly gave me complete control and final right of approval over all remixes and edits. I, in turn, would not approve a remix or edit unless Alan and Pauly were both happy with it. The fact the UK remix was poor underscored one of my core philosophies: always start from the assumption the major record company is wrong because, as experience proves time and again, they often are.

'On The Run' was a minor hit around the world and found its way into a few movies, but its failure to go further led to mild panic in PolyGram's Sydney office. Alan's opinion was that he had not been able to properly finish the song – Pauly's vocals were substandard, the lyrics uncomfortable, and he had been left with little to work with. If OMC were to have another hit he needed to go back into the studio, and on his terms.

In early December I was told that Pauly and OMC were confirmed for the trans-Tasman Big Day Out shows in January and February 1997. But first, at Victor's insistence, Pauly had been lined up to sing at the huge Christmas in the Park concert in Auckland's Domain. PolyGram thought it would be a good idea to launch the new single 'Land Of Plenty' the same week.

At the Christmas concert Pauly would need to perform 'Land Of Plenty' to a backing disc. I wasn't sure about this: putting Pauly on a stage with dozens of perfect voiced and experienced singers and professional bands would show up his vocal limitations. However, I was talked into it by a label eager to find a way of selling more copies of an album that was moving rather too slowly out of record stores. And Taisha would be there to sing with him.

The day of the concert was swelteringly hot. Late in the morning we did a cursory soundcheck without Pauly and all seemed fine, although we had little more to rely on than me chanting 'Check, check' a few times into the stage mike and an audio engineer pushing play on the backing CD.

That afternoon I drove Pauly to The Domain. With the car windows down, he leaned out and smiled as we swept into the backstage carpark, where he was feted by the guards and waved and squealed at by dozens of families queuing to get in. We were given passes and ushered into a backstage pavilion where numerous household-name stars were waiting their turn onstage. Dalvanius Prime, a mountain of a man in every way – not least because of his warm personality, which, with his roar of a laugh, always made him a pleasure to meet – came over and said, 'Simon, introduce me to your friend.'

He took Pauly by the arm and said graciously, 'Welcome. We have a lot to talk about.' Pauly smiled broadly. Dalvanius carried immense mana in both the Māori and Polynesian communities. He told Pauly with great sincerity how much he loved his work.

Standing on our left was the Māori entertainer Howard Morrison. Notorious for his crankiness and slightly unpleasant attitude towards those he regarded as lesser beings, the ageing and recently knighted Morrison was still indisputably one of the greatest entertainers New Zealand had ever produced

Dalvanius called him over and said, 'Have you met Pauly and Simon?'

I had met Morrison several times, but I said, 'It's a pleasure, Howard' and put out my hand. Pauly smiled and also put out his hand. Morrison looked at us both, said, 'It's Sir Howard to you' and walked away.

As Pauly and Taisha went on to the stage I watched from the sound desk with Greg Peacock, the front-of-house sound technician. What followed was horrible. Pauly was not only vocally flat but forgot many of his words and mumbled into the microphone. The huge crowd were mostly silent. They seemed bewildered by the performance. Taisha covered for Pauly as best she could but the whole thing was abysmal.

Pauly was supposed to go back onstage for a grand finale but as he came off he looked at me and barked, 'Let's go.' As we left Dalvanius was being carried out to the stage in his Māori Santa Claus outfit in a large waka, crying out, 'Merry Christmas! Merry Christmas!' The crowd roared. They had already forgotten about 'Land Of Plenty'.

Just after New Year, Grant Thomas rang and asked who was in Pauly's band for the Big Day Out. Their first show was in Australia in less than two weeks.

'How should I know?' I said. 'You're his manager.'

I hadn't seen Pauly since the fiasco at Christmas in the Park. I had been on holiday and assumed his new management team had the band – and some intensive and much-needed rehearsals – in hand.

It turned out nothing had been done. After a long silence Grant, in a tone verging on panic, pleaded with me to help. I said I would see what I could do. I called Nathan Haines. Could he urgently put together a band for Pauly? I realised it was a huge call.

An hour later Nathan called me back. After some hustling, he would be able to do it. I rang Grant and gave him Nathan's number. I put down the phone, wondering where in god's name this was all going to go.

The live notices from the Big Day Out shows in Australia were brief. There were no raves like Clinton Walker's few lines in 1995 that had helped launch OMC into the spotlight. Indeed most reviews of the Big Day Out didn't mention OMC at all.

Grant and Bill, though, appeared relieved to have professional musicians at hand and decided to continue to use the band for OMC's upcoming European dates. As well as Nathan on saxophone, Pauly now had Rob Paterson on bass, Taisha Khutze on backing vocals and Manuel Bundy on turntables.

In early January 'How Bizarre' went to number one in Canada, a country that had always been friendly towards New Zealand-originated music, with acts such as Split Enz, The Mutton Birds and Crowded House enjoying success there. The album was selling well too and was now marked down for US release on February 25.

In the middle of February I flew to Sydney with Victor for another meeting with PolyGram. The initial discussions centred around the costs of the forthcoming European shows. The figures being tossed around for tour support dwarfed all expenditure on the OMC project to date and seemed to indicate a change of tack for Pauly. Whether the programme was being driven by Grant and Bill, by the Australian record company or, as was most likely, a combination of them all, it was now clear that Pauly was to be pushed as a working rock 'n' roll musician in a traditional way. Victor and I were uneasy about this. The tour would come at huge financial cost to Pauly since tour support, if advanced by a record company, is usually charged back to the artist and extracted from his or her royalties. If we had a record currently being pushed by the record company in the territory and an artist who shone in concerts, this would not be unreasonable. But in February 1997 we had neither. 'How Bizarre' as a single was a spent force in Europe.

That night I rang Alan and talked over my worries. We agreed that sending OMC on the road as a working band would probably be a disaster. Unless OMC developed a substantial and credible live show that complemented the album and developed Pauly as a strong and commanding performer, the strategy was doomed to failure. Alan's final words to me, spoken slowly and with resignation, were, 'You can only open the door for him. In the end he and he alone has to walk through it.'

I had a sinking feeling. Pauly was now buying into the hype we had helped to create. This is a dilemma that happens with almost every successful act. How do you stop an artist believing the bluster and ballyhoo the publicity machine has produced on their behalf? And if they don't believe it, their partner, family and friends certainly will. The puffery, spin and PR bullshit more often than not comes back to bite you.

Like the Big Day Out, the European gigs passed largely without notice and made little or no impact on album sales. Once 'How Bizarre' had dropped off the radar there, the album was only ever going to sell more copies if another hit single got the sort of massive airplay the earlier record had benefited from. It would not be helped by expensive live performances from an artist not equipped to play live.

From the US, Mercury asked us about dance remixes and I put in a hopeful list of people I thought would do a good job. Within a few weeks I was presented with a finished 12-inch disc of remixes by two people I had never heard of and could find no record of online. On inquiring, I discovered one was related to a man who owned a chain of important radio stations across the US South; getting him to do a remix was a way of edging the single on to those radio stations.

Despite this the remixes were fairly passable and they began to pick up a bit of club play in the US, even though they were not commercially released and only available on a promotional 12-inch single. In reality, pressings of dance mixes tend to be distributed to dance specialist shops and services even if not 'released'.

To capitalise on the increasing demand for dance mixes on vinyl from retailers around the world, I compiled a fairly cool-looking 10-inch four-track semi-transparent green vinyl EP of the best of the UK and US remixes. I pressed 2,500 copies in Los Angeles and sold the whole run to a New York vinyl distributor, Watts Music, where the chief buyer was my old friend, New Zealander Harry Russell.

That was supposed to be it but the demand was so high I eventually pressed another 1,500 for other wholesalers, plus 100 for DJs, before deleting the record forever. I did this outside the PolyGram system and paid a percentage to PolyGram in New Zealand as a royalty. The EP became collectable and is now rare.

Mercury had decided to release the 'How Bizarre' single in the US solely to media and radio as a promotional disc. The public would be able to buy it only as a track on the album. This ploy to boost financial returns was an increasingly common practice in the US, and is now seen as a contributing factor in the perceived collapse of the record industry in the decade that followed. The big labels were with some justification seen as screwing their customers.

There were obviously substantial upsides to the strategy. The biggest was that we all stood to make an awful lot more money in the short term from selling albums to people who couldn't buy the single. Secondly, it might accustom people to seeing Pauly as an album artist rather than a single artist – or so I was told by PolyGram. I treated this with cynicism.

It seemed the company had blindly convinced itself that Pauly was some sort of South Pacific Bruce Springsteen.

The downsides were just as profound. There was every chance the public would refuse to pay fifteen dollars or more just to acquire a single track they liked. And if they did hand over that sort of cash, they might feel ripped off if the album as a whole didn't click. This was likely to damage Pauly's image. It's the artist most people see when they buy a record, and Pauly could be perceived as greedy and not particularly fan-friendly. The last bit worried me especially: if Pauly couldn't connect through live shows he needed to connect any other way he could.

There was, too, a selfish motive: both Alan and I were keen to have a number one US single. It was the sort of thing you dreamt of when you started out in the record industry. Now we were to be denied a shot at *Billboard*'s Hot 100. Today, with iTunes and ringtones, it's relatively easy to sell several million tracks of a song. Smallish hits in the US do it all the time, and indeed New Zealand rapper Savage sold two million downloads and ringtones in 2007 of a track that was only ever a medium-sized hit in the US. But in pre-digital days getting a single into the Hot 100 on physical sales was a notable achievement.

In March Alan and I flew to Sydney for more meetings with PolyGram. Pauly was back in Australia after his initial European dates and one morning we met up with him. He calmly told us he'd decided the album needed radical remixing to turn it into more drum and bass style, along the lines of the music Nathan Haines had been playing to him over the past two months.

As an alternative he wanted to go into his own studio, a place nobody seemed to be previously aware of, and immediately record a new album that would be drum and bass and would replace the existing album in stores worldwide. People who had bought the earlier album would be allowed, in fact encouraged, to swap versions. Alan and I looked at each other with the same thought: had anyone told PolyGram about this?

Wandering into East Sydney, we ran into Grant Thomas at the famous coffee institution Bill & Toni's. Pauly sat down and said, 'Grant, my new records are all going to be drum and bass.' Grant, perplexed as only a rocker can be by things electronic, said, 'Yes, sure, Pauly, most records have drums and bass.'

Pauly then regaled us with stories about the *Top of the Pops* shows. None of the stories matched up with the trip I had been on.

26

IN SYDNEY SUE DEBENEDETTE gave me a video compilation of some offshore footage. I didn't look at the video until I was back in New Zealand, but when I did I called Victor and Alan to come and watch a particular few minutes of it. They comprised Pauly with several of his band, including the gloriously voiced Taisha, in a radio studio doing a magical live acoustic take of 'Never Coming Back', the almost folk Polynesian song on the album.

'Never Coming Back' had originally been written about Pauly's friend and sometime Otara Millionaires Club DJ Soane Filitonga. During the recording process the song had been changed, with lyrics being rewritten on the spot. The band had now transformed it into a gorgeous swaying soft rocker that screamed out 'single'. To me, it demanded rapid re-recording in that style. This could be the big single we needed to follow 'How Bizarre'.

Alan and Victor agreed although Sue seemed less convinced. A new song was in the offing for a movie soundtrack. That, she thought, could be better for a single. However, putting on my label owner's hat I pushed ahead and a small budget was allocated for Alan to completely re-record the track.

Immediately we hit a snag: Pauly wanted to record and produce the song himself. This promised to be a debacle but his management backed him, as did PolyGram Australia, which was keen to give him a chance to prove himself artistically. Alan agreed to hire him the studio. Pauly would make, record and mix the single, bringing in any guest musicians he thought he needed.

We played the result without Pauly present. The track was unlistenable. The vocals were flat. The instruments were out of tune and out of sync with each other. They seemed to have been randomly placed on the recording.

Grant Thomas turned to Alan and said, 'It's complete shit.' I asked Alan if there were anything he could do to rescue it. He thought for a moment and then said he could perhaps put the vocals through a pitch-shifter, and cut and paste the usable parts of the backing, adding new overdubs where needed. Grant cut him off. 'It's shit, and no matter how much you polish it, it will still be shit.'

The recording still lives on a hard drive somewhere. It was never released.

Sue DeBenedette's video compilation also included early live performances, and clips from European television shows. The TV clips were mostly interviews and were fine: Pauly was doing the job; the band was performing cut-down or mimed versions of 'How Bizarre' or 'Right On' and keeping OMC in the European public eye.

One Italian interview had us perplexed. Pauly was asked exactly what was so special about New Zealand.

'We have four seasons,' he replied.

The host looked confused. 'We too in Italy have four seasons.'

'But ours are all in one year,' Pauly said.

This strange comment aside, the videos underscored how hard Pauly had worked in the twelve months since the single of 'How Bizarre' had taken off in Australia. He was charming and charismatic in the interviews, even though they were probably far too late to influence the sales of the singles and the album in Europe.

The live footage was less impressive. Everyone who looked at it came to the same conclusion: it was not to Pauly's advantage to do live shows as a promotional activity.

In April the touring band played the 1997 New Zealand Music Awards, which were again held at Aotea Centre. By now Pauly's brother Tony Fuemana had replaced Rob Paterson on bass after Pauly took a dislike to Rob and physically threatened him.

Pauly won the International Achievement Award but in his short speech he upsettingly failed to thank Alan, although Alan was the primary reason Pauly was on that stage. Afterwards he and the band played 'A Friend', the song Pauly had played to me in his hotel room in London nine months earlier and later on MTV. They dedicated it to Pauly and Tony's father Takiula Fuemana, who had died in 1989. A fairly messy presentation was held together by the musical prowess of the musicians and the backing vocals of the talented Taisha. The song, however, seemed to have lost some of the quiet, gracious beauty it had had when I heard the acoustic guitar demo at the Metropole.

In the US, radio response to the single of 'How Bizarre' was very slow, but from early April various cable television channels, including the important BET – Black Entertainment TV – picked up our video. BET would eventually play this video almost 500 times, as would MTV. In 1999 we received a final tally. The video had been played 14,474 times on American television, which was not bad given it had been made for only NZ$7,000.

In May I walked into Roger Grierson's office in Sydney. He was on the phone and seemed unusually animated. When he put it down, he said, 'Mate, do you know who that was? Allen Klein in New York. He's heard "How Bizarre" and thinks it may have breached Phil Spector's copyright in "Spanish Harlem".'

Allen Klein, Phil Spector's manager, was one of the most infamous figures in the global music industry; in his time he had managed both The Rolling Stones and The Beatles and ended up fighting them in court.

'Spanish Harlem', which Spector co-wrote with Jerry Leiber for Ben E. King, had been a huge global crossover hit in the early 1960s. We had talked about the similarity with 'How Bizarre' and compared the two songs, but had decided they were different enough for there to be no problem. Moreover, Roger was grinning. Why? I asked him.

'Because,' he said, 'Allen Klein wouldn't give a damn about our record unless he could smell a huge hit in the making.'

A few days earlier I, too, had taken an odd call, this time from an American called Kim Fowley. Depending on your point of view, Fowley was a famous or infamous name in rock 'n' roll history. He had been writing or creating hits (and countless flops) since he was a teenager. In the 1960s he had produced a string of throwaway pop hits that included the novelty disc 'Alley Oop' by The Hollywood Argyles, essentially Fowley and singer Gary Paxton, and 'Nut Rocker' by the anonymous B. Bumble and The Stingers. In the 1970s he had been the Svengali behind the manufactured pop-punk girl group The Runaways, which had included Joan Jett who went on to achieve success in the '80s with The Blackhearts.

When the phone rang in my office I had casually picked it up. 'This is Kim Fowley in New Orleans,' a nasal voice said. 'I want you to tell me all about this Polynesian stuff. Any more hits there? Any more Māoris?'

I tried to gather my thoughts and work out if this was really Kim Fowley. I had met Fowley once: in 1979 he had come into a small record store in Auckland where I was working. He had been looking for Zero – real name Clare Elliot – the female lead vocalist of a punk band, The Suburban Reptiles, which I was managing. Naïvely thinking there could be something in this for Clare career-wise, I thought about putting him in touch with her, until I worked out that he had a less than professional desire to meet the attractive blonde singer.

We talked for about half an hour but he rapidly lost interest when he learned the artist he had been hearing was already signed to Mercury. I gave him Phil Fuemana's phone number in case he had an urge to delve further into the sounds of South Auckland. If anyone could handle Fowley, Phil could. Phil never heard from the lanky hustler.

The US and European promotional schedule for the next few months was laid out by Grant Thomas in April and May. Despite contractual requirements there was little consultation with me or PolyGram New Zealand. The schedule effectively put Pauly on the road with his band – Nathan Haines, Tony Fuemana, Manuel Bundy, Nick Duirs and Taisha Khutze – for much of the rest of the year.

The next single would be a cover version of the Randy Newman song 'I Love L.A.' and would appear in the Rowan Atkinson film *Bean: The Movie*. I was informed – because PolyGram Australia had to, not because they wanted to – that it would be released in late September to follow 'How Bizarre' in the US, and as the next single worldwide.

The idea was that Pauly's recording of the song would be tagged on to the end of the *How Bizarre* album in the US as a bonus track, and hopefully give him another hit. It reeked of desperation and I had an instant bad feeling about the idea. However, I decided to try and make the best of it and avoid ruffling Mercury, which was selling a lot of records for us. I said I'd go to Alan and try and timeline a recording.

Back in Auckland we listened to the original song and Alan worked out a rough arrangement that would be sympathetic to Pauly and potentially strong in its own right as a song and a possible single. His take was a little cheeky but it had humour and a Pacifica edge that would sit comfortably on the album as the bonus track. Importantly, it didn't sound like a parody.

When Pauly came into the studio he was completely uninterested in Alan's ideas. We heard little more about the song until Pauly returned to the US and we were told, again contrary to my label agreement with PolyGram, that a decision had been made in Australia, in conjunction with Pauly's management, to record it in the US with a local producer.

It was becoming obvious there was an attempt by PolyGram's Australian management and Pauly's management, urged on by Pauly himself, to extract him from Alan, PolyGram New Zealand and me and establish him as an artist in his own right. I had no issue with his going out on his own but I was aware of the artistic pitfalls he would face if this happened before he was ready.

In late May, out of the blue, I received a letter from PolyGram Australia's business affairs department wanting to amend my contract with them. Had I agreed, I would have been relinquishing any further claim to the OMC project. It was another harbinger of the greed starting to envelop the project. I tore up the letter.

After Pauly spent a period in the US rehearsing and recording 'I Love LA.' he set out on a second round of European touring, beginning in Cologne, Germany, on June 8. After three weeks in Europe, during which every show lost money, the band went back to L.A. for the making of a video of 'I Love L.A.'.

All this required 'tour support' from PolyGram, and at the end of the day Pauly would have to pay for all or most of it. In the music industry, tour support is the money required to support a live touring band, including musicians, crew, buses and much more. It is advanced by the record label against the artist's income from music sales, usually called their recoupment account. The reasoning is that the tour is essentially promotional, designed to help the artist or band build a solid fan base that will grow album by album.

This can be a massive burden and cut a huge hole in an artist's future royalty stream, but for many it is the only way to attract fans – or was before the internet turned up. The artists hope that in time the live shows will not only pay their way but become profitable enough to cover any losses incurred on the way up. This is a huge risk, but since only a tiny percentage of bands have ever made serious money from the major-label royalty system, it can be a risk worth taking – if you are a band with the live chops.

Pauly Fuemana and OMC were not such a band and should not have been put on the road. Even though PolyGram agreed to make 50 percent of the support for the US tour non-recoupable, these adventures were to cost Pauly a small fortune. They would play havoc with his already volatile state of mind and make no appreciable positive impact on his record sales. Far more would have been achieved by sending Pauly and

Taisha out to do TV, media, radio and the odd showcase, and this was something the US label would have covered cost-wise.

This was not the view, though, of those who had taken the reins. In September Pauly's co-manager Bill Cullen told the *New Zealand Listener*: '[Mercury Records] did the same thing in Canada, and that's helped establish him as more of an album artist. … [PolyGram] are looking at OMC as an album act rather than a pop thing aimed at teenagers.'

Both statements showed a failure to understand OMC and what had led to the group selling over a million copies of the album and single to date. It looked as though the successful creative process and partnership was set to be destroyed by Pauly and his managers.

In his defence, Bill was not alone. His statement highlighted a failure of the whole recording industry across the last part of the 1980s and into the 1990s. The power structure controlling the way music was sold seemed not to realise that most people simply want the song they've fallen in love with on the radio. It's always been about the song and always will be.

In the same interview Grant Thomas claimed, 'The reason this thing is working is because we have a shitload of synchronicity on all levels. … [Pauly] is working hard to take that one song and turn it into a career.'

He was wrong. The thing had been working because two people, Pauly Fuemana and Alan Jansson, had made a hugely infectious, radio-friendly record and then a bunch of other people had worked hard to take it around the world before Grant and Bill were involved.

27

AS MAY ROLLED INTO JUNE there was a growing sense of gloom at PolyGram. Despite the early video play on BET and a couple of other networks, 'How Bizarre' had been slow to be picked up for American radio playlists. Eventually we received an email telling us that while Mercury was still working on it, it had deprioritised it in favour of a single by an Irish band, The Cardigans.

Although this was depressing news, Alan and I remained confident. We knew the record had a will of its own. As if to prove us right, a radio station in Buffalo, New York picked up 'How Bizarre' and began championing it. My email address was on the back of the CD. One morning I received an enthusiastic email from the programme director; the song was causing the station's phones to ring constantly every time it was played.

The station passed on this information to its New York City affiliate Z100, which began to air the record with similar results. It would go on to be named the sixth biggest single in New York City in 1997, a notch ahead of The Spice Girls.

With Mercury re-enthused, the single started to spread steadily. Stations from Dallas to San Francisco picked it up. We began to see a radio frenzy, just as we had in Australia, New Zealand and the UK.

By early July 'How Bizarre' had started to climb the American airplay charts. By the middle of the month it was headed towards number one on several of them, including those in New York City.

With this buzz, Mercury edited the part of the song being auditioned to programme directors across the country. Customarily, the directors were played just 15 seconds of a song, and the song had to work in that window. Before Mercury boss Danny Goldberg intervened, the pluggers were playing them the 'how bizarre' part and getting a blank response. After consulting radio people he trusted, Goldberg moved the 15-second focus to the 'Oh baby, you're driving me crazy' segment. 'The song worked everywhere else in the world. It will work here if we do it right,' he told me.

Sure enough, programmers lapped it up. The song continued its rise and in the first week of August Sue DeBenedette rang from Australia and squealed loudly down the phone, 'We're number one. Number one!' Nearly twenty years on, I still have to pinch myself. 'How Bizarre', a record we had made almost two years earlier with an instinctive belief in the song and how far it could go, had conquered the most important music market in the world.

That day 'How Bizarre' was number one on the US Top 40 Mainstream Airplay chart. It was also number two on the R&B Airplay Chart, and number five on the Adult Top 40. The next week it reached number four on the Billboard Airplay Hot 100 and number one on the Billboard Pop Charts. It sat on the pop chart for some eight months. The US accounted for around 40 percent of the global music market and our single had soared to the top of its charts. This was something no other New Zealand act had done from New Zealand.

The feeling bordered on surreal. Alan and I and the crew at PolyGram New Zealand wanted to scream out the news. I wandered out on to High Street and randomly told people. I then rang the newsdesk of *The New Zealand Herald*, thinking it would be something they'd want to report. The person I spoke to told me they had covered OMC before but would run a short notice. The next day it was tucked away on a corner of the front page. Neither Television New Zealand nor TV3 returned my calls.

In July and August 1997 'How Bizarre' was played on US radio almost 500,000 times. No New Zealand record, before or since, has come close to that staggering figure in two months. Indeed, few hit records in the US ever come close. It would be 17 years before another New Zealand-made record, Lorde's 'Royals', reached the top of the US charts.

The album, too, was slowly rising, driven by the increasing airplay and Mercury's heavy advertising on both MTV and regional media. By late July it had reached the mid 50s of the US Top 200. Every week Mercury's office would fax through page after page of incredibly detailed Soundscan sales data. This broke down album sales not only by states but by towns and even major stores in these towns. For an industry nerd like me, it was fascinating to watch how local radio play and promotional activities and deals matched the ebb and flow of sales. We would, for example, be told of a co-op deal – a joint advertising campaign between a label and a retailer – in a state or with a retail chain and then be able to watch sales bump upwards the following week. On top of that I had friendly Mercury staffers firing me all sorts of trivia.

The digital audio tape of Pauly's US-recorded cover of 'I Love L.A.' arrived at PolyGram's Auckland office. Victor, Alan and I put it on and listened. There was silence as it finished. The track was appalling. Produced by a New Yorker called Peter Zizzo, who had worked with Celine Dion, it sounded like a half-baked parody of the sound Alan had created for 'How Bizarre'. The vocals were not just out of tune, they were completely tuneless. Pauly hadn't even been able to reach the required notes. The song plodded along like a Mexican funeral dirge.

I faxed Sue DeBenedette and pleaded with her to kill the release. Contractually, I had the power of veto but nobody was listening. Insisting on using the veto would cause a fight we didn't need just as the *How Bizarre* album was taking off in the US.

The video that arrived shortly afterwards was even worse. Pauly had often expressed his Hugh Hefner fantasy of hanging out at the Playboy mansion in the pool with the babes. Here he was in a pool in a Los Angeles mansion in the hills, which he later swore was owned by Hefner, with babes. Directed by someone called Evan Bernard, the video made Pauly look ridiculous.

This was an artistic catastrophe in the making. If 'I Love L.A.' happened to be a hit, however unlikely that was, since it was a crude facsimile of 'How Bizarre' it would tag Pauly forever as a novelty act. If it was a failure, which was much more likely, it would go a long way towards convincing Mercury that OMC was a one-hit wonder. Either way it was a career killer.

To make things worse, the recording costs and half the video costs of 'I Love L.A.' would be debited to Pauly's recoupment account. If the movie's soundtrack didn't sell, PolyGram New Zealand would still bill him.

Not surprisingly the record was a commercial disaster. It was not added to a single radio playlist in the US, Australia or New Zealand, and its worldwide sales were virtually nil. It was not used in the *Bean* movie, although in a few territories it was added to the end credits.

There was a longer-term problem. Sue DeBenedette and Pauly's managers were very good at negotiating deals and handling other business matters, but they were now making the sorts of decisions that had previously been made by creative people, and especially by Alan Jansson.

28

IN AUGUST 1997 ALAN AND I were back in Sydney. At Polydor, Sue DeBenedette played us a series of videos that had arrived from New York. The first was a Canadian clip of Pauly and the band playing outdoors with a crowd in the snow earlier that year. Manuel Bundy seemed to be expertly spinning backing tracks off vinyl as Pauly, strutting along the raised stage, improvised vocal snippets of the album tracks. It seemed to have little to do with the music Pauly had made with Alan but he was very good. His performance exhibited the raw magnetism of the New Zealand-made videos and his second *Top of the Pops* performance. He wasn't trying to sing or be hugely innovative but he had a complete command of the crowd despite the freezing cold, just as he had had in the London pub a year earlier.

The next video was of an extended live show in the US. Whereas the other video was inspiring, this one was heartbreaking and depressing. Pauly and band had decided to rework the songs into an extended drum and bass set. Their performance not only bore no resemblance to the music we wanted to sell in the US but was poor. Nathan Haines would go on to make quite brilliant drum and bass records in the UK and the band was on form. This, though, was just wrong. Over frantic staccato bass rhythms, Pauly muttered or shouted fragments of his recorded work in a confused quagmire.

Sue looked at me and said, 'Isn't it wonderful?'

'It's awful,' I replied, 'truly awful.'

Alan walked away without saying a word.

How this had been allowed to happen was beyond our comprehension. Such music would be a hard sell even in a territory where the styles had some currency. In the US, and especially in middle America, which had for decades been a conservative backwater as far as new musical styles went, performing niche underground UK dance styles would not only confuse potential buyers but probably completely alienate them. Worse, people who had bought concert tickets thinking they were going to hear music in the vein of 'How Bizarre' and the other tracks on the album would be stunned and disappointed. Nothing on that stage would encourage them to buy another OMC record.

As the band headed back out on the road the blowback from these gigs began. The reviews I was sent by Mercury directly, not the filtered ones that came via Sydney, were uniformly terrible. The *Village Voice* headlined its review 'OMC Live: Dead'. The *Los Angeles Times'* coverage was wholly negative and *The New York Times* ended its review of the show, which had been at the famed Supper Club, with this:

'Mr Fuemana … proclaimed that he wanted everyone to dance and proceeded to recast his songs as thumping moaning club music. Taisha Khutze wailed like a house music diva; Nathan Haines, on saxophone and flute, played perky lines. And Mr Fuemana rushed unintelligibly through verses so he could repeat choruses more often. What made the songs distinctive … was buried in weak, second-hand beats.'

The reviews from other cities were even more dire, and because my contact details were on the album sleeve I began to get a stream of complaining and sometimes abusive emails and letters. Many people were angry and a few asked for refunds. Most simply expressed disappointment in an artist they said they would no longer support.

I personally answered every email and printed them all out for Pauly. He didn't ever pick them up.

The album continued its upward path on the US charts and in August jumped into the Top 50, which meant it was selling 50,000 copies a week (today these sorts of numbers would get a record into the US Top 3), but sales fell dramatically in every town where OMC played. This stood out as I pored over the Soundscan figures faxed through every week. The awful live shows and the hugely costly touring, complete with buses and crew, were doing exactly what Alan had predicted two years earlier. In the towns and cities that OMC didn't visit, sales were growing steadily in line with the airplay, video play and advertising campaigns.

On the August 30 US chart the album peaked at number 40: it had sold just under a million copies. Eventually it would sell nearly 1.5 million before dropping out of the US Top 200 almost six months later.

Behind the good news, though, things were unravelling and getting uglier by the day. In November 1996 Pauly's lawyers Russell McVeagh had given PolyGram's lawyers a written instruction, to which Alan was also party via his solicitor. Attached to it was the original agreement signed by Pauly and Alan in my office, with me as a witness. This specified clearly how the income and profit from the master recordings was to be split between the two of them. The document was fairly straightforward. It had been discussed endlessly over the months before and after. There was no mistaking the intentions of the two parties. PolyGram was to pay Alan his split pursuant to that document and it was Pauly's intention that this should happen.

In February 1997 PolyGram asked for clarification. That was under-standable: although the document was unambiguous it was the company's responsibility to ensure it executed it to the letter. By the middle of March 1997, however, PolyGram had received new instructions from Russell McVeagh. It seemed Pauly was no longer willing to pay Alan without a radical renegotiation of the terms and income split.

Both PolyGram and Huh!, as the record labels to which Pauly was signed, needed to deal with this at a distance. We could neither give advice nor be seen to be doing so.

Huh! and PolyGram New Zealand observed this. However, intelligence I was getting from PolyGram Australia suggested some staff at executive level were offering Pauly informal advice.

Alan's lawyers decided the best way to force the issue was for Alan to sue PolyGram for its non-payment pursuant to the original instruction from Pauly. By the end of July letters were flying back and forth between PolyGram New Zealand, Pauly's lawyers and Alan's new barrister, John Wain. Alan was angry at what he saw as a grave betrayal of trust, good faith and an honourable agreement.

On July 25 a meeting was held in PolyGram's Sydney boardroom of all Australian and New Zealand interested parties. A range of things were discussed, including the future direction of Pauly's career.

Given what was going on in the US, and the looming breakdown in the creative partnership between Alan and Pauly, I made a statement I would repeat to Alan a few weeks later. 'Pauly Fuemana,' I said, 'will likely never make another album.' There was nervous laughter, followed by silence. Then someone changed the subject and started talking money.

The costs to Pauly and PolyGram of the tours and the impending 'I Love L.A.' debacle were laid out by Sue DeBenedette:

1st European dates: $49,000 (100% recoupable)
2nd European dates: $88,000 (100% recoupable)
US dates: $166,000 (50% recoupable)
'I Love L.A.' recording: $29,450 (100% recoupable)
'I Love L.A.' remix: $7,350 (100% recoupable)
'I Love L.A.' video: $148,000 (50% recoupable)

The bulk of this, $330,800, would come directly from Pauly's royalties. In addition to his publishing advance, he had also taken personal advances of close to $100,000 over the previous 18 months.

By the middle of 1996, before 'How Bizarre' had been released outside of Australia and New Zealand, the single, the album and the videos had more or less broken even. This had meant both Pauly and Alan stood to make a profit after this: even the cost of the extra videos would be well and truly covered by the first rush of sales out of Europe.

Now Pauly was in a hole again. And the debt was his alone: Alan had no liability for the touring costs or the 'I Love L.A.' blowout. Worse, the money would come out of Pauly's income after his management fees had been paid. The industry standard was that a manager received 20 percent of the gross before costs. If this applied to Pauly – and I was not privy to his arrangement with Grant and Bill – he would be paying the 1997 touring and recording costs from 80 percent of his agreed 75 percent of the returns from the 'How Bizarre' sessions. This perhaps explained why Pauly and his managers were so reluctant to pay Alan his due: in July 1997 there was little money left.

While the OMC tour continued to burn money across the US, PolyGram turned on Victor Stent. In mid September, when the company's regional boss Tim Read and lawyer Sue Cohen arrived in Auckland, the writing was on the wall for the New Zealand managing director.

Victor was widely disliked in the company and I felt any excuse would be used to remove him. After a series of interviews with people inside and outside the company, myself included, Victor was sacked with immediate effect. He kept his benefits but as a condition signed a non-disclosure agreement.

I was told by someone in the Australian office that its business affairs department had been digging into my company. This was undoubtedly related to the piece of paper I had refused to sign, which would have removed Huh! from the income stream and label role for OMC. It seemed part of an ongoing move to take full control of the project, and loosely tied to the problems Alan was having getting paid. To remove us, Victor obviously had to go too and there were now millions of dollars in potential future revenues in play.

Victor was not a hugely likeable person. Things such as his 'sooties' comment rubbed people the wrong way and he had some odd personal quirks and habits. His continual failure to understand where the boundaries lay between creatives and marketers caused us endless difficulties. But for all that he could sell records like few others, and there were those who suggested he was poorly treated by PolyGram, given that the label he signed had brought the global corporation an artist who had given it one of its biggest records in years.

Part of it was the culture of backstabbing that defined the music industry. While there were many talented and forward-thinking executives, including in PolyGram, there was also a tradition of ruthless infighting and outmanoeuvring. Ed Bicknell, who managed Dire Straits to their phenomenal global success, experienced continuous legal brawls with PolyGram over royalties and artistic control. He later said, 'I got through sixteen or seventeen managing directors … they're incredibly inefficient and absolutely hopeless to deal with.'[11]

We were told that in the US Victor's firing was greeted with cheers on the tour bus. Pauly was pleased the executive he had regarded as 'the man' just eighteen months earlier had been dumped but by this time Victor was having little impact on Pauly's career: PolyGram New Zealand had moved on to new domestic signings.

With Victor gone, Ian Watson, the local sales manager, was appointed to head the New Zealand company. Paul Dickson became the boss of PolyGram Australia and Tim Read, who could now claim his company had signed the multimillion-selling hit, was promoted to head PolyGram Asia-Pacific.

For us, the only bright spot was that Adam Holt had been promoted back to Sydney to replace Paul Dickson at Polydor. Adam understood exactly where 'How Bizarre' had come from. When Alan visited Sydney in October, Adam took him aside and asked him whether there was

---

11 Quoted by Simon Napier-Bell in his article 'The life and crimes of the music biz' in *The Observer*, January 20, 2008.

any way he would work with Pauly again. Alan declined: he had still not been paid.

In September, a couple of new recordings produced in the US arrived by courier from New York. I knew nothing about these and had not been consulted. The first was a cover by Pauly of an old Julie Andrews' tune, 'My Favourite Things' from *The Sound Of Music*. It had been recorded for a Christmas album, *A Home For The Holidays*, the profits from which were going to Phoenix House, a drug rehabilitation charity. Pauly's rendition was passable if a little flat.

The other track was more problematic. 'Friend' was the song Pauly had played me in London and that his band had played earlier that year at the New Zealand Music Awards. The song now seemed to have had the life sucked out of it. An enclosed note said it was a new song, written by Pauly for a potential next single.

As I played it in the PolyGram offices the new A&R boss, Mark Tierney, came over and said, 'That's a Matty J song.' Matty J Ruys, a New Zealand singer and songwriter, had made several quite credible blue-eyed soul records. He had a long, close history with the Fuemana family, playing and writing with them as a member of both Houseparty and Fuemana, and sharing strong religious beliefs with Philip Fuemana. Mark had produced Matty J's one solo album for EMI and worked on demos for a second one that was never released.

Mark told me the song now was a Matty J Ruys composition and had been demoed for his second record. I rang Matty and he confirmed it. I then rang Phil Fuemana, who verified that it was Matty's song, although, he said, he himself might have contributed a line or two. Pauly, he said, had had nothing to do with writing the song.

If Pauly was going to release the record as a single with accurate credits, there wouldn't be an issue. However, if he passed off the song as his own there would be – especially as Mercury was touting it as evidence of Pauly's new writing prowess, as was Sue DeBenedette in Australia.

I phoned Sue. She was completely flustered by the news and seemed at a loss for words. I then called Bill Cullen in the US. He wasn't around but I got through to Pauly's brother Tony, whose response, before he hung up on me, was a taut, 'If Pauly said he wrote it, then he did.' Later, Bill rang and admitted this posed a bit of a credibility problem for Pauly: he had been pushing the song as his own for a long time when it seemed fairly clear it wasn't.

Next morning Phil Fuemana called to say he had been mistaken. Matty hadn't written the song, Pauly had. Later that day I was told by a third party that Phil Fuemana had decided the family would close ranks. Whether this was true I had no way of knowing, but either way the song was never released.

Worse was to come. The stories being fed back to Auckland from the American tour were not good. By all reports, Pauly was acting and playing every bit the rock star, and was increasingly volatile. This volatility had repeatedly tipped over into violence. His victims now included Bill Cullen, Nathan Haines (over Nathan's request for a wage rise), a bus driver in Tennessee who had gone to the police after Pauly threatened him for not following his suggested route, and finally, and most damagingly, a senior promotions person from Mercury in San Francisco. After this man had made a remark about how difficult Pauly was to work with, Pauly had knocked him down and torn his shirt. The incident had made the pages of *Rolling Stone* magazine.[12]

Pauly was not yet at the place in his career where hitting a person from his record label would be overlooked as the whim of a highly strung artist. There was talk of Mercury dropping him but eventually the company's head, Danny Goldberg, said it would keep him on the roster. Almost immediately, however, the company pulled the plug on extra

---

12 In an interview with *The Sunday Star-Times* in October 2006, Pauly said he did an 'All Blacks tackle' on a man in San Francisco, sending him through a plate-glass window. The man had, he said, called him and his entourage 'sheep shaggers'. 'Unbeknown to me,' he continued, 'he was the head of some record company, Universal or PolyGram or something. They sent me a bill for the window.'

expenditure on the album, and a large promotional push was quietly shelved after word came down the chain that it was time to step back. Coupled with the failure of 'I Love L.A.', a few seconds of violence had caused massive career damage. Tentative plans to issue 'Right On' as the next US radio single were dropped.

In October Pauly arrived back in Auckland. Alan and I met up with him at Columbus Café in High Street – ironically in the space previously occupied by the bank to which I'd taken him two years earlier to open his account. It was a scorching hot spring day but Pauly was dressed in winter clothes, including what looked to be an extremely expensive wool-lined jacket.

Our meeting was uncomfortable from the beginning and Pauly sweating profusely did not help. Without much ceremony he launched into Alan and demanded money. He aggressively explained he had gone out on the road with a live band to sell the record while Alan had sat in Auckland and done nothing. If Alan wanted to see any money from 'How Bizarre' he would have to pay a chunk of the enormous tour support bill that he now faced as a deduction from his royalties for his extended treks across Europe and North America.

Alan was at first surprised. As he gathered his thoughts, this turned to anger. 'I told you I wanted no part of that. The touring was all yours,' he said. 'The reason you get 75 percent against my 25 percent is because you are the frontperson. You agreed to be the face of OMC.'

Alan had made it absolutely clear, as had I, that touring was not something we saw as a part of the OMC project. 'How Bizarre' was a radio record and written and produced as such. Pauly was welcome to tour a band anywhere in the world if he wished, but the touring was at his discretion and his expense.

I had also repeated many times over the years – verbally and in writing – my view that touring an OMC band was not only artistically unwise but fiscally insane. In Australia in early 1996 I had told PolyGram management I could see no reason to put OMC on the road. I had reiterated this to Grant Thomas later that year, and again in 1997 to Sue DeBenedette. Such advice had been dismissed out of hand, and yet Pauly was now demanding Alan pay a share of his and his management's folly.

Incensed, Alan got up and left. I tried futilely to convince Pauly he needed to stick to the agreement but he became increasingly agitated. He had done the work, he said, and he had sold the record. If Alan wanted to get paid he needed to put his hand in his pocket. This ignored the obvious. First, without Alan there would have been no hit and no OMC. And second, the touring had hurt the record much more than it had helped it.

I reminded Pauly of the agreements and the conversations that had taken place among the three of us. He was not interested: it was simply time for Alan to pay his way. He looked at me. 'It's his call, bro.'

Letters went back and forth between Alan's lawyers, Pauly's lawyers, and Sue Cohen at PolyGram. This was at huge cost, especially to Pauly, whose team from Russell McVeagh was led by a noted barrister.

PolyGram argued the dispute was between Pauly and Alan, and put pressure on Pauly and his managers to sort it out. However, the company was vulnerable since some of its staff may have played a part in encouraging Pauly to walk away from Alan and Huh!. The mechanism used by Alan's lawyers, John Wain and Noel Agnew, of suing PolyGram rather than Pauly directly, could possibly open the company up to embarrassing revelations about any machinations that may have taken place.

Eventually, after a great deal of time and money had been spent, all the parties agreed to arbitration. This was set for mid 1998. As I was the person who had written the 1996 agreement I got prepared, thinking I might be called as a witness to counter any argument that the agreement had been made under coercion and was thus void.

When the day arrived, Pauly stood outside the court and told Alan and his astonished lawyers that none of this was his idea. He wanted to pay Alan but 'others' simply wouldn't let him. He looked at Alan. 'You and I both know, bro, the only reason we are here is because of the success of 'I Love L.A.'

After the lawyers had put their arguments, the arbitrator called Pauly to the witness box. 'If you received a million dollars, how much would you think Alan Jansson was due?' he asked.

Pauly immediately replied, 'Half.'

The arbitrator asked Pauly's lawyers if they thought their client really understood and agreed with the arguments they were so forcefully and at such great expense making on his behalf. It was clear the case being made by Pauly's legal team was in tatters. Pauly left the stand, broke down in tears and said to Alan, 'I'm sorry, bro. I didn't want to do this.'

Alan received a substantial settlement from Pauly and walked away.

29

THE CASE MAY HAVE BEEN SETTLED but the lawsuit and the events of the previous twelve months had destroyed the team that had created 'How Bizarre', the single and the album. Pauly and Alan's relationship would never fully recover. The trust was gone and so was the magic. Pauly would never again replicate, or come close to replicating, the success of his first hit song. Without Alan he was unable to write or produce a record that would enter charts or gain radio play anywhere in the world. Alan, on the other hand, would write and produce a large number of artistically and commercially successful records, including number ones and iconic New Zealand tracks, with a variety of artists.

During this period Alan had been heavily involved in making an album for Sina, the former OMC backing vocalist. I had signed her to Huh! in April 1997, part of our agreement to recompense her for the more than a year of hard work she had put in on 'How Bizarre' for little more than a session fee.

Alan also took his first break in years – a road trip across the US with his friend Rick Huntington.

Early in 1998 I spent the best part of a month in the US. At a meeting with A&R staff at Mercury in New York it was made clear to me that, unless something radically interesting turned up, OMC was no longer on the map for the label. In May, less than nine months after the song had taken America, the Mercury-hosted OMC website disappeared from the internet.

Sina's debut single 'Don't Be Shy' was released in September, went to number two in New Zealand and was certified gold.

Pauly, with Soane Filitonga to keep him company, spent a month in Mexico playing a small role as a gangster called Mr Scary in a thriller directed by Mathew Modine. Despite good reviews and Pauly's credible performance, *If... Dog... Rabbit* sank without trace after its release in 1999.

Meanwhile, 'How Bizarre' took off in South America and Pauly was sent there by PolyGram for promotional work.

In 1998 PolyGram Australia and the Grant Thomas organisation began a seemingly endless stream of attempts to revive Pauly's moribund career. Over the next few years demos would be recorded in collaboration with a variety of producers and writers across the world. One early set was recorded in New York with Michael Mangini, a top US producer who would have a huge smash two years later with 'Who Let The Dogs Out' performed by a Bahamas-based group, Baha Men. The songs on the set were not bad in themselves, just poorly constructed, monotonously delivered and unimaginatively recorded, all at quite some cost to Pauly.

There was an air of resignation at PolyGram as I was handed the CD. Paul Dickson asked to see me and inquired whether I could reconcile the two OMC creators. There was growing recognition at the company that it had backed the wrong horse.

In May that year Seagram bought PolyGram from its parent company Philips, the Dutch electronics empire, and merged it with its subsidiary Universal Music Group, and the whole messy game changed yet again.

The sale of PolyGram came as a huge surprise, both to the industry as a whole and, closer to home, to the staff and management of PolyGram in New Zealand and Australia, whose lives were turned upside down as they were forced to battle for their immediate futures. Universal took over large parts of the PolyGram system intact but stamped its own management team on top of the PolyGram structure; staff duplications led to redundancies, effective almost immediately.

Some in lower and middle management kept their positions and were absorbed into Universal, including Alister Cain, PolyGram New Zealand's popular, well-regarded sales manager. However, Ian Watson, Mark Tierney, Paul Dickson and Roger Grierson lost their jobs. Mark was replaced by Universal's Grant Kearney, an old friend of Alan's and mine. Ian's replacement was George Ash, who had headed Universal Music New Zealand since its establishment in 1995.

Adam Holt lasted a little longer before he too was given the push and returned to New Zealand to work for an independent music publishing house. Sue DeBenedette had already left and was working for Grant Thomas, among others, as a freelancer. She would later return to the US.

What this upheaval meant for Pauly and OMC was that every person who understood the project at an A&R and artistic level was gone. This included those at PolyGram in Australia who had come to the realisation that the project and Pauly were in deep trouble in the wake of the bungles and lawsuits of 1997 and '98. A new generation of label people were now in charge.

Some thought OMC might be a project worth hanging their hats on. In New Zealand this included the new managing director George Ash, who wanted to maximise what he saw as an asset of the company. Over the next two years Universal continued to fund demos and recordings, all of which were billed back to Pauly. They included sessions with the English act White Town, who had had a number one single in the UK in 1997 with a song called 'Your Woman'. Even Pauly would admit these sessions were a waste of time and money: the musicians sat in a room for long periods, smoked dope and produced nothing of musical worth.

Around the middle of 1999 Grant Thomas called and asked to meet. We had coffee in the foyer of the Regent Hotel in Albert Street, where he was staying. I guessed the topic would be how to bridge the Pauly–Alan gulf and bring the two back together. I knew Alan's attitude. He and I had talked endlessly about it. The phrase we used most often was: 'The madness has passed.'

Not having Pauly in his life had allowed Alan to relax and live again. He was working with a mix of friends and new artists at Uptown and building a house he had designed himself. He was spending more time with his family and enjoying his freedom after a decade of being driven to create the hit that was 'How Bizarre'.

Pauly's life, meanwhile, appeared as tumultuous and confused as ever. When he should have been sitting back, a wealthy man, he seemed to be forever battling the world. He was living in the largely white suburb of Beach Haven on Auckland's conservative middle-class North Shore, close to Kirstine's family, and constantly falling in and out with his South Auckland relatives.

Grant came straight to the point: would Alan be interested in working with Pauly again, and if so under what conditions? I almost replied that if Pauly were happy to rescind the agreement made at mediation the year before and pay Alan the full sum of the money he owed him under the 1996 deal, we could talk. Instead, I simply said I would ask.

I went outside, phoned Alan and put the question to him. His answer was cursory: 'Do I want the madness back? Tell him to get lost.'

I went back to Grant and was stunned when he blithely asked if Alan wanted to have more than one track on Pauly's greatest hits album. Did Pauly want more than one track on Alan Jansson's greatest hits album, I retorted. He never spoke to me again.

A few months later, Universal's Grant Kearney also approached Alan. George Ash had authorised him to offer Alan $50,000 to produce one track for Pauly. It was a crazy and desperate idea. Alan declined. He simply didn't need the grief.

Although there were no new hits, little real likelihood of new hits, and the bulk of his income from 'How Bizarre' had already been banked, Pauly was spending wildly. He was buying cars, motorbikes and watches, taking groups of friends to Rio, and lavishing large amounts on studio gear, much of which was never used. I got regular calls from my record store staff telling me Pauly had been in, picking up hundreds of dollars' worth of records he grabbed almost randomly from the shelves and banged on his gold credit card.

Over the previous two years Pauly had earned massive amounts of money, mostly publishing returns for 'How Bizarre'. Although these royalty streams were now diminished, they still flowed steadily. If Pauly were smart he could have a comfortable income but his world was spiralling out of control.

30

AFTER 2000 I SAW PAULY every few months. He would ring me and we would have dim sum at his favourite Chinese restaurant, The Rendezvous in Hobson Street. He would always bring generous gifts for my daughter Bella. There was an ever-changing stream of cars – Volvo, Range Rover, black BMW 540i, Hummer – long after I knew he couldn't afford these things. He would tell me he had bought cars and paid mortgages for members of his family in South Auckland. He would talk about the demos he was recording and how the Germans or the Americans or the Dutch wanted to tour him again shortly and were offering huge money.

In 2001 George Ash was promoted to head Universal's Australasian office, and Adam Holt was appointed managing director of Universal Music New Zealand. He found himself working with Pauly again and was invited to hear works in progress, essentially demos. The address given was a tower block in Symonds Street, near the Sheraton Hotel.

Adam arrived to find that Pauly had rented a whole floor and filled it with a huge array of expensive gear, including Yamaha samplers and high-end Apple computers. Pauly pressed play on one of the machines and triggered his latest recordings. After listening, Adam told him he would pass but would be happy to hear anything else he produced in the future.

Pauly exploded. Screaming at Adam, he told him he had made Universal 'millions'. Adam nervously looked for an exit and realised he was trapped – Pauly had the only key. He slowly and carefully defused the situation and managed to take his leave, informing Pauly he would be happy to release him from his contract. This was a mere formality: the contract had effectively already expired.

Arriving home, Adam found a huge gift parcel from Pauly on his doorstep. He never saw him again.

Early in 2002 I was approached by Colin Hogg, a journalist and friend, to help with a project he was working on for a Television New Zealand arts show. The show was planning to do a brief, neutral piece on 'How Bizarre' and wanted to work out what exactly had happened to Pauly and why he had gone so quiet.

Alan was agreeable. I passed Pauly's email address on to Colin, who sent him a friendly but professional email asking if he was willing to be interviewed. Pauly told Colin to get lost – or, more precisely, to 'fuck off'.

After talking with me, Colin sent another polite email telling Pauly he was interviewing Alan, the story would go ahead either way, and he would be keen to include Pauly's side of it. Pauly's answer was to threaten to come after Colin's family if he 'tried anything'.

Colin rang and invited him to lunch to talk it over. Pauly turned up at the restaurant, SPQR in inner-city Ponsonby, on a large motorbike and wearing full leathers. A man in the restaurant couldn't take his eyes off him. Pauly leaned over to him and said, 'What are you looking at, cunt face?' He then stood up to hit him.

Colin managed to diffuse the confrontation. Pauly continued to refuse to be interviewed. Colin completed the story, focusing primarily on Alan as a songwriter and producer, and it was broadcast later that year.

From 2002 and 2005 money became tighter and tighter. Pauly stopped phoning me. I was told later that he and Kirstine had lost their house in a mortgagee sale. Creditors closed in. Staff at Universal New Zealand reported repeated requests for advances from Kirstine, who was now acting as Pauly's manager. Universal Music Publishing, the successor to PolyGram, tried to help out but the requests for money usually had to be declined: there wasn't enough income to justify them under Pauly's contract.

New Zealand on Air received applications for grants for the same tracks over and over again. These, too, had to be declined: Pauly was neither a new artist nor eligible for an album grant.

Mike Chunn, the former Split Enz bass player who had revived APRA – the Australasian Performing Right Association – hawked Pauly's demos around record labels in 2003 but found little interest. He also arranged for Pauly to appear in a charity television show but he failed to turn up. I'm guessing Mike found it too hard after that and lost interest.

In late 2004, Pauly was touted as being about to record under the wing of Neil Finn at his Roundhouse Studios but nothing came of it.

In early March 2005 Pauly's brother Philip died of a heart attack. Phil Fuemana was a huge guy physically and vulnerable to heart problems, but his early death caused a shockwave through not only the South Auckland music scene but South Auckland as a whole and the entire New Zealand music industry.

I had liked and admired Phil and appreciated the way he would quietly update me by phone or face-to-face on how Pauly was doing in the years after 2000. And I was always grateful for the public thanks he repeatedly gave Alan and me over the years for the OMC project and for working with Pauly.

His funeral at Te Tira Hou Marae in the south-east Auckland suburb of Panmure was a mammoth affair, filled with legions of family, friends, admirers and workmates. When it ended Pauly came over, hugged me and thanked me for coming. He then looked into my eyes and quietly said, 'I'm sorry, bro.'

A few days later we met for dim sum at The Rendezvous. Pauly gave me a couple of demo CDs. They contained some 40 items – songs and fragments of songs. He kept apologising. 'It wasn't me,' he said several times. 'There were others in my ear.' I told him an apology wasn't necessary. It was eight years in the past. I couldn't see any benefit in going over it.

He also apologised for the violence. 'I'm past that in my life,' he said. 'I don't drink or take any drugs and I'm in control of my anger. There are so many people I need to say sorry to.' All that mattered, he said, was his immediate family and making music. Grant Thomas was completely out of his life and his business.

I asked him if he would be interested in working with Alan again. He said no, there was too much bad feeling, given the court case. He wanted to be his own man, make and produce his own records.

I had heard large parts of this many times before, especially the apologies, but I still felt drawn. I noted that he was driving a much older car. More seriously, his speech seemed to be badly afflicted by something: he had a bad twitch and a stutter. I asked him if he were physically okay. He said he was fine and gave me that huge disarming grin – the one that had sold all the records that day on *Top of the Pops*.

Later there would be speculation that his health had been damaged by drug use. I saw no evidence of that. In all the years I knew him, aside from the fracas on the *Rip It Up* boat in 1995, I never saw him take hard drugs. What I now understand I was seeing were the early signs of a disease that would take his life five years later.

I told Alan about the meeting. He and I had set up a new label, Joy Records, and a joint publishing company. We had our hands full with a couple of new signings, most especially a band that would later release its Alan Jansson-produced debut as the eponymous *The Others Requiem*. For the first time since 1998 Alan was not ardently against recording a track or two with Pauly. However, he had no desire to deal with the baggage of Pauly's management and hangers-on, or the arduous task of extracting an album from the process.

I gave him copies of the demos. He listened and said there were some germs of ideas, although he could hear nothing substantial enough to turn into a finished song. I felt the same: the only track that was close to complete and had any real commercial legs was, ironically, a rather appealing acoustic take of 'How Bizarre'. It was almost good enough to release as a single in its own right.

The rest was a patchwork of the good, the okay and the really dire. In his lyrics Pauly seemed to be continually recycling the themes of earlier songs, particularly 'Land Of Plenty'. One of the pieces used the well-known 1971 recording 'L.A. Woman' by The Doors as a backing track. Another took an instrumental version of a song called 'Love Me With Feeling' by the Jamaican reggae singer and songwriter Gregory Isaacs and layered a vocal over the top. And that was a huge problem because the vocals were almost all flat and somewhat listless.

Some tracks, Alan explained, were just Pauly singing over keyboard presets – the sounds that come with a keyboard. There were some interesting drum and bass rhythm tracks. One called 'Planet Phat' was a paean to an overweight lover: 'You're my fat girl / my elephantitis / my hippopotamus.' Pauly had touted this as a potential single. I was aghast.

Alan felt nothing could be retrieved from the material and his brief spark of interest waned.

I received an email from Kirstine telling me that one of the tracks, 'Tropicana', had been picked up by the Tropicana Film Festival in Brazil as its theme song. I wondered if the organisers knew this – especially as the Tropicana Film Festival was in Australia, not Brazil. Kirstine added that Pauly was in the process of mastering his new album – by which I guessed she meant the demos we'd heard – and had put together a band out of Australia to tour it. Perhaps some of this was true although I doubted it.

I wasn't willing to give up quite yet. There were at least half a dozen tracks on the demos that had the hint of a usable melody or lyrical idea, although they would take a masterful collaborator to realise. To date, the only collaborator who had been able to take Pauly's fractions of ideas and meld them into something was Alan.

I saw a fair amount of Pauly over the next few days, and on March 18 he emailed and suggested he re-sign to my Huh! label and we put a new recording studio downstairs where my old club had been, a space I had vacated years back, so he could record for me.

It was a pleasant enough email but it was clear he was still living in a world somewhat divorced from reality. He had also asked if I would DJ for him on his next tour, but I hadn't done any deejaying of note since the late 1980s.

We had a couple more lunches but it all seemed to be going nowhere. It was obvious I needed to force the situation one way or another. Was something possible? Or was this all a waste of time?

I was out of the country for a few weeks. When I arrived back in May I emailed Pauly and suggested as diplomatically as possible that he needed to team up with a producer and I thought it should be Alan. Pauly phoned next day. He was unwilling to work with Alan unless he was in control and Alan little more than a paid engineer.

I took an all-or-nothing leap. I rang Pauly and asked him to check out a new dim sum place in downtown Auckland on me. He was eager so I pencilled in a time for the next day. I then called Alan and invited him to the same lunch without mentioning Pauly. He too accepted.

Neither knew the other was coming and they arrived at almost the same time. There was a moment of hesitation, then both smiled. They grabbed each other tightly. There were tears.

Over the next few days Alan Jansson and Pauly Fuemana, the team who had written and created the biggest selling record ever made in New Zealand, agreed to work together again. I knew this was Pauly's last chance. Almost every bridge had been burnt – thoroughly demolished – but one: the original team was creating again. People in record companies would be interested. So would the media.

There were a few ground rules that Alan and I needed to establish. First, there was to be no management in the picture. Primarily this meant absolutely no involvement of Grant Thomas. Second, Alan was to be the producer – absolutely. He was to have the final say. Third, we would release any record through our new label, Joy; this meant it would be sold and distributed by Sony, with whom we had an excellent relationship. Fourth, Alan and Pauly would write completely new songs. Alan had decided there was little on Pauly's demos that was worth keeping.

And fifth, the recording would happen during normal business hours. There were to be no more of the all-night sessions that Pauly used to love and insist on, no long nighttime drives around Auckland, and no extended aimless sessions where no work was done. The process had to be professional and productive.

Pauly enthusiastically agreed to all these terms. He wanted to sign a contract that day and declared he had no need to run it past a lawyer. I had a horrendous case of déjà vu and quickly rejected the offer.

Part of my commitment was that once Pauly had some music recorded I would try to find him a music publishing deal, with an advance to alleviate some of the intense financial pressure he was under. To push things along I sent out a press release saying he and Alan were working together again and an initial single on the Joy label would be released by Sony later that year. Sony had yet to agree to this in writing but Malcolm Black, the A&R manager, had expressed enough interest that I felt reasonably comfortable saying this. Malcolm was enough of an old industry hand to understand that a little bravado upfront played a big part in getting things off the ground.

The press release had an immediate effect. Mike Bradshaw, the managing director at Sony Music, called to say I had jumped the gun a little. I had expected that. More importantly, the media came calling. Grant Smithies, one of the most respected names in New Zealand music journalism, emailed asking for an exclusive. As I trusted him and he wrote for *The Sunday Star-Times*, the most respected of the national Sunday newspapers, I agreed and put him in touch with Pauly.

The other approach was from Haydn Jones, a reporter on Television New Zealand's *20/20*. Haydn committed the show to an extended piece on Alan and Pauly that would coincide with the release of the single.

Both journalists understood the potential public interest in OMC's rise to riches, crash, and then attempt to rise again, but I believed they were likely to treat the story in a balanced and sensitive way.

There were a series of other calls over the next few days. Many came from the trash media, who could smell blood and would sensationalise the story. I didn't reply.

31

I BEGAN TO GET A TIGHT KNOT in my stomach and woke at night wondering what on earth I was doing. Within a few weeks it had become clear that things were not working out. Pauly was spinning unbelievable stories and increasingly fantastical ideas. He was also getting steadily more demanding and combative. 'Where is my advance?' he would demand. 'I want to record my songs. Alan needs to understand he's not in charge any more.'

Alan had his own doubts. He decided to work on two tracks and then step back and decide if he wanted to go any further.

Out of the blue, Pauly started laying out his plans for a band to tour the US and the festivals of Europe. I was to be the DJ. Alan was to do the live sound and play keyboards. Lee Baker, long since disappeared into Europe, would be on guitar. George Chisholm, who had played the signature trumpet on 'How Bizarre' and was perhaps the least likely person to want to go on a gruelling coast-to-coast bus tour of the US and Europe with Pauly, was to revisit that role. Sina was to sing backing vocals – she could bring her children. Nathan Haines, though, would be blocked from the tour for having tried to rip him off and other imagined misdemeanours.

We would shoot a video for the single with our children – my one, his five, and Alan's two – running around in front of Auckland Museum, with Polynesian dancers swaying down the steps. Kerry Brown would again direct.

I tried to speak but could only open my mouth numbly.

Shortly after this Pauly attempted to schedule regular meetings in the studio for after eleven at night. This, he said, was the only time he was able to leave home because the kids had gone to bed. The kids, however, didn't seem to interfere with the random calls I repeatedly received, requesting we eat dim sum. Nor did they interfere with the ongoing plans to tour the planet.

I discussed my reservations with Alan again. He said he would continue working on the two tracks they had managed to write, one of which used a few lyrics from a track called 'Aotearoa New Zealand' on Pauly's demos. However, work in the studio had dropped to glacial speed as Pauly was refusing to cooperate. He was now citing himself as co-producer and wanted to return to the mostly unusable demos as the basis of an album.

Both Kirstine and Pauly complained to me via email and phone that Alan wanted to redo the vocals over and over again. I listened to the takes and understood exactly why this was but I refused to interfere. It was not my job to make production decisions.

In early September 2005 it all came to a head. I was overseas and flew back earlier than planned to hear three tracks so we could meet a NZ on Air application deadline for what was called a Phase Four Album Grant of $50,000: I was holding out hope an album could somehow be produced.

Pauly failed to make three meetings in a row and then threw a tantrum when I refused to set up a fourth meeting – at midnight. He informed me Grant Thomas was again handling his business affairs and had advised him to sign whatever deal we were offering.

My patience was exhausted. In early 2006 I told Alan I wanted out. With Pauly having broken three of the key conditions and talking all sorts of nonsense I wanted no part of it.

I had countless emails and phone calls from Pauly after this but no face-to-face meetings. It seemed, though, that I was not forgotten. In the middle of 2006 he announced to Alan late one night in the studio that he had decided to have both Adam Holt, with whom he had had no dealings since 2001, and me killed. In 2007 he would tell Alan he had a gun in his car. That time it was just Adam who was going to be 'taken out'.

Pauly was also fighting with his South Auckland family. One evening he asked Alan if he knew anyone who could give his brother Tony 'the bash'. Tony was running their brother Philip's Urban Pacifika label and had announced via Juice, a TV video channel, that he was shortly releasing a new OMC single. Pauly, who claimed to know nothing of this, hit the roof. Despite having recently told Alan he was going to have me killed, he sent an email asking me what he should do about it. I told him to ignore it. This would be my final communication with Pauly.

Alan, too, pulled back. Between December 2005 and April 2006 he did no more work on the project. However, in May 2006 Harvinder Singh, a man who had been in and out of the music and technology industries over the years, approached him. He wanted to work out a way to move forward with at least the few tracks that had been recorded in 2005.

Alan was reluctant. Singh then brought another person into the mix. Glenda Wynyard was the owner of The Media Council, a high-flying independent advertising agency, and had an extensive and illustrious family involvement with both Māori and Polynesian music. As a teen in the 1970s she had sung with several of the iconic Māori show bands that played the Pacific and Asian circuits. Her lineage also included Wahanui Wynyard, a producer who had been a major figure in the Australasian recording industry in the 1960s.

In June 2006 Pauly was declared bankrupt. Kirstine joined him in July. What had happened to the millions of dollars Pauly had earned from 'How Bizarre'? The simple answer was that he had spent most of it.

Most of the money had come from songwriting royalties. For two years running, 1996 and 1997, 'How Bizarre' had been awarded plaques for airplay in the US in excess of one million plays, something achieved by very few songs. Added to that, the airplay across Europe was massive. In territories such as Germany and the UK, where airplay royalties from radio can be considerable, the song is still today a radio staple, as it is in the US. In Europe and the UK the highest rating stations pay several pounds or euros per play. In 1996, when 'How Bizarre' was at its peak, Britain's Radio 1 was paying £39 a daytime minute.

Other income from 'How Bizarre' did not, as many assume, dry up after the record dropped off the charts. Money still flowed in from advertising placements and movie and television synchronisation licences: the song was in at least a dozen sitcoms and half a dozen major Hollywood movies, including one that showed much of the video in the background during a scene. This one use alone paid tens of thousands of dollars. Then there was software, games and all sorts of other uses. One strange one by the Walt Disney Company was for a toy hippo; when the hippo's head was patted, it said, 'How bizarre, how bizarre.' Not everything was agreed to: Pauly turned down a Chipmunks' cover of the song.

If Pauly and Kirstine had handled their finances prudently they would probably have been well off forever. It was not to be. Pauly's spending was legendary throughout the New Zealand music industry. There were not only the cars and endless toys and almost everything else that money could buy but a retinue of hangers-on, all with hands out. Many hung in right to the end. When Pauly and Kirstine's company FFFF.Com Ltd., formerly Otara Millionaires Club Ltd, was dissolved in August 2003 the liquidator's report noted: '[They] lived extravagantly on the early royalty proceeds but their lavish lifestyle had not contracted when the royalties began to diminish.'

It had been only six years from the first big royalty cheques to the company's liquidation. They lost their house a year later. However, the spending did not stop.

The media called me when Pauly was declared bankrupt. I gave a short comment to *The New Zealand Herald* but mostly I refused to say anything. There was really nothing I wanted to say and I was no longer involved.

Harvinder Singh helped Pauly through the negotiations with the official assignee and managed to preserve his royalty stream as income for his family to survive on. He argued that it was not appropriate for Pauly Fuemana to have to get a job as a dishwasher, and he was not musically equipped to do what many other musicians might do – namely, pick up a guitar and start playing in public.

Alan settled down to try and finish the tracks he had started on. He and Harvinder had initially decided to form a label, Unco, but when Glenda Wynyard came on board that mutated into Orpheus. By the beginning of 2007 this was just Alan and Glenda: Harvinder had opted out.

Orpheus was to release the final OMC record. I handled the contractual paperwork for the label and passed on details of many of the things I had been working on, including the *20/20* story.

Through Glenda's contacts, the comeback single, '4 All Of Us', was tied to the Human Rights Commission's annual Race Relations Day and released on March 21, 2007. Both the song and the video clip featured Lucy Lawless, a New Zealand actor known internationally for her title role in a New Zealand-US television series, *Xena: Warrior Princess*.

It was a lovely song, lilting, optimistic and well-produced by Alan, but it suffered from the limitations of Pauly's vocal performance: he had wanted to sing rather than use his unique rapping style. I can't listen to it without feeling a sense of pathos.

A second finished song 'Please', also featuring Lucy, had been Alan's preferred choice for the single, but '4 All Of Us' had been chosen because its lyrics were appropriate for the charity. 'Please' remains unreleased, beyond a limited sampling of an early mix to commercial radio in 2008. In my last communication with Pauly he told me it was his favourite OMC song, although I didn't feel the same – my favourite will always be 'Land Of Plenty'.

The single of '4 All Of Us' made little commercial impact but the video, beautifully shot and directed, caused a flood of questions about Pauly's health. He appeared unsteady and visibly unable to lip sync. To cover this, most of his appearances were limited to non-performance. Those that had him singing or playing guitar were brief, and edited so as to appear ambiguous and cover up the increasingly obvious physical effects of his still undiagnosed illness.

The video is upsetting to watch. Pauly is clearly not well; he looks like a ghost of his former strong, confident self. There is little of the magnetism and raw charisma that grabbed viewers of the original clips for 'How Bizarre', 'Right On' and 'Land Of Plenty', the second *Top of the Pops* show, and the stage strut in Canada. He looks broken, nervy and unsure of himself. In retrospect, it's obvious that the problems he was having performing were a manifestation of neurological issues that were getting progressively worse.

Lyrically, the song is almost a thematic rerun of 'Land Of Plenty'. Alan had wanted to continue working on the lyrics but Pauly had insisted there be few changes to his words. The original take of 'Please' contained many of the same lyrics, forcing Alan to bring in a rapper, Chris 'Mighty Boy C' Maiai from West Auckland hip-hop group 3 The Hard Way, to replace the duplicated verses on later mixes of the song.

There were few interviews during this time but one of the more curious was with the New Zealand women's magazine *New Idea* in January 2007. Pauly claimed to have 'performed duets with the late Frank Sinatra'. Sinatra had suffered a heart attack in January 1997, six months before 'How Bizarre' stormed the US, and was a recluse, seeing no one beyond his immediate family until his death in May 1998. In the same interview Pauly claimed to have written music for Drew Barrymore and worked with Wesley Snipes. There is no evidence any of this ever happened.

The *20/20* story took a long time to come to fruition; it would finally appear long after I had walked away. Haydn wanted to keep the idea alive, and when the piece was finally broadcast it was probably the most honest, insightful and sympathetic media overview of Pauly and Alan's

229

relationship to have appeared in mainstream media. Together with Jock Lawrie's *Pavement* feature it stands as the definitive OMC story, even if, like everything else, it sidestepped the less pleasant things about Alan and Pauly's relationship and Pauly's volatile character. This had shown itself when he got into a fight with another driver after an incident involving his vehicle. In a rage, he had pursued the other car and menaced its driver.

Another time he had threatened the life of an engineer who worked for him. After the man quit, saying he had no wish to be a paid servant, he was treated to a visit from a fuming Pauly, who stood outside his house shouting and promising physical retribution.

And there was the callout to the North Shore Police armed offenders squad, complete with helicopters, when Pauly ranted and discharged guns at neighbours' houses in his quiet suburban cul-de-sac.

Eventually in 2008, after a series of peculiar communications from Pauly and Kirstine, Alan and Glenda decided enough was enough. Glenda had begun to see OMC as a bottomless money pit with little possible light at the end of a long and traumatic tunnel. She told her staff to cease work on the project. Alan felt he had come as close as he was ever going to get to achieving the closure he was missing after the '97 breakdown in the creative partnership and the '98 arbitration. He was able to answer, at least in part, most of the questions he may have had about what might have been if it hadn't all fallen apart a decade earlier. An album was out of the question. Even if Pauly had had enough material, he was no longer emotionally or psychologically equipped to make one. Alan Jansson and Pauly Fuemana would never meet again.

On the morning of January 31, 2010, I received a call from a friend. RadioLive had just broadcast the news that Pauly had died that morning. The neurological condition that had afflicted him for several years had taken his life. He was eight days shy of his forty-first birthday.

32

AS I WALKED OUT OF THE FUNERAL I saw Nathan Haines and walked across to say hello. Nathan whispered that Pauly had not wanted Alan at his funeral. If that was really his wish, I said, why had no one bothered to tell Alan?

As we stood outside the church, Alan was approached by a member of the original Otara Millionaires Club. The man had had nothing to do with Pauly's recording career since. In a crude stand-over attempt, in front of at least a dozen witnesses and the media, including a TV crew filming the mourners, he physically threatened Alan. Claiming to be representing Pauly after his death, he said it was time for Alan to 'pay up'. He then handed him his business card.

The incident felt like a discarded scene from a B-grade gangster flick. Were it not for the threat of violence, which included a promise to firebomb the schools Alan's children attended, it would have been comic.

I was then subjected to the same treatment. He knew exactly where in Bali I lived, he said. He had friends there who would 'pay me a visit'. It was an absurd threat: I didn't live in Bali and hadn't done so for some time.

He wasn't the only one to make a fool of himself that day. Other people at the funeral staunchly declared there were serious questions for the record company to answer. Anyone who had any understanding of 'How Bizarre', the history of the record, and the course Pauly's life had taken over the last decade and a half knew there were questions that needed answering – just not the ones these men wanted to put.

Over the years, as the money ran out, conspiracy theories had proliferated among Pauly's family and inner circle. These revolved around the notion that Pauly had been screwed out of millions by someone somewhere. Victor Stent's name was often mentioned. There was no evidence to support any of the theories, quite the opposite: Pauly's lawyers and managers had ruthlessly audited PolyGram and Universal over the years and found no glaring discrepancies or wrongdoing.

The finger was pointed at Alan and me from time to time, and the amount deemed to be missing grew by the year. On the day Pauly died the family claimed in an interview with Wellington's *Dominion Post* that fifty million dollars had gone AWOL. For this to be correct each record sold would had to have generated seventeen dollars' profit, to be shared among all parties. In reality, a single sells at retail for only five dollars. The artist royalty is about twelve percent of wholesale, less packaging deductions – a figure of about 30 cents a single. An album yields, in US terms, about $1.30 per sale. Pauly had received well over five million dollars; the fifty million was nothing more than a fantasy.

In the end what remained was a song. As I write, 'How Bizarre' has sold in excess of four million copies worldwide as a single or on the album. It has appeared on almost a hundred different artist compilations, which have taken it into many million more homes.

These sales are just a small part of the song's global currency. Its worldwide airplay tallies are immense. It has become a radio standard in virtually every territory where there is a radio station broadcasting. In 2014 the logs of airplay were stronger than they were in 1999 at the tail end of the record's initial chart run. Until Lorde's success with 'Royals' in 2013, 'How Bizarre' was by a massive margin the most successful popular song ever recorded in New Zealand. It is a ubiquitous part of not just New Zealand's popular culture but global popular culture. It can be heard in malls, in muzak, in TV shows and on games and toys. There is rarely a week when at least one request for its use isn't received by Universal Music or me from somewhere around the world. Some weeks there are more.

I still look back on those few chaotic years with disbelief. In early 1995 I was running a record label in Auckland and hoping that our debut release, 'Shift Left' by the young and untried Nathan Haines, would be a success in New Zealand and, at best, in Australia too – critically if not in sales. Two years later Huh! was the most successful record label in total sales in New Zealand's history of locally recorded popular music. We had released what is still the biggest record ever to be released by a New Zealand-owned label. It had gone to number one not only across the world but also and uniquely in the world's largest market, the United States. And we had done it from New Zealand, something conventional wisdom said was simply not possible.

'How Bizarre' was written in a kitchen and recorded in a small, privately owned studio in Auckland, the result of Alan Jansson's unwavering self-belief and faith in what was possible and the unique talent and raw passion of Pauly Fuemana. They had proved that when making music there are no rules, no cannot-dos, unless you impose them on yourself.

Of course, none of it had happened in isolation. Adam Holt, Paul Dickson, Roger Grierson and Mark Phillips in Australia were all significant players, as was Victor Stent and the tireless Sue DeBenedette. The trip Alan and I took to Australia, where we successfully pitched the song to Polydor, was perhaps the most significant single step towards turning 'How Bizarre' into a global record.

However, the industry also consumed the record, and in a way it consumed Pauly too. The initial network of players who'd created the hit unravelled. This was partly of Pauly's doing but also of offshore parties who clambered for position as the record took off worldwide. Pauly should not have been sent on extended, exhausting, money-losing tours. Every effort should have been made to ensure that his working partnership with Alan Jansson could breathe and prosper. If it had done so, there is plenty of reason to believe Pauly would not have been cast in music history as a one-hit wonder.

Today, I still have a plaque on my wall with a dozen flags on it. Each has the tag 'Number One' below it.
We did it.
How bloody bizarre.

Epilogue

ALTHOUGH IT WAS ANNOUNCED on February 6, 2000 that Pauly Fuemana had dispensed with the services of both Grant Thomas and Bill Cullen, in reality Bill had left some time before, after Pauly had accused him of 'stabbing Grant in the back'. In September 2000 Bill and his wife Edrei set up One Louder Entertainment; they would go on to become among the most respected artist managers in Australia.

Grant, no longer managing Crowded House, was handling the group Bardot, the manufactured stars of the Australian version of the New Zealand-originated Popstars franchise, a precursor to reality television series' such as *Idol* and *The X Factor*. When Screentime, the production company behind the show, fired him he took it and the band to court, winning a settlement of $129,000 in 2004.

Victor Stent never again entered the PolyGram or Universal offices. He later ran Mai Music, a record label specialising – ironically, given Victor's earlier attitude to such music – in Māori and Polynesian acts. Mai Music ceased trading at the end of last decade but Victor still controls many of the copyrights generated by the company.

In 1998 Roger Grierson was named managing director of Festival Records in Australia and took Paul Dickson with him as general manager.

In 2001, Paul took Roger's position when Roger moved to the UK to run the Rupert Murdoch-owned company News Corp Music. Both men have since retired from the music industry.

Mark Tierney left New Zealand in 2000, took up residence in London and then Los Angeles, and began to produce television programmes and feature documentaries. His first dramatic feature film, *Moving Target*, appeared in 2011. He also makes music videos.

George Ash, as managing director of Universal Music New Zealand, spent a small fortune on a Europop trio called Deep Obsession who did little, signed Hayley Westenra who did lots, and in 2013 became president of Universal Music Asia Pacific.

Adam Holt, perhaps the most capable record man I have ever known, is today chairman of Universal Music New Zealand, liked and respected by the whole industry. Also a director of Recorded Music New Zealand, he deserves much of the credit for the way New Zealand's local music industry has grown in recent years.

In 1998 Ian Watson left PolyGram New Zealand and retired from the industry.

Sue DeBenedette eventually returned to the US. In 2003 she became director of marketing and public relations with the Tucson Symphony Orchestra. She is currently director of communications at the Tucson Jewish Community Center.

Alan (and briefly Pauly's) gracious and much respected lawyer Noel Agnew died in 2003 from a brain tumour.

In 1996 I bought Tom Sampson out of our businesses and the following year I sold Cause Célèbre. Tom became a live music promoter of some reputation in Auckland. He now lives in the Bay of Plenty.

James Pinker also remains a good friend. A producer, percussionist and sound engineer, he is currently Auckland Council's senior programme leader for arts and culture.

Lee Baker moved to Paris.

Mark Cathro formed Brand Events in 1997 and works as an artist and talent coordinator in Auckland.

Matty J Ruys had a long spell as A&R head for Universal, signing among others Sani Sagala, who, as Dei Hamo, had a smash hit single, 'We Gon' Ride', in 2004. He now lives in Singapore.

After she was dropped by Universal, Sina Saipaia retired from active involvement in music to raise a family. She still records and writes with Alan Jansson from time to time.

Grant Kearney is a working DJ in Auckland.

Nathan Haines is one of New Zealand's most highly regarded musicians and composers, with ten albums and a global reputation. After several years living and making albums in the UK, he now divides his time between New Zealand and London.

Mark Phillips is living and working in Australia but is no longer in the music industry.

In 1999 Peter Urlich joined me in a partnership to release albums. In 1996, he and DJ Bevan Keys had begun running *Nice'n'Urlich*, a popular radio and club show. Peter and I released a series of *Nice'n'Urlich* albums and also put together a *Room Service* series and about ten other compilation albums on the Huh! label. We sold around 200,000 albums in Australasia, including 60,000 of *Nice'n'Urlich* and over 110,000 of *Room Service*.

Alan Jansson and I continue to work together; we have two active record labels and music publishing interests. In 2015 Alan produced the second album of singer Aly Cook; the debut single, 'No Phone No Mail No Internet', became an Australian country top five hit. He is also active in film soundtrack and advertising work. We remain close friends.

Soane Filitonga, Brother Pele in 'How Bizarre', died unexpectedly in November 2014. His funeral at St Benedict's Church in Newton, Auckland attracted over a thousand mourners. Pauly would have known and felt close to almost everyone there, including many raised in his old South Auckland neighbourhoods and who knew him most of his life.

Kirstine Fuemana and her children live in South Auckland; Pauly's and her sixth child was born after Pauly's death.

Timeline

1969

February 8   Pauly Fuemana is born, the fourth child of Merelyn Fuemana of Ngāi Tūhoe and Takiula Fuemana, a Niuean immigrant. The family lives in Parnell, Auckland; Merelyn Fuemana later leaves them and moves to Australia. At some point the family moves to Ōtara, South Auckland but Pauly remains in central Auckland with his grandmother. In his early teens he rejoins his family in Ōtara.

1987

Alan Jansson sets up Module 8 recording studio in Waverley Street, Auckland with Gary Smith and Tommy Fergusson.

1991

Fuemana family band Houseparty releases a single, 'Dangerous Love', on Murray Cammick's Southside label.

Alan Jansson sets up Uptown Studios in Drake Street, Auckland.

1993

Pauly Fuemana becomes a regular at Cause Célèbre, a High Street nightclub run by Simon Grigg and Tom Sampson.

Alan Jansson works with Tim Mahon, events manager at Manukau City Council, to record an album of new South Auckland bands. Jansson and Andrew Penhallow, owner of Australian indie label Volition Records, set up a new label, Second Nature, and enter into distribution deals with EMI New Zealand and CBS Australia.

1994

February	Simon Grigg founds record label Huh!.
May	Second Nature releases *Proud – An Urban Pacific Street-soul Compilation*. The album contains fourteen tracks from ten acts, including 'We R The OMC' by Pauly Fuemana, his brother Philip Fuemana and Paul Ave. The trio call themselves Otara Millionaires Club.
July	*Fuemana – New Urban Polynesian*, an album written, produced, directed and mostly played by Philip Fuemana, is released on Kane Massey's Deepgrooves label.
December	Simon Grigg signs a contract with PolyGram New Zealand and agrees to offer the company first option on any promising acts he finds. Releases that PolyGram picks up are to go out internationally, via Polydor, on Grigg's Huh! label.
	Philip Fuemana signs a label deal with BMG Records for his Urban Pacifika Records.

1995

January	Otara Millionaires Club, now known as OMC, secures a place in the Big Day Out tour. A band is formed; it includes Pauly Fuemana, Sina Saipaia and Ned Roy.
	Alan Jansson and Pauly write 'Doof It Up' and 'Big Top', early versions of 'How Bizarre'.
July	PolyGram New Zealand agrees to release the single 'How Bizarre'; Alan Jansson and Simon Grigg fly to Sydney to persuade PolyGram to also release the record in Australia.
August 3	Pauly Fuemana signs a recording deal with PolyGram in Sydney; 'How Bizarre' will be released by Huh! and PolyGram Records.
September	The finished master of 'How Bizarre', produced at Alan Jansson's Uptown Studios, is delivered to PolyGram.
October	Gideon Keith and Marcus Ringrose of V-8 are commissioned to produce a 'How Bizarre' video; this is later rejected and a new video shot by Lee Baker.

November	Music writer John Russell predicts in *Rip It Up* magazine that 'How Bizarre' will go 'at least Top 10'.
	Mai FM programme director Ross Goodwin adds 'How Bizarre' to the station's playlist. No other radio stations are interested.
December 14	'How Bizarre' hits New Zealand record stores. *The New Zealand Herald* runs a front-page story on Pauly Fuemana in its entertainment section; TV One and TV3 carry stories about the song on their six o'clock news. The record goes gold on its first day; the following week it enters the singles chart at number 15.

1996

January 28	'How Bizarre' goes to number one in the New Zealand Top 40. It will stay in the Top 50 for five more months.
February	A parody record, 'Stole My Car', appears.
	'How Bizarre' is released in Australia. In March Pauly Fuemana appears with Sina Saipaia and Willie Boaza on Channel Nine show *Hey Hey It's Saturday*.
April 13	At the Clear Music and Entertainment Awards Pauly Fuemana wins Most Promising Male Vocalist and OMC Most Promising Group; Alan Jansson and Rick Huntington win Engineer of the Year; 'How Bizarre' wins Single of the Year in a public vote.
April 14	'How Bizarre' jumps to number one on the ARIA Australian Singles Chart; it will remain there for five weeks. Pauly Fuemana appears for the second time on *Hey Hey It's Saturday*.
May	OMC follow-up single 'Right On' is released in New Zealand; certified platinum, it charts at number 11 in the singles chart on June 2 and never goes higher.
June	*Pavement* magazine runs a cover story on Pauly Fuemana.
July	'How Bizarre' is released in the UK by PolyGram subsidiary Polydor Records; on July 20 it enters the singles chart at number 22; midweek sales show it is likely to climb into

Top 20. On July 24 Pauly Fuemana and Simon Grigg fly to London, where Pauly appears on BBC One's *Top of the Pops.*

August	OMC single 'Right On' is released in Australia.

Pauly Fuemana and Simon Grigg fly from London to Melbourne for Pauly's third appearance on *Hey Hey It's Saturday.* On their return to Auckland they are immediately recalled to the UK for Pauly's second appearance on *Top of the Pops.* 'How Bizarre' is number 11 on the UK charts; it will subsequently go to number five.

September	TV3 broadcasts a story about Pauly Fuemana by reporter Anita McNaught on its current affairs programme *60 Minutes.*
October	'How Bizarre', the single, is released across Europe.

How Bizarre, the album, is released in the UK and Europe.

Pauly Fuemana does a promotional tour of Europe accompanied by Mark Cathro.

November	Grant Thomas becomes Pauly's manager; the following year Bill Cullen will become co-manager.

Pauly does a promotional tour of Asia accompanied by Tom Sampson.

How Bizarre album is released in New Zealand.

December	Pauly performs a new song, 'Land of Plenty', at Christmas in the Park in Auckland.

1997

January	*How Bizarre* album is released in Australia.

OMC single 'On the Run' is released in the UK.

January	'How Bizarre' reaches number one in Canada.
Jan–Feb	Pauly performs at Big Day Out concerts in Australia.

February	'Land of Plenty' is released in the first week of the month; on February 12 it charts at number 4.
February 25	'How Bizarre' is released in the US – the single to radio stations only, the album to record stores.
March	Pauly plays at festivals in Europe.
June 8	Pauly begins a second European promotional tour.
Jun–Sept	Pauly tours the US.
July	'How Bizarre' starts to climb US airplay charts.
August 16	'How Bizarre' reaches number one on US Top 40 Mainstream Airplay chart, number two on R&B Airplay Chart, and number five on Adult Top 40. The following week it reaches number four on US Hot 100 Airplay and number one on Billboard Pop Charts.
October	Pauly Fuemana returns to Auckland after the European and US tours.

1998

| April | 'How Bizarre' takes off in South America; Pauly is sent on a promotional tour. |

2005

| March | Alan Jansson and Pauly Fuemana agree to work together again. |
| December | Alan pulls out, concerned at Pauly's erratic behaviour. He will later agree to work with Pauly again. |

2006

| June 20 | Pauly is declared bankrupt; the following month his wife Kirstine Fuemana is also declared bankrupt. They will both be discharged from bankruptcy in 2009. |

2007

March 21   Pauly releases a single, '4 All Of Us' for the Human Rights Commission's Race Relations Day. The single, recorded on Pauly's Orpheus label and produced by Alan Jansson, features actor Lucy Lawless on backing vocals. Pauly Fuemana gifts the track to the commission; Lucy Lawless donates her proceeds to the hospital Starship Children's Health.

2008

June   Alan Jansson leaves the writing partnership permanently.

2010

January 31   Pauly Fuemana dies of respiratory failure after nearly two years battling progressive demyelinating polyneuropathy, an auto-immune disorder also known as chronic inflammatory demyelinating polyneuropathy. He is 40 years old. His sixth child, a boy, is born in August.

Acknowledgements

I began writing this book shortly after Pauly died. It was never my intention to see it published. Rather, I thought of it as a private memoir and a way to somehow excise the pain I felt after Pauly's far too early and, although I knew he was ill, unexpected death.

As perhaps the most complete witness to the phenomenon that was 'How Bizarre', having been there from the beginning and central to much of what went on day to day, I also felt there was a need to set the record straight. There had been, and continued to be, so many misplaced and erroneous statements and rumours about Pauly, 'How Bizarre' and the other people involved in the record's creation. I was in a privileged position. Not only had the record been released on my label but I had an almost complete set of documents from the period, including many internal PolyGram documents – including financial records – long lost by the company. This would allow me to present the first accurate account of this profoundly interesting event in New Zealand – and international – music history.

This book is not intended as a biography of Pauly Fuemana and should not be read that way. All the events surrounding both him and the journey of his song are seen from my personal perspective and experience.

In many ways this is a universal story. Hopes and dreams still fuel countless hours in recording studios, in home studios and on stages for people with the same sorts of aspirations that Pauly Fuemana, Alan Jansson and I had. And yet sometimes those dreams can go badly awry, even when you achieve what you've hoped for. So it was with 'How Bizarre'. While I have sometimes held back on sensitive details, I have also tried to tell the truth, unpalatable though it may occasionally be.

I have Nick Bollinger to thank for the book's ultimate publication. Nick read the manuscript as research for his profile of OMC on the *AudioCulture* website and suggested to publisher Mary Varnham that it would be of interest to a wide audience. I thank Mary and her colleagues Sarah Bennett, Kylie Sutcliffe and Emma Wolff at Awa Press for believing in me and in the power of the story.

I wish especially to thank Alan Jansson. It was Alan's relentless belief, exceptional skill and musical genius in pulling together the disparate elements that he and Pauly penned over late-night coffee and drives that gave us the song we took around the world.

The people I respect most in the recording industry, Chris Caddick, Adam Holt and Brendan Smyth, have been very supportive and I thank them for their honest opinions and advice. These mean a lot. Adam was also a key player in the record's international progress. Without him, Paul Dickson, Mark Phillips and Roger Grierson there would have been no global hit. There are many others to thank but I hope they will recognise their key input and support within the book's pages.

Finally, there would, of course, have been no record without the unique talent of Pauly Fuemana. He and the Fuemana family have left an indelible impression on popular music and its ongoing life.

Simon Grigg
August 2015

Index